# Olivia's Only Pretending

## REBECCA JO JACKSON

# Olivia's Only Pretending

SWEET RIVER SERIES
BOOK THREE


REBECCA JO JACKSON

# *Playlist*

I always make a soundtrack for each of my books to listen to while writing. Below is a peek at what was playing in the background while Olivia and Victor tried to pretend they were just pretending.

*(You can also find this playlist on Spotify at the link in my Instagram profile, @AuthorRebeccaJoJackson).*

1. End of the World by Kelsea Ballerini
2. One Foot in Front of the Other by Griff
3. Begin Again by Taylor Swift
4. Bulletproof by FARR
5. Now I'm In It by HAIM
6. BOY by Charlie Puth
7. We're Not Just Friends by Parks, Squares and Alleys
8. Peer Pressure by James Bay and Julia Michaels
9. Make You Mine by PUBLIC
10. Crash My Party by Luke Bryan
11. Dress by Taylor Swift
12. I Like Me Better by Lauv
13. Close to You by Gracie Abrams
14. we can't be friends by Ariana Grande
15. late night thoughts by shy martin

*For those armed with their lists and logic— your heart all locked up —you deserve to find your safe place. And so much more.*

*And to Ivy Jo, my sweet eldest daughter.*

# One

Of course, I knew Victor Hernandez had a crush on me, at least when we first met. There was a particular way my friend Victor Hernandez's amber eyes crinkled when he was looking at something he really liked, and that was exactly how his eyes crinkled at me the day my younger sister, Lucy, introduced us months ago.

The day we met, I'd stopped by my small-town coffee shop,

Coffees and Commas, in Sweet River to meet my sister and her then-work partner, Adam. It was hard to ignore how Adam's rakish assistant, Victor, lit up when his warm brown eyes landed on me. And then there was that crinkle—like he was looking directly into bright sunshine, creased at the edges but not looking away, half grinning.

That summer afternoon, Victor immediately offered to wait in line with me to order our lattes. Beneath the sunlight gleaming through the tall café windows, he excitedly asked me everything—about my summer, the old house I'd just moved into, and how I like my coffee. His focus was on me the whole time, not wasting a single second getting to know me.

His full attention, eyes aglow, was enough to draw me in. Victor had a way of roping *everyone* in like an irresistible lasso.

He'd given me his full attention every single time we met since then. It felt good, but I wasn't about to get lost in those crinkly eyes. I didn't need any more heartbreak. I had to remind myself over and over of that fact when it came to Victor.

But a girl could always use a good friend. So, instead of a romance, Victor and I grew a friendship. Anything more wasn't something I ever *really* entertained.

One of the biggest reasons was that he was younger than me, twenty-four to my twenty-nine. I was ready for something serious, even marriage, while Victor was still in his "dating around" phase. Another reason was that, as weak in the knees as those crinkly brown eyes could make you feel, they were not reserved for me. They crinkled over a lot of things—his golden retriever puppy, a cold bottle of Coke on a hot day, a fresh batch of his mom's salsa, or when he was blowing sawdust off a completed woodworking project, proud of what he'd made.

*And me*, one of his best friends.

He was grinning at me on this late September afternoon as I walked through the door into my house after a long day at work.

"Olivia," he said, his wavy jet-black hair flopping over his eyes.

He was there, as he often was, working on one of the renovation projects for my fixer-upper house. He was standing in my kitchen in a white T-shirt and jeans—so casual in comparison to my work attire of a black pencil skirt and a white satin blouse.

"Hey there," I said, dropping my cardigan on the coatrack in my entryway. Late September in Texas meant it was finally cool in the mornings, but by the afternoon, the sweater always ended up bundled in my bag.

Victor's golden retriever, Watson, panted up to me as Victor leaned his shoulder against the doorway between the entryway and the living room. Furry ears were under my hand.

"You've got to see the deck out back. It's finally done," Victor said.

I'd bought this old, historic house in my hometown of Sweet River five months ago, only weeks before meeting Victor. It was one of the first things we talked about, standing in line at Coffees and Commas—his love of renovation and woodworking piquing his interest in my fixer-upper project. He'd offered to help a few times before I finally accepted.

I was in love with this old house, but I was in over my head, which had me overwhelmed, so his woodworking skills were an answer to my prayers.

We connected over our love of fixing broken things right away. Like me, Victor didn't see a chore when he looked at this fixer-upper, but instead, he too saw something beautiful waiting for the right eyes to look at it in the right way.

Over the summer, he came over nearly every day to work on my floors, my kitchen, my walls, my yard. We'd created our own rhythm and routine, working together over the past few months. Our friendship caught quick, like striking a match.

We had heart-to-hearts while painting walls and made inside jokes as we tore down another. I'd learned the rumble of his laughter, the way his brow furrowed in concentration when he was working, and a list of his favorite songs.

I ditched my ankle boots in the entryway before Watson and I followed Victor through the living room and out the glass doors leading to my backyard. I placed my bare feet on the warm wood of the deck Victor had been working on for the last several weeks. I grazed a hand across the railing.

"Wow," I gasped, glancing around. He'd set up my patio furniture—a terra-cotta sofa with matching chairs and a round black table. "It's a dream. I can't wait to sit out here under the stars."

His chest puffed a little in pride. His cheeks were pink under his dark stubble. "It looks pretty good, huh?" He knelt down to scratch Watson's belly.

"Pretty good is an understatement." I shook my head. My auburn hair fell out of its ponytail. My historic house came with rules and regulations for renovations, so not only had Victor become my volunteer renovation buddy, but he'd also pored over historic home rules and codes with me and made sure to honor them.

I'd probably only have half the progress we'd made if it wasn't for him.

"You owe me a bottle of Coke out here." He grinned up at me from his spot on the ground with Watson. My big living room windows opened behind us, curtains tripping in the early autumn breeze.

I crossed my arms, biting my lip. "Deal."

"What's left on the to-do list after this?"

I swallowed. Over the last five months, we'd spent nearly every evening and weekend together, sweaty, dusty, paint on our clothes, laughing hysterically over messy, drawn-up plans going sideways but in the best ways. I loved coming home and finding him and Watson here. I was basically Watson's co-parent now.

I licked my lips. "Um." I wasn't sure what else I could afford after paying for this deck, but I wasn't ready to let him go. "Maybe ..." I squinted into the house. *Should I repaint something?* I glanced back toward the yard. *Maybe ...*

Working with him had become a sort of addiction. My sister, Lucy, kept asking, *How's the Victor habit going? What new job have you come up with for him today?*

Victor broke into my thoughts. "You know we talked about how you need a bookshelf dedicated to all your schoolbooks?" Victor had been teasing me since he caught me unpacking my multiple boxes of textbooks on history, classical antiquity, and languages like Greek and Latin. I'd gotten a PhD in history and classics and refused to let go of any of my books. *I pored over those,* I'd defended my stacks. *Each one holds a different memory. Plus, I still come back to them for different lesson plans.*

I'd recently finished my degree while working as a professor at the college where I was completing my program. I'd been Professor Rhodes on campus for years, and it still felt like a happy little shock when I was referred to as Dr. Rhodes.

He'd nodded and told me they needed their own shelf then.

"That's right," I said now, the wind rustling through the elm trees lining my backyard. I felt my body relax, knowing that this bought me more time with him. "A shelf for my textbooks."

"We also need to get you one for all those cartoons," Victor said, his grin playful. He referred to my romance collection as cartoons because of their animated covers.

"Ah, yes, my *cartoons*." I sat down beside him and Watson on the deck.

Victor scooted closer to me, bumping his shoulder against mine. My stomach flooded with warmth.

"So, two new bookshelves?" Victor looked sideways up at me, under his dark lashes. "Oak? Walnut?"

"Walnut," I said. The temperature was dropping as the sun set. I rubbed my arms. "My sisters are going to want to have our margarita night out here tonight."

"Aren't margarita nights usually on Fridays?"

Victor knowing my schedule and routine made my chest squeeze. I'd memorized his, too. Somehow, over the summer, he'd wiggled his way into becoming one of my most important people.

"Yeah, but I'm swamped. The history department's Fall Seminar Series kicks off this week. And I have a fancy faculty dinner on Thursday and the Fall Festival on Friday, so we had to move margarita night up."

"Fancy dinners for my fancy baby girl," he said, messing up my copper hair.

My ponytail was barely hanging on now. I shoved him.

"Not the baby girl thing again," I groaned playfully. It was a nickname he'd given me just to get under my skin.

"It ain't going anywhere." He squeezed my side, making me erupt into laughter.

"Am I interrupting?" Lucy said, apparently having let herself in through the front door. She leaned against the glass door to the porch, with the curtain rippling in the breeze. Her wild red hair was piled atop her head in a messy bun.

"Just interrupting Victor being annoying." I shrugged.

"Ouch." Victor grasped his chest.

I tried to ignore how his T-shirt pulled tight across it.

"How can you burn me like that?" Victor said, trying to suppress a grin. The way his whole face lit up when he smiled, even just a small half smile, did something to my heart.

I glanced over to Lucy, shaking my head at Victor's drama. She simply raised a bottle of tequila in the air, and then a bag of limes.

M om, Lucy, and I stood in the kitchen on the shiny hardwood floors, blending our margaritas, while my younger sister Gracie's big blue eyes and strawberry-blonde hair filled up my phone screen, propped up on the kitchen island.

"Lucy, did you tell Adam that he has to come with you to my spring show?" Gracie asked. She was a senior in college, gearing up for her final dance performance.

"Adam? I thought it was going to be a *girls-only* trip." I

scrunched my freckled nose at the phone. Adam was Lucy's boyfriend and Victor's boss.

Gracie laughed. "As if Victor won't somehow end up there, too."

"Seriously," my mom chimed in.

I opened my mouth to respond, but then Victor, who was measuring spots in the living room for the bookshelf, let out a loud cackle. "I'm taking that as an invitation."

And I felt a tiny thrill at the idea of Victor cementing himself in our group.

"For all we know, Mom is going to have some guy she's bringing along by then." Lucy elbowed Mom in the side. "You should see the number of DMs she's gotten since we set up her account on that dating app, Love Local."

"The question is, have you replied to any of these *many* DMs?" I asked.

"I have." Mom's eyes twinkled. "I've replied to a few."

"She's replied to *four*!" Lucy said, scandalized. Lucy was only three inches taller than me at five foot three to my five feet and had scooped the phone up and was holding it over us. I wondered how our tiny redheaded crew looked to broad-shouldered, six-foot Victor.

"Four?" I gasped. I couldn't imagine Mom flirting with one man, let alone four.

Gracie groaned. "There's enough man drama in this family. We don't need more."

"Is that flaky Austin still giving you the runaround?" Mom said, her voice full of concern, while holding the pitcher in her tight grip. Austin was a tense subject for Gracie.

"I don't want to talk about Austin." Her voice dropped, with all the fun and energy zapped.

*Not Austin again.*

"Did he message you again?" Lucy asked, ignoring Gracie's attempt to avoid the subject. We all leaned closer to the phone screen.

"He called." Gracie rubbed her forehead.

"Did you answer?" Mom asked.

Gracie just sighed, which in Gracie language meant she definitely answered.

"Do not meet up with him, Grace." I grabbed the phone and stared her down as seriously as I could through the tiny phone screen. Austin and Gracie had been off and on for two years now. "I know when he reaches out, it always includes an invitation to get coffee or dinner and talk things out—"

"You've given him enough time already! He's maxed out on chances!" Victor called from the other room. He'd been privy to the Austin drama. He had some strong opinions.

Gracie just mumbled that she knew. It wasn't very promising.

My mom poured our glasses. "Before we lose Gracie to rehearsal"—she took a sip—"tell us how you're feeling about creating your new course, Olivia?"

Excitement bubbled in my stomach. After years of teaching courses with topics given to me, my department had room for a special topic class, and I'd been invited to design the class and teach it. I was putting together a proposal for review by a committee. *A class designed by Olivia Rhodes*—the only thing for it that wouldn't be chosen by me was the registrar number.

For years, I'd had so many ideas, but now that I was about to start working on my proposal, I wasn't sure what direction I wanted to go. "I've been going over old classes to get an idea of what the department would like or need. There's also a class topic that one of our tenured professors, Dr. Lewis, is really pushing for me to go with."

"What ideas have *you* come up with?" Gracie asked. She slipped on her sneakers while balancing her phone in the air overhead. "I don't care about old classes or your fellow professors."

I took a sip, my mouth sour and salty. "I have a few ideas I've toyed with, but none sound like something the department would like—"

"But what would *you* like?" Victor shouted from the living room. His measuring tape snapped shut.

I closed my eyes. I'd like to teach something that made my students think about history in a new way. Like this old house did for me and Victor as we researched why the crown molding was so important or why the original windows were significant.

I loved what I did because you could study history through the lens of anything. I'd taken a course in school that studied American history through vampire literature, taking notes on Bella and Edward like a textbook and learning what it told us about our culture at that time.

While surveying old class descriptions, I hadn't found any classes like that. But I wanted to teach a class that got the students' eyes lighting up like we did in that vampire class.

"I'd just like to have a successful new class!" I shouted so Victor could hear. "I have to get it approved *and* have a certain number of students sign up if it's going to make it." What I wanted couldn't be at the forefront of my mind. I didn't want to get my hopes up just to get shot down on my first try.

The sun had fully set outside my kitchen windows, while Victor packed up his toolbox in the living room. "You're coming up with it, Liv. It's going to be successful. You never miss," he said.

"All the kids will sign up," my mom said, giving my arm a reassuring squeeze.

"Of course they will. Everyone has a crush on Dr. Rhodes," Lucy added, shimmying her shoulders as her wild red curls bounced. Her red was a shade brighter than my own darker auburn. Her hair was curly and wild to my sleek and straight.

"Of course they do," Victor said, popping his head into the kitchen, like he hadn't been eavesdropping the entire time, always playing this overly charming game with me.

I just rolled my eyes.

"Good night," I said, lifting my margarita high in the air. "See you later."

"I'll be by the next couple nights to start work on the book-shelves," he said casually.

Lucy chuckled under her breath, then mouthed to Mom, *Bookshelves now?*

"See you then," I said quickly, not wanting him to see Lucy's reaction or the way my mom was nodding in agreement. I didn't want anything to throw off the happy little equilibrium of our renovation world.

LUCY

so, what's your plan for Victor after he finishes
the bookshelves?

ME

those were his idea, actually

LUCY

poor guy, he's got it bad

I knew he wasn't ever going to call it quits
when he decided to build you a new kitchen
table and a bench to match

but that fancy deck is top tier

ME

this is his passion!

LUCY

you?

ME

WOODWORKING

LUCY

and you

ME

we're just FRIENDS

he's my YOUNGER FRIEND

LUCY

don't know any guys your age who would
build you a fancy deck

The morning air was crisp, breezing through my kitchen window, making my blue bonnet vintage curtains dance. I was pouring the rest of the coffee from the pot into my travel mug when there was a knock on my door.

I glanced at the microwave clock: 7:12. I furrowed my brows as I shuffled to the door. *Who would pay me a visit before working hours?*

I pulled the door open to find Victor standing in my doorway. "Good morning," he said with a big grin. His caramel eyes looked sleepy.

I was incapable of anything but grinning back. "Well, good morning. What're you doing here so early?"

"I left my work bag here last night," Victor said. He wore a black hoodie with the hood pulled on, a few dark waves curling at the edges. "I need it for a meeting. I was hoping to catch you before you left for work."

I worked in a little college town about twenty minutes south of Sweet River.

I went inside to finish packing my work tote, while he grabbed up his bag from the living room. He wandered into the kitchen with it slung over one shoulder. The bag hung open un-buckled, and I glimpsed a book spine poking out—*Wheelock's Latin*.

"Are you learning Latin?" I asked him as I dug through my tote.

He glanced toward his bag self-consciously, then flipped it closed. "I might be dabbling."

"Am I rubbing off on you?" I put my hand to my chest proudly.

He didn't answer, looking over my shoulder distractedly. "Liv, I'm going to close this window for you."

"Thanks, I always forget. You know, a bird even flew in once," I said, slipping my arms into my cardigan as he grabbed an apple off my counter. "Grab me, one too?"

He dropped the apple into my tote as I hung it over my shoulder. "A bird literally flew in before, and you were *still* about to leave it open?"

"Well, I don't want the birds to think they're not welcome," I joked. Though I did love how they filled my trees and sang by my windows. "I really love them making a home in the backyard. I think they should have their own spot out there."

"Their own spot?" Victor chuckled, following me out of the kitchen. "I think you mean *a birdhouse*?"

"Something like that, yeah. There's a little bird family out in the elm trees that could use a house," I said.

Victor opened the front door for me. As I turned the lock, Victor leaned back against the door, his hood still on.

"You wear hoodies into the office?" I asked, raising a brow.

He grinned. "I wear hoodies to the gym. I'll change after my workout."

I nodded, stepping onto the porch. "Got to get your gains, huh?"

He shook his head, eyes crinkling. "You mock, but you like the results."

My face went hot. Scenes from yesterday ran through my mind: Victor's tight white T-shirt, sweaty and clinging to his chest, his biceps flexing as he wiped his forehead with the back of his hand.

I cleared my throat, suddenly nervous. "Someone's feeling cocky."

Victor's eyes dropped to my blush. "I meant *for renovation purposes*. You know, the heavy lifting I've done around your house." A grin cracked across his face as we crossed the rocky ground to our cars. "But, if you appreciate more than that, even better."

I palmed my forehead with one hand, pulling my shiny white Prius's door open with the other. "I'll see you later, Victor."

"See you, Liv," he called, sing-songy as he sauntered to his black Silverado.

I turned the key in the ignition, and a metallic clanging sputtered from the engine. My heart sank. I knew that sound all too well. I tried again, turning the key again, but got the same sound.

"No." I hit the steering wheel.

*I'm in the middle of renovating. Busy with the Fall Seminar. Preparing my proposal. I don't have time for car trouble and definitely can't afford it.* I turned the key once more—same splutter.

"Need a ride, baby girl?" a syrupy sweet voice asked outside my window.

I glanced up at Victor leaning over my car door. I pushed the door open. "I think my car is broken," I whimpered.

"Pop the hood," he said, walking to the front of my car.

I sat in the passenger seat of his truck, listening as he told me what he thought might be wrong. I nodded along.

"You won't know for sure until it's checked out professionally, though," he said. "I could tow it over to the Rogers' auto repair shop, but I'll call 'em first. They might pick it up."

He pulled out his phone and started dialing.

He helped me with my broken house one day, then helped me with my broken car the next. The man was multifaceted. I smiled to myself. It wasn't hard to see why women fell all over themselves for him.

Silly, playful Victor one moment, and then confident and caring Victor the next, helping me like it was second nature.

I felt lucky about our friendship. That I'd walked into the coffee shop the day we met.

Lucky that even though we were years apart—missing each other's groups and circles in school—God had brought us together now at just the right time. My heart had needed a friend like him.

Victor and I arranged for the auto shop to come pick up my car over the phone, then I pulled up my mom's number to see if she could give me a ride.

He put his hand over the screen of my phone, shaking his head. "Hey, I'm right here. Let me take you."

My chest twisted in guilt. I felt like he was always going out of his way for me. I didn't want to interrupt his morning now, too. "Are you sure? You were here working on my deck last night. Now you're going to mess up your morning by driving me out of town?"

He started his truck. "Happy to help," he said casually. "Buckle up."

"You're always helping me," I said softly, reaching for the buckle. "How can I help you?"

He ran his hand through his hair thoughtfully. "Stop scratching up the new dining table."

"Victor."

"Okay, okay. How about one of your famous grilled cheeses?" He hit the turn signal.

"I'm serious."

The car slowed to a stop at an intersection. He swallowed. "I've been working on business plans, actually."

"What?" I twisted toward him in my seat.

Victor had toyed with the idea of starting his own carpentry business a few times before, but noncommittally. He was hesitant, like he wasn't sure he could pull it off.

"It's still in the early stages, low-key. But I would love a second opinion." He paused, his eyes darting over to me. "And your opinion means a lot to me."

"I'd love to see your plans. I'm excited you're doing this." I'd been quietly trying to encourage him, without pushing too hard. A few mini pep talks when he mentioned what he *could maybe do someday.*

I'd seen his work over the past few months. It had the potential to be big.

*A few weeks ago, we'd stayed up late in my living room talking after working on some reno project. The conversation took a serious turn, toward the future.*

*We were sitting on my tan sectional. I was facing him, a soft pillow to my chest. It was dark, only a couple of table lamps on.*

*I'd opened up to him about how I dreamed of teaching new classes that excited me. I wanted to challenge myself and pour into my students in a new, fresh way.*

*He cleared his throat and told me he wanted to do something new, too. He wanted a carpentry business of his own. "I've thought about it. Maybe I would start small, just something on the side. But it'd be cool if it grew over the years. I'd start with furniture, tables, and chairs like I've done for you, then maybe one day ... renovations." His eyes stayed on the pillow beside him, toying with the loose thread. "It's just an idea, though."*

*Victor's eyes always turned downcast when conversations turned toward his potential in a way that made my hands ball into frustrated fists. He couldn't see all the good I saw in him. I wished I could fight his doubts away.*

*"Victor, what's holding you back from starting your business?" I leaned forward from the other end of the couch, my hair brushing across my shoulders.*

*"Starting a business is a lot of paperwork—"*

*"You can handle paperwork. I'll help you with that. But is that really what's stopping you from taking the leap?"*

*He swallowed, eyes still downcast. "I don't want to try and flop. Be the only Hernandez flop of the family."*

*"The only Hernandez flop?" A lump formed in my throat. The late summer sun dipped below the horizon outside the glass doors, casting a warm glow. Elm trees swayed in my backyard.*

*"Have you noticed that everyone in my family does these great things, makes these great lives my parents are so proud of, and then ..." He took a long inhale.*

*I tapped his foot with mine across the couch. He pulled his eyes up to mine.*

*"Then there's me."*

*"Then there's you—the one who can build the most beautiful things with his own two hands." I reached toward him, grabbing his hands in mine and shaking them. "Who the city department would be lost without. Who makes everyone laugh. Who shows up for your family and friends every single time. The one everyone can rely on. No one else can say that."*

*His hands stayed in mine, hanging between us. There was a small smile under his five o'clock shadow, those dark eyes searching mine. "Everything I do feels small in comparison to my siblings."*

*"Then dream bigger." I let go of his hands, but the warmth from his stayed like smoke from a fire. "But nothing about you doesn't measure up. I don't think you understand how significant you are."*

*"I'm significant to you?" His voice was rough.*

*I could nearly feel it against my skin. He grabbed my bare foot in his hand. My heart quickened. We didn't touch like that.*

*"Of course," I whispered.*

*The way he looked at me shifted the energy in the room, like we were standing on the edge of a big expanse. I needed to step back to safer grounds.*

*"You've become one of my best friends."*

*"You're my best friend, too." He pulled me toward him by my feet, making me squeal.*

*I was laughing and out of breath, with my face inches from his. His hands were still wrapped around my ankles.*

*Gulping for air, I said, "Start the business, if you want to. Don't think about what your siblings are doing, or what you think you should or shouldn't do, or if it could fail. Only think about what you want."*

*"I do want it," he confessed, releasing my ankles.*

*I pulled my legs close to my chest, back to safety, my heartbeat returning to normal. "Then I say go for it."*

Now we were pulling into the campus parking lot. "Just don't mention the business plans to anyone yet. I'm waiting to tell my folks," he said.

"Okay, but I know they'll be proud." He didn't see how his mom beamed when he entered the room, or the hearty way his dad laughed at his jokes. How his siblings' eyes shot straight to him at the dinner table, hanging on his every word.

But since he'd let me into his world, I saw.

I hung on his every word, too. I beamed at his smile. It was just the Victor effect.

I slid out of the truck and onto the pavement of the parking lot, stopping to say bye to Victor. But then he cut the engine and climbed out of the truck, too. *He was supposed to drop me off and go on to work.*

"What are you doing?" I asked from the passenger side.

"Getting out of my truck?" He cocked his head, as if I'd asked a ridiculous question. He slammed the driver's side door behind him.

The air was cool. I tugged my sweater close around me. "Why? You don't work here?"

"'Cause I'm curious about this place." He wiggled his brows. "I want to see Liv's world."

# Three

Tall trees with autumnal leaves freshly turning scattered the campus. We walked the sidewalk paths, weaving through the green lawns peppered with students hauling thick books and shouting across the way to one another. Red brick buildings surrounded us.

"Our campus is pretty small in comparison to big universities," I said, leading him toward the history building where I taught. "But I love it."

"I can see why. It's charming." He grinned. "You walk this way every day?"

"Every day." I nodded. I tipped my chin toward the building ahead. "That's where my office is and where I lecture."

"I want to sit in on one of your lectures," Victor said, pushing back his hood and running a hand through his hair. "What if I crashed one of your classes one day?"

"Please don't. I can only imagine the chaos you'd cause."

"Like interrupting class to confess my undying love?"

I elbowed him. "Shut up."

We passed the fountain in the center of campus, weaving right toward a patch of grass shaded by a big oak tree. Its leaves were just starting to crisp, the colors fading. I came to a halt in front of it.

"This is my favorite tree." I patted the trunk fondly.

"It's a mighty fine tree," Victor said, giving it a once-over.

"It's where I come to work sometimes. I eat my lunch here. Sometimes, I read. My book club meets under it."

"The cartoon book club?" Victor asked, crossing his arms.

"My *romance* book club, yes," I corrected him. A few students and I had bonded over our affinity for romance novels, so we started meeting to talk about them. Word got out, and the club kept growing.

Now, it was a big book club that met once a month outside the history building by the oak tree. It had become a respite for all of us during the ups and downs of tough semesters and dense reading assignments. I even had a couple of students write me a thank-you letter for starting it, even though it was kind of an accident.

"I like that you share your favorite tree." He reached up and rubbed a leaf between his fingers.

"I'm happy to share it. You can come sit by my tree anytime, you know." For a moment, I imagined how nice it would be to have Victor invade all the areas of my life—not just renovations and friendly hangouts, but getting to have him everywhere.

His eyes landed on mine, making me feel like the sun was shining directly on me.

"Oh, next you have to see my coffee stand!" I grabbed his hand and pulled him down the sidewalk to the little coffee cart outside the steps of the history building.

"Today is fun," he said, trailing behind me.

We chatted in line waiting for coffee, and I told him more of the school's history than he'd probably wanted to hear. Eventually, it was our turn to order.

A new barista stood behind the counter—someone I'd never seen before. "Hi," I greeted her, but her big green eyes weren't on me.

"Victor?" she squealed, tucking a long strand of blonde hair behind her ear.

"Hey there," Victor said, all friendly. He paused, just for a second, scanning her, and only I could tell he was trying to remember her name. "*Annie!*"

"What are you doing here?" she demanded flirtatiously. "What got you out of Sweet River?"

"I'm here with Olivia." He slung an arm around my shoulder. "She's a professor here."

Her face fell. He made us sound like a couple. Before I could clarify or say something about how we were just good friends, Victor blew right past it, asking her how long she'd worked here and how she'd been. They chit-chatted while we ordered, typical small talk.

I smiled along, but inside, I felt like a balloon with all the air sucked out of it. Totally deflated.

My sisters were always asking why I didn't date Victor. There was an evident attraction between us. I'd never pretend there wasn't. We obviously got along.

*He's younger*, I'd say, like that explained everything.

But there was also the fact that I'd sworn off guys like him. I'd been a notorious sucker for the boys who made you feel like the sun was shining on you when they looked your way ... but then left you asking where he'd been when you ran into him at the coffee stand while he tried to remember your name.

I'd been the girl whose name was forgotten.

Not anymore, though. I was too old for that now. I'd learned to spot the signs and head in the other direction.

Victor was playful, flirty, achingly gorgeous ... *and* had a reputation in Sweet River for breaking hearts. So, I safely kept him in the friend zone.

I enjoyed him, adored him, but all from a safe emotional distance, where he couldn't wreck my heart.

Victor grabbed his wallet and paid for both our coffees before

I could even unlatch my tote. I thanked him, and he shot me a wink.

"I'm this way." I jogged up the steps toward my office, my nude ankle boots clicking.

Victor reached around me to pull the heavy door open, his scent of sawdust and strong coffee whirling around me. I let it envelop me as I walked through the door with him right on my heels.

I glanced up to see someone in front of me who stopped right in my tracks. I took an immediate step back, crashing into Victor's chest.

"You good, baby girl?" Victor asked teasingly, oblivious to my internal meltdown.

I looked up at him with what must've been a look of despair, because his smile faded into furrowed brows of concern, and he opened his mouth to say something.

"Olivia?" a voice I knew all too well said.

Ryan Callas. Tall, dark, and handsome. Standing just a few feet away was the man I'd once thought I was going to marry.

"Ryan," I choked out, then awkwardly, as almost a question, "*Hi*?"

Ryan was supposed to be across the country right now.

Victor stayed pressed against my back, thankfully. I burrowed into him for moral support.

"You look surprised. I should've called or emailed. I was a late addition to the Fall Seminar. I'm attending as a guest lecturer for the next six weeks," he said in a fast tumble of words.

I was trying to keep up.

*Six weeks.* He'd be here for six weeks.

"Someone fell through?" I wondered aloud, my voice a tone of clear disappointment. I felt Victor's warm hands rest against my shoulders.

Ryan nodded, then cleared his throat. "Dr. Morris. She had some family matter come up. I was called only a few days ago."

*But he loved his job at his new school. How could he take off for six weeks?*

His eyes kept skittering toward Victor behind me, and Victor's hands on my shoulders. "Oh, um, this is Victor." I patted Victor's hand. "Victor, this is Ryan." He knew who Ryan was. I'd told him the story.

"Nice to meet you." Ryan scratched at his chin.

Victor nodded toward him. "Yeah, man." Then he dropped his voice, putting his lips against the side of my head above my ear. "Ready to finish the tour?"

We stumbled into my office. I felt confused and slightly nauseous.

*Ryan is back for the fall.*

We had only spoken a few times since our breakup, mostly emails about things he needed me to mail him, and each time left a bitter taste in my mouth. Things I'd ignored for the sake of our relationship were now blatant and annoying in hindsight. Plus, there was my favorite pumpkin-shaped mug that he'd "accidentally" taken with him to Minnesota and never mailed back to me, even after I'd asked him to.

Anger swelled in my chest every time I thought of that mug and all the warm cups of coffee I could've drunk out of it over the past two years. Coffee I'd had to sip out of far lesser mugs.

"This is so you." Victor chuckled, picking up a framed photo of me and my sisters in matching sweatpants from my desk, pulling me out of my thoughts.

"The last stop on the campus tour: my office." I waved around my cramped office. The walls were lined with stuffed bookshelves, there was a dark walnut desk with notebooks and framed photos littered across it, one of me and my late nana arm in arm at our lake house front and center, and an old desktop computer.

He pointed toward the large poster maps on my walls. "What

are these?" He squinted, peering closer. "Paris. Greece. London. Ireland."

"Maps of places I want to visit." I walked behind my desk for a closer look. "I got them years ago as sort of inspiration. I've been saving for a while, but I've yet to get the gumption to buy a ticket."

He nodded.

"Plus, distractions arise. Like beautiful old houses that need renovating," I said, when my phone buzzed in my pocket. It was a text from one of my fellow history professors and closest friends, Gabby.

GABBY

Office rumor is that you have a new BF you're prancing around campus right now

Do you have a man with you? I know you don't have a BF (right??)

I gasped and quickly shot back a message.

ME

It's just Victor! My car broke down, so he gave me a ride and was Victoring and demanded a tour. Don't know why anyone thinks he's my bf??

I put my phone down and tried to put my focus back on Victor, who was rummaging through all my stuff and asking questions about everything he picked up.

A few seconds later, Gabby poked her head into my office, with her black, braided hair falling over her shoulders. "Hey."

"Gabby is here!" Victor called from his spot by the shelves, flipping through my books.

"Vic," Gabby said, giving him a quick side hug. "You've got the office talking."

"Do I?" There was no missing the pleased grin that spread across Victor's face at this news. "How so?"

I leaned back against my desk. "Yes, how so? I just gave the guy a brief walk around the campus."

"*The guy?*" Victor slapped a hand against his chest. "That's all I am to you?"

Gabby bit her lip. "I think Ryan started the rumor. He's told a few different people in the last, like, half hour that he met your new boyfriend. People were like 'oh, that explains why she gave him a tour and why they were all giggly.'"

Victor snorted. "*All giggly.*"

I shook my head. "Did you set them straight?"

"No, I mean, I was wondering if I'd missed something. Someone said they'd heard him call you *baby girl*, and he'd bought you a coffee. It just—"

"Baby girl is true, but it's a joke," I said, shooting an accusatory glance toward Victor. "I told you that nickname was too messy."

Gabby raised a brow to Victor. "You trying to manifest?"

His cheeks blazed red.

"Well, go back to your office and set people straight, please?" I clasped my hands together.

"Don't worry about it, Liv. It'll blow over, anyway. No reason to stress," she said on her way out.

Victor set the book back on the shelf and turned to me. "Sorry I started rumors," he said, raising his shoulders in a sheepish shrug that made my insides melt a little.

Of course people were talking. Bringing my alarmingly handsome and far-too-flirty friend was bound to start rumors. If they weren't whispering about him, people would probably be asking me if he was single and trying to snag his Instagram handle.

"It'll pass," I said, waving a hand as if it didn't matter. "By the way, Lucy said she'd pick me up after work, so I'm all set."

He tapped my desk as he turned to go. "Let me know if that changes. I'll come get you."

And just like that, he was gone. And I hated the fact I could feel his absence after only a few moments.

*Four*

I let out a long, slow breath as I sat in my comfy desk chair. I brought my coffee cup to my lips, savoring it a moment to collect myself after the emotional whirlwind of this morning, when there was another knock at my door.

"Come in?" I called out.

Ryan sheepishly popped his head around the corner, pushing open the door. He glanced around my office, presumably to check if Victor was still there. "Hi there."

"Hi?" I resisted asking, *What do you want?*

It was the start of my office hours, and I had a packed schedule of meetings with students starting soon.

"I wanted to come by and, well, apologize for not giving you a heads up that I was coming for the seminar." He walked toward the two chairs in front of my desk and plopped down.

"You don't need to apologize—"

"But I do. I know it's hard on you to have me here. You've been adjusting to everything, and then I storm in here. And it'll probably awaken a lot of memories for you. And as a guest speaker, they'll be pasting my name everywhere. I just ..." He shook his head. "I just feel sorry about it. I should've checked with you first."

I felt nauseous again. It had been an adjustment over a year ago, sure, but now it felt nice to have carved my own place here in the history department, without his name always tied to mine. "I'm fine, *really*."

"Hey, if it helps, I'll be sure to talk you up. Give your name a boost, yeah?"

*Oh, how generous.*

"I'm fine, Ryan. No worries." I plastered on a smile. He was right; this did awaken memories—memories of how he'd always acted as if our relationship was a favor to me. As if our relationship were a joint account, and what he deposited had higher value.

"Also, not to pile on, but someone I'm seeing might be coming out to visit for a few days. I didn't want to take you by surprise. I'm not sure if that guy who was with you was someone you're seeing or just a student with a crush or something? But I thought I should warn you so you could prepare yourself." He gave a small half smile. "You've been a real champ through everything."

*A real champ.* For what? Being able to handle being broken up with? Or for sharing the campus with him for an hour this morning?

I fought the urge to roll my eyes.

"Well, congrats," I offered, blowing past his curiosity about Victor. *A student with a crush?* Victor was so much more than that, even if he wasn't my boyfriend. "You've got the job. And a relationship. I'm happy for you."

He stood up, and I did, too.

"You'll get there, too, Livvy."

*Livvy.* This time, I didn't resist rolling my eyes.

I used to wonder if Ryan and I would ever run into each other again. I'd assumed we might bump into each other at a conference —neutral ground. I'd imagined a friendly, polite conversation. I would ask about his new position at the university. The position that was the first domino in our breakup.

Now that he was really standing in front of me, in my office, I didn't want polite small talk. I didn't want closure. I didn't want anything except for him to *go*.

"Well, I'm sure I'll see you around." I gestured toward the door.

Victor came barreling back into my office. "Hey Liv, I left my coffee—" He stopped in his tracks, looking between Ryan and me.

I had my arms clasped tight around myself, and his gaze tracked it, his brows furrowing in concern.

Ryan looked annoyed. *What? Is he irritated that the student and his silly crush are back?*

I set my eyes on Victor and blurted out, in a voice as sweet as syrup, "You know you're welcome here anytime, *sweetie*."

Victor's eyebrow shot up so far it almost blew through the roof. I gave him a big smile and silently begged him to go with it.

Whatever *it* was, I wasn't sure. I just wanted Ryan to realize how wrong he was to dismiss Victor, to feel uncomfortable with how he spoke about him, to feel uncomfortable sitting in my office.

Victor slid behind my desk, beside me, reaching for his coffee, which I'd moved there after he left, planning to steal it. I slipped my arms around his waist, clumsily, unsure of my movements. Victor grinned down at me with his head cocked in question. I gave him a small, sheepish shrug.

A slight chuckle escaped his lips. He had to realize what I was doing.

"I was just on my way out." Ryan thumbed back toward the door, tripping over one of the chairs.

"Oh yeah, I'm running out, too. I'd forgotten—" Victor started.

I grabbed his sweatshirt in my fists and pulled him closer to me. His eyes went wide as his chest pressed against mine with each rapid intake of breath.

Our lips were millimeters apart. I felt myself leaning in for a kiss, his eyes tracking my lips.

"Not without a goodbye ..." I couldn't bring myself to say *kiss.*

I'd always teased my sisters for their chaotic impulsivity. *Why not think before acting?* Yet here I was, shocked by the words coming out of my own mouth.

Ryan cleared his throat awkwardly, standing in the doorway.

Victor looked at me with a mix of wonderment and amusement as he replied, breathlessly, "Of course; I wouldn't dare."

The way his hands slid around my waist made my body flood with heat, waking me from this dangerous game I was playing.

*Olivia Rhodes, you don't have anything to prove to your crummy ex.*

*And Victor is your best friend. Kissing him would be trouble.*

I blinked, pulling my face a few millimeters away. "You don't have to," I whispered, barely audible. I'd almost made a very stupid mistake. I was starting to pump the brakes.

Victor pulled me closer, whispering warmly in my ear, "Happy to help."

Goose bumps erupted down my shoulder.

"I'm—" Ryan was saying something from the doorway. Maybe goodbye? I couldn't hear a thing.

Victor had crossed the millimeters between us with his eyes dropping to my lips, then back to my eyes. Now I felt mine go wide as he slowly, tentatively brought his lips to mine.

I could've pulled away. Stopped him.

Instead, I lifted onto my toes to bring us closer. His lips were warm and tasted like maple latte and mints. He dropped his coffee cup back onto my desk so he could drag his hands against my waist, pulling me closer, eager and hungry.

There was a jolt of electricity between us, sending my hands around his neck, into his hair.

What I thought would be a small goodbye peck felt like opening a floodgate I couldn't contain. Our kiss was frenzied and feverish. As he deepened the kiss, pushing me against the desk, a moan escaped me.

I'd lost all control the minute we'd made contact.

Victor rasped my name into my mouth in a way that made the hairs on my skin raise.

*What are we doing?* It felt like stepping out of a strong current, but I pulled away from him. Dizzy and dazed, I touched my fingers to my lips and looked up at him.

He looked temptingly undone: hair a mess, lips red, swollen. The urge to pull him close again hit me hard.

He swallowed. His gaze narrowed, examining me like he was watching for a tornado on the horizon during a storm.

My feelings were the tornado, wreaking havoc.

Victor cleared his throat. "He left already," he said, gesturing toward the door.

*Oh yeah, Ryan.*

"Oh, good. We scared him away," I said, trying to keep my voice steady and ignoring how my hands were trembling. Even my stomach was trembling.

"Was that what was just happening? Were we scaring Ryan away?" Victor ran a hand through his hair. "Not that I'm complaining, *at all*. I'm just curious about what you're thinking."

"I don't know what I was thinking." I glanced toward the doorway, realizing it was wide open. So much for the rumors blowing over.

Sonny, an older lady who was the secretary for our history department, was right in sight line of my office. I squinted at her for a better look. Her lips were pursed, and she was actively looking away. I rushed over to close my door, and she turned her head toward me for a moment, trying to suppress an obvious grin. *She'd seen.*

I closed my door and rested my head against it with my eyes closed. I had a student coming in eight minutes. "Victor," I groaned.

He chuckled. "I'm liking these new sounds I've been eliciting from you the last few minutes."

I narrowed my eyes. "Victor Hernandez. The office is going to think—"

"That we just made out, and now you've hurried over to slam the door shut?"

"This isn't a joke. We need to figure this out." My heart was racing. Victor showed up on campus and turned my world upside down. *Of course.* He was like ivy growing wild in every area of my life I gave him access to.

"Figure what out?" He propped himself halfway onto my desk. Normally, that'd bother me, but on him, it gave me an ache of affection. I liked seeing him comfy in my safe places. "Annoying ex thinks you've moved on—"

"I have moved on."

"Annoying ex thinks you have a *hot younger boyfriend.* Your department thinks maybe you're having a fling of some kind. I don't think it's that bad." He shrugged. "Nothing to figure out. Let it fizzle. Later, if anyone asks, tell them we decided we were better as friends." He cleared his throat. "Which we are. Right?"

"Right." Victor's perspective brought my heart rate down. I took a deep breath, resting my head against the door.

"Problem solved."

"Now, I only have to deal with Ryan being at all the Fall Seminar activities I was looking forward to. We have the faculty dinner this weekend." I stepped away from the door.

"Sorry, Liv." Victor walked over to me, meeting me in the middle of the office.

He reached for my arms, and my skin flushed, remembering how his hands felt on me only moments ago, like an engine that had just been running and was still hot.

"I'll be fine. I'm a big girl."

He gave my forearms a gentle squeeze. "How about I come with you?"

"Oh," I said, taken aback by his offer. As the eldest daughter, I was used to facing problems by myself. I'd grown up taking scary steps first, so my sisters had footsteps to follow in. I'd checked under my own bed for monsters along with theirs.

Asking for help was not an instinct for me. It was an after-I'd-already-figured-it-out thought. I was our family's pioneer. The captain. Always on the front lines.

"Everyone thinks we're together anyway. I can be your distraction," Victor said. "Might make it more tolerable?"

I chewed on my lip. "My distraction?" Victor *was* skilled at distracting me.

"More than that, though. I can help you navigate everything, be by your side, so you're not dealing with Ryan and office gossip alone. Like a copilot."

"You want to be my copilot?" My chest tugged.

"Anytime. I help you fix up that old house. I help you deal with annoying exes. I buy you good coffee," he said, grinning down at me and warming me all the way down to my toes.

"Okay." I nodded. Just the idea of having him there dialed back my anxiety. "I think that sounds like a good plan."

"So, that's the plan? We let everyone keep thinking we're dating?" His voice dropped, low and warm.

The words sent a rush through me that I didn't want to investigate too closely.

"Yeah, it sounds like a good plan. Right?" I felt like I'd woken up this morning in some messy romcom movie.

"Right." His eyes searched mine. "We can handle that."

Victor left, leaving my office door wide open. I avoided Sonny's nosey gaze from across the hall and slid back behind my desk. I realized one of my notebooks was soaked from where Victor had spilled his coffee during the frantic haze of our kiss. Neither of us had noticed in the heat of the moment. I grabbed a few tissues from a nearby box and tried to sop up the mess before anyone arrived.

But all I could think about was the way Victor had dropped the cup, like nothing else mattered, in a hurry to get his hands on me. The taste of maple latte and mint lingered on my lips the rest of the day.

*Five*

Ryan and I had dated for two years. He was the first guy I'd dated who felt like *this could really be something*. We'd met at the university. Both of us started working there around the same time, and he asked me to lunch to discuss the department and how we were feeling about our new jobs. I was still finishing up my PhD while he was further along in his career. Over lunch, we bonded quickly over how much we had in common, how our goals so perfectly lined up. Our friendship quickly turned into dating.

Ryan was tall with floppy brown hair and a confidence that made people want to follow wherever he was leading. Or sometimes made people want to put him in place. I really loved doing both.

He helped me feel comfortable on campus, right by my side as I found my footing in my new professor shoes, which was a bonus that still made me feel grateful as I looked back on our relationship.

It felt perfect in the way things going exactly the way you'd always imagined sometimes did. What would make more sense than me falling in love with a fellow history professor? It was what I'd expected my future love story would be like.

We worked together and could share office lunches and coffee breaks. It became serious between us quickly.

He met my sisters and mom, and they thought we made sense, too.

I showed him around Sweet River, taking him to the summer festival and ordering him the best coffee on the menu at Coffees and Commas, telling him how much this town and my family meant to me, and he told me he was falling in love with it, too.

Much like his love for me, he only loved it while it was useful to him.

*We should buy one of those historic houses in downtown Sweet River*, he'd said, after I'd told him owning an old house was my dream. My heart swelled. Everything was going so perfectly. I felt afraid to make a wrong move or say the wrong thing.

Because, as *perfect* as it looked, it felt precarious for some reason. Like I could smell the smoke, I just couldn't see the fire.

Ryan and I made plans to save for a future home together, talked about engagement and wedding timelines. I saw and heard all of it with my own eyes, but something about it didn't feel real.

My body always tensed like I was waiting for the drop on a roller coaster during our entire relationship. Tense *and* hopeful, because I loved our little campus love story so much until finally ... the drop I'd been awaiting arrived.

He got offered a job in Minnesota. He'd told me he wanted to settle in Sweet River with me. We were saving for a house. We'd looked at rings. So my jaw dropped when he told me he'd taken the offer.

No conversation. And no invitation.

But I'd been honest when I told him I wanted my life here in Sweet River, so I wouldn't have moved with him if he'd asked. Maybe he'd known that.

*"I just don't feel anything growing here," he said, his voice tight. No growth? I thought our relationship was growing.*

*I wasn't throwing out accusations, though. I felt numb. I silently nodded.*

*"There's no development if I stay here. No upward mobility. My time here has served its purpose,"* he said apologetically.

*Was I just part of that purpose?* I looked at my hands, tangled in my lap. He hadn't said anything about our relationship, just on and on about his career, his goals.

For me, it'd been so much more than that. I'd loved Ryan and his always-organized desk, his brown, scuffed-up loafers, and the way he wanted to dream with me.

I'd thought I'd finally found someone who would stay.

*"There's got to be more to us than that, though,"* I said. *My voice was so quiet, he didn't even respond. I was too disappointed to even cry.*

On top of the shock and the heartbreak, I felt so embarrassed. *Had he always known he didn't mean it? Or was I just that easy to blow off for something better?* I couldn't decide which stung less.

In the year that followed, as I extracted Ryan from the beautiful life I'd built here in Sweet River, I realized I could keep all the beautiful parts. I didn't need Ryan, or anyone else, to make those dreams come true. I wanted to stick with the plan—my plan—with or without him.

So, I kept saving for that old house.

Last June, a year later, I finally joined the Sweet River Historical Society we'd talked about joining together. I sat in a plastic chair in a room of fellow Sweet River lovers and watched a slideshow go by of a historical house downtown. It looked like a dream come true.

I toured the house that day and saw rooms for me to decorate, a yard for me to barbecue in with my friends, shelves to paint, and walls to break down. I could already envision the light coming in through the back windows as I turned the pages in a good book.

Yes, *this* was what I'd wanted all along.

This dream was mine to begin with. I'd only briefly shared it with Ryan. When he left, I felt freedom in knowing he hadn't taken anything of mine with him. Not my dreams, not my heart.

Okay, he did take my favorite pumpkin mug.

# Six



Not sure what exactly Sonny saw happening in your office…but whatever it was, is not helping dial back the office gossip…

"Wait, wait, wait." Lucy dragged a french fry through ketchup. "Do you really think you can maintain lying to the whole school *for weeks*?"

We were in the shiny red booths at the old burger joint near Lucy's apartment. It had been a frequent dinner spot for us back when we still lived together. She'd picked me up from work because my car wouldn't be ready for me to pick up from the auto shop until the next morning, and since we hadn't adequately discussed the fiasco that was my morning, we decided to head straight for burgers and fries to finish hashing it out.

"Okay, first, *the whole school* doesn't even know who I am. Second, we're not lying. We're just letting people think whatever they want."

"Sure, if you make out with someone, it isn't technically

saying you're dating, but you can't deny that it does send a certain message, Olivia." Lucy raised a judgmental eyebrow.

"We won't be making out anymore," I said quickly, feeling my cheeks heat. And my chest. And my stomach.

"How was it, though?" She leaned in, elbows on the table. "The kiss?" she added in a whisper.

"Oh, I don't know, Luce." I let out a breath, trying to stay cool and collected, even as my body still felt Victor's hands on my waist like an imprint.

"Was it a peck?"

"Definitely not," I said without thinking.

Lucy squealed, bouncing in her seat. "I've been waiting for this."

"No, hold on." I placed a firm hand on the table. "Do not get your hopes up. This is pretend. The kiss was ..." But I couldn't get myself to call that kiss *pretend*. It felt as real as the heartbeat pounding in my chest.

"Sure, sure." Lucy grabbed another fry. "*Sure.*"

"Lucy, it'd be tougher at this point to try and explain to everyone on campus that we're not together. Plus, this way, I have a copilot with me through everything." I tried to recall the great points Victor had made when we schemed up this plan. It was convincing when he said it with all his charisma and confidence.

"A copilot?" Lucy's brows furrowed.

"Yeah, he can be like my sidekick. Since everyone thinks we're dating, he can tag along with me to every event and help me out with Ryan."

"You think Ryan will be that much of a nuisance?"

I suddenly felt defensive of my and Victor's plan. *Of course*, I needed Victor to accompany me to everything. "Maybe. I didn't expect him to show up this morning, so obviously, the man is full of surprises."

"Uh-huh," Lucy said slowly. "That's totally a valid reason to experiment with taking Victor along as your date—"

"No, no!" I nearly shouted, making Lucy break into giggles. "Don't make this a thing."

"You and Victor literally made this a thing all by yourselves."

"We're just ... you know ... He's so ..." I grabbed my sweet tea and took a long, sugary sip. "Anyway, whether you think it's a silly idea or not, I'll at least have some company with me on Friday. I can't believe these fall events I've been excited about will now include Ryan."

I wasn't sure Ryan would be that much of a nuisance for me on campus, but one of the upsides to his fleeing to Minnesota was no awkward ex run-ins. Now, I was guaranteed run-ins *at work*.

Lucy reached her arms across the table, covering my freckled hand with her own. "Do you want me to go give him a talkin' to?"

I snorted.

"Or I could go key his rental car or something. And, I mean, I don't think we should resort to violence, but I would kick his butt for you. If that's what you really need."

"I appreciate the offer." The idea of Lucy kicking Ryan's butt did bring a smile to my face. "I'm a big girl. I can handle it."

"You always do." Lucy gave me a small smile.

I felt my phone vibrate in my purse and slipped it out to find a message from Victor.

VICTOR

Mind if your new BF is working in your backyard when you get home?

That night, the sun was already starting to set by the time Lucy dropped me off in my driveway—the time of year when autumn ushers in dusk.

I immediately noticed Victor's truck was still here. My shoulders immediately dropped. That instant comfort Victor's presence brought me seemed to work even via his vehicle. Knowing he was near always settled my nerves.

I didn't see him at first. I crossed my deck and squinted toward the backyard until I spotted him beneath one of the big elm trees, surrounded by yellow and red leaves.

"What are you working on over there?" I asked, dropping my bags with a thud.

He popped his head out from behind the leaves. "Giving the birds somewhere to hang out other than your open window."

My mind flashed back to our conversation in my kitchen this morning. "Victor, I didn't mean for you to actually ..." My chest was feeling that familiar Victor tug, that sweet kind of ache.

"I know, I know, but ... you had a bad day. You looked so sad when you saw Ryan this morning." He shrugged. "I was thinking about you all day and thought this might ..."

"Be way too much?" I said, walking across the yard to him.

"*Make you feel better,*" he said, with those caramel eyes crinkling. "Come on over and check it out."

It was a small birdhouse in blonde wood nestled in my tallest elm tree. He'd put it together this evening while I ate burgers with Lucy. I could imagine him out here picking just the right tree and hanging it up carefully.

He'd even painted a message on it in thick black strokes: *bird families welcome here*. My own words this morning, *I don't want them to think they're not welcome here,* rang in my ears.

I rested my head on his shoulder. He smelled like sawdust and his spicy cologne, the scent he always wore. I had to resist the urge to wrap my arms all the way around him.

Over the last few months, he'd become one of my favorite people.

Not many people got to see this side of him—the birdhouse builder, the guy who knew what to fix before you even realized it was broken, a man who always showed up for everyone around him ... but I did. And I appreciated it more than he realized.

"This does make my day better," I said softly. I smiled, thinking of the little bird family out here in my trees this fall.

"Mission accomplished," he said, pulling me in for a small hug.

I hated, and loved, what that did to my heart.

We sat outside on my deck for the rest of the evening under a blanket of twinkling stars, talking about everything but the kiss and the campus charade. We talked about reality TV, his brother Gabe's upcoming wedding to Emma, and my mom joining the dating apps. It could've been any other night from the past summer, and maybe my heart needed just a normal night like that.

I wrapped my arms around my knees and let out a big yawn.

"Okay, sleepyhead, time for bed. You've had a long day," Victor said, standing up and stretching his arms behind his head. His biceps flexed under the sleeves of his shirt. "We can finish debating who really deserved the First Impression rose later this week."

I stood up with the words forming in my mouth— about the kiss, our friendship, pretending, how unsettled I felt about everything—but before I could say anything, he pulled me in for a tight hug.

"Get out of that head of yours," he said, reading me instantly.

I shook my head at him, smiling despite myself. He could always tell when I was anxious.

"Deep breaths, Liv. In and out," he said, modeling it dramatically for me as we hugged.

I could feel his chest rising and falling against me. I playfully shoved him away. "If only I could be as chill as you."

I didn't want to burst our safe little backyard bubble just yet, so I swallowed the worries and told him goodnight.

After he left, I tiptoed barefoot across the cool grass to the old tree where the birdhouse now hung. I knelt down, grabbed a handful of twigs and grass, and carried them over to the birdhouse, just a little something to help any future house guests get started nesting.

Then, I took a few steps back, smiling to myself as I took in the view of it swaying gently in the branches.

It felt like something was shifting in the air—a change blowing in with the breeze. I felt it in my bones, like something was also shifting in me.

# Seven

"I can't read second chance romance. It always makes me want to throw my Kindle across the room," one of the students in my romance book club explained passionately, rubbing their temples. "The female main character says she remembers how his lips used to feel, and all I can think is how remembering kisses with my ex makes me feel the *exact opposite.*"

I nodded along as we sat in a semicircle under the shade of my favorite tree. I agreed with this student. There was nothing I wanted less than a second chance with the ex I'd been dodging on campus this morning.

"Are you kidding? Second chance romance gives you the best pining!" another student nearly squealed.

A trope debate was on the horizon again. I could appreciate pretty much every trope, even if my own ex felt like an annoying gnat I wished I could swat away.

The conversation was a murmur around me. I let my eyes roam the campus.

*Was it really only yesterday I was carefree and leading Victor along these sidewalks? Kissing him in my office?*

*Was there some way I could exchange Ryan for Victor's presence on campus?*

Later, after the club dispersed, I headed straight to my favorite coffee cart. It was a cool, overcast morning, with the trees blazing in rusts and golds against the gray sky. I kept my cardigan wrapped tight a little longer.

I stepped up to order my coffee, and the blonde-haired barista from yesterday was grinning back at me.

"Annie, hi," I said, remembering her name even though Victor hadn't exactly introduced us yesterday. She seemed to be burned into my brain for reasons I didn't want to examine.

"Hi," she said, her eyes squinting, head tilting, like she was trying to place me.

"Victor Hernandez's friend from yesterday," I offered. "I'm Olivia."

I guess I wasn't burned into her brain in quite the same way.

She nodded. "Yeah, yeah, that's right." She opened her mouth like she was about to say something else but then quickly pressed her lips back together, before asking for my order instead.

A few moments later, she handed me my hot chai latte. As I wrapped my hands around the warm paper cup, she blurted out, "Olivia, are you and Victor together?"

I took a step back, taken aback by her directness. "It's ..." *New? A ruse?* I swallowed. "Complicated?"

She buried her face in her hand. "I don't know why I asked. I'm sorry."

I shook my head, with auburn strands breaking loose from my ponytail. "Don't worry." I turned to leave but hesitated. Annie had popped into my mind several times since yesterday.

*Was she Victor's type? Did they text? Had they kissed? Had he met up with her after hanging around my house, painting with me all day?*

I didn't want to care about any of that, but as much as I tried to fight it, a part of me really cared.

I turned to her. "Did you and Victor ...?" I winced, hearing that question in my own voice, as if the words left my mouth of their own accord.

Her eyes dropped as she shook her head. "No," she said. "For a minute, I thought we might."

"Oh," I said, annoyed at the relief flooding my body.

"I should've known better." She rolled her eyes. "He's Victor Hernandez, you know." She said the last part as if I'd commiserate, as if I knew exactly what she meant.

*He's Victor Hernandez* rang in my ears the whole walk back to my office.

I plopped down in my office chair, dropping everything on my desk. Annie's remark was like a little alarm bell waking me up from this silly fantasy I was about to let myself get swept away in. Because I did know exactly what she meant.

I knew Victor's reputation. He was young and carefree. He was one of the handsome Hernandez brothers from Sweet River —the one who notoriously broke hearts. *He's not into serious relationships*, was something I'd often heard people say about him when chatting with my friends, back before we'd developed our own friendship. *He's not the type of guy you'd hang your hopes on*, they'd sigh, and I'd nod along.

Now that I knew Victor better, I did notice that his reputation was right. He was never seriously dating anyone, or dating anyone *at all*, for that matter. Maybe he just wasn't interested right now. He was still young and figuring out the next steps in his life.

Yet, there was a part of my heart that tugged toward him. But if he was the type of guy who didn't get into serious relationships, I was the type of girl who couldn't ignore alarm bells. I'd watched my own dad walk out when I was a little girl; even my straight-laced, safe-as-they-come boyfriend had left. If I were guessing, young and playful Victor would definitely have an expiration date in my life.

Even if he kissed me in my office in a way that I couldn't get out of my head

"Do not let this get you all confused, Olivia," I chastised myself in a whisper. I was nearly thirty. I knew better by now.

My phone vibrated on my desk, jolting me from my thoughts. A message from Victor appeared on the screen.

VICTOR

am I still the talk of the campus today?

I typed up a quick reply. *Definitely. It misses you already.*

But then I let my fingers hover over the screen for a moment, rereading it before tapping delete until each letter was gone. I let out a slow breath. *That was too flirty, right?* I chewed on my lip.

*Since when did I overthink my messages to Victor?* I was letting the kiss get my insides all twisted.

I pushed my phone away, deciding to worry about the reply later, waking up my computer screen instead.

V ictor didn't come over the next few days, which I tried telling myself was a good thing. I could use that time to make sure my head was in order when it came to him and whatever our arrangement was going to be, stacking up my thoughts and feelings like loose paperwork.

I also used that time to research classes and workshop ideas, printing out syllabi and reading lists. One rainy evening, they were scattered around my feet as Julia Roberts filled my TV screen and a half-drunk glass of red wine sweated on my coffee table.

"None of these courses feel right," I told Gracie, who had FaceTimed me in the middle of my messy evening. I twisted my phone so she could see the papers everywhere.

"I'm sorry you're still stuck," she sympathized, sticking out her lower lip.

"I can't imagine my students getting excited about any of these."

"Well, I'm sorry. I know you, Liv. You won't settle until you find just the right course," she said encouragingly before switching gears. "How's everything else going in your life? How're things *on campus*?" Her voice was higher as she finished the sentence.

*Was she probing?*

I sank deeper into the couch. Rain pattered against the window. "Campus life, huh? Well, the romance book club met up today. It turned into a venting session for some college romance drama."

Gracie sighed. "I personally don't have any time for college romance."

"You're not letting yourself get too overwhelmed again, are you?" My voice went nearly maternal. Gracie had a history of overworking herself and cramming her schedule to breaking point. Where I built nearly too many boundaries in my life, people-pleasing Gracie tended to forget boundaries altogether, especially with her time.

I pulled the phone close to my face and narrowed my eyes.

"No, no," she said in a soothing tone. "Don't worry about me. I've just plugged practice in where dating would normally go."

"I don't even know where dating would normally go in my own life."

"Hey, how's Vic?" Gracie cut in, her brows raised.

My palms felt instantly sweaty. *My palms do not need to sweat over Victor.* "He's fine, why?"

"Because he's become your best friend over the past few months, and you care about him?"

"You're not asking about any of my other friends." I sounded way too defensive.

"Why are you feeling defensive, Liv?" She raised a brow.

I took a long gulp of my plummy cabernet to stall.

"I mean, I'd be defensive too if I'd made out with my hot best friend on my office desk."

I nearly spit out my wine. "*On* my office desk?"

Gracie fell off her bed laughing.

"Freaking Lucy Rhodes!" I shouted. "We were not *on* the desk." But I could imagine us on the desk. And my stomach dipped.

"*But you did make out in your office.* We've been talking for nearly an hour—were you just not going to tell me?"

"Did Lucy say it was on the desk?" I demanded.

"Olivia! Focus. Why didn't you tell me about the kiss?" She held the phone close to her face, like she was trying to get a better view of me.

I sighed. My little sisters were exhausting. "I didn't want to get your hopes up. Or have to explain why it didn't mean anything, you know? *Because it didn't mean anything.*" Then I added, "Plus, why tell you when I know Lucy will do that for me?"

Mom would probably be calling to sniff around for more details soon.

"So, it doesn't mean anything?" Gracie said. "You kiss your best friend in what Lucy said was *definitely not a peck,* and ... somehow, it means nothing?"

"It was an accident," I said. "I'm sure you've heard the whole story." She probably heard the whole story, *plus* Lucy's added embellishments for dramatic flourish.

"If it didn't mean anything, I guess that means you didn't feel anything? No sparks?" Gracie asked.

I remembered his hands on my waist, his lips rough against mine, his warmth and woodsy scent. I remembered everything it made me feel. Like he'd started a wildfire across my skin.

"It's Victor. It's not about feelings or sparks with him."

"Why not?" Gracie nearly shouted.

I reached for the soft gray throw blanket Grandma Rhodes had knitted for me years ago and pulled it around myself for comfort. "Because he's my best friend. Okay? I don't want to ruin that." I hesitated, looking down for a beat. "Plus, he's not ready for anything serious. He even broke the coffee cart girl's heart!"

"The coffee cart girl?"

"There's a new server at my favorite coffee cart. Victor had like a thing with her, and she told me how she should've known better since he is *Victor Hernandez,* after all." I made air quotes around his name with my fingers. "Gracie, even the coffee cart girl knows you can't let yourself get caught up in feelings when it comes to him."

"But the coffee cart girl doesn't know Victor the way you do."

I open my mouth, but a response evades me. I let out a breath.

"You've gotten to know him over the past, what? Six months? He's your best friend. You know him better than that. He's over fixing your freaking deck, not out breaking hearts." Gracie laughed as if it were the silliest thing she'd ever heard.

I nestled deeper into the couch, because that was the problem. He *was* the sweet, dependable Victor who fixed my deck and knew me better than any best friend I'd ever had ... but he was also the one person who could absolutely demolish my heart.

# Eight



De nocte cenae nostrae excitatur!

...was any of that right?

(it's supposed to say I'm excited about our dinner tonight)



That was mostly right. I'm proud of you!!

I can't believe you're actually learning Latin.



you inspire me

you make me want to learn more

plus, now I've gotta keep up with my pretend gf's coworkers and all the languages they've studied

Friday came, and I could barely focus at work. There were lectures to give and essays to read and grade, but in the background, my mind kept sounding the alarm: *call off the charade.*

If this fake date with Victor managed to not blow up our friendship, it could easily blow up my work life. I wasn't living in some silly romcom movie. I'd worked too hard to start playing make-believe in front of my colleagues.

I spent my entire lunch break anxiously chewing through my salad, on the precipice of calling Victor and telling him the plan was off. That I'd suck it up and go to my work dinner on my own like the full-grown woman I was.

But I didn't.

Because I was torn.

Until a few days ago, I hadn't seen Ryan since our breakup. And this next time would be with all my coworkers, all of whom had known us as a couple when we were *Ryan and Livvy.* I shuddered at the memory of that old nickname he'd given me. I'd tried so hard to make myself like it.

And Victor had a way of calming me down and making everything more fun. He made things that were usually hard, like knocking down a wall or having tough conversations with my family, feel easier. I knew having Victor by my side would make so much of my anxiety around this evening fizzle out.

So, I put off calling him, even as it ate away at me the rest of the afternoon.

Finally, on the drive home from work, I knew it was time to call him and put an end to the insane plan we'd concocted in our post-kiss haze.

"Hey, you." His voice echoed through my car. "You getting ready for our big date?"

"I'm just driving home from work, actually," I said through the knot in my throat.

"You know, I'm actually pretty excited. I can't wait to see you all fixed up and meet your boss."

"Meet my boss?" I choked. *What would Victor even say to my boss?* I couldn't handle bringing her into our scheme. This was such a bad idea.

"Of course. That's at the top of my list." His voice muffled on the other line for a second, like he had the phone propped between his shoulder and ear. "How're you feeling about it?"

"I ... I don't know. I'm rethinking it."

"*Rethinking* it?" His voice sharpened. "Why?"

"I've been thinking about what a wild idea it is to bring you as a fake date to my workplace," I said. "I don't know what I've been thinking. I can handle seeing Ryan on my own. I don't need to drag you into drama and risk our friendship ... or my job—"

"Olivia," Victor cut in, voice steady and calm. "I'm not your fake date. I'm your *real* date. I'm your best friend. Why not bring your best friend?"

I nodded along, listening from my driver's seat.

"Our only plan is not to correct anyone. That's it. We're not making a scene. We're just letting them call us whatever they want to. I don't think you're risking your job—or us—by bringing your best friend, someone who really cares about you, to your work dinner."

I sighed, hitting my blinker as I took the exit. He made it sound so simple and harmless compared to the dumpster fire my brain was creating.

"Besides." He broke through my thoughts. "I want to go. I'm excited. You dump me now, and *that'll* cause some drama in our friendship."

"Really?" Maybe I was simply overthinking the whole thing.

"Really," Victor said, a car door slamming on his end of the line. "And, admit it, you're nervous to see Ryan. That's normal. That doesn't make you weak or immature, it makes you human, and your friend wants to be there for you—let him. *Let me.*"

I swallowed, my grip tight around the steering wheel. "Okay."

"You need to take a deep breath," he said, reminding me to

inhale and exhale, my chest expanding and contracting underneath my seat belt. "I think tonight will be fun, honestly."

I stood in the middle of my closet, surrounded by dresses, jackets, and sweaters, but I still didn't have anything to wear to the fancy work dinner. I'd had a couple of options in mind—a slinky green dress, maybe a red jumper, but now, under pressure, neither felt right. And Victor would be here in less than an hour, so I had no time to waste.

I had an idea, so I pulled out my phone and called up Lucy. The moment she picked up, I blurted, "Can I borrow a dress?"

"Do you have a specific dress in mind, or do I need to bring over options?" she replied without missing a beat. Her blinker clicked, and the low hum of her car buzzed in the background.

I closed my eyes. A couple of weeks ago, we'd gone shopping, and I'd talked her into buying a silky black slip dress. I ran my fingers across the clothes hanging around me, the material rough underneath my fingers. "That black dress you bought the other day?"

"I knew you wanted that dress for yourself." She chuckled. "I'm heading home from work now. I'll grab it and bring it over."

"You're doing that deep breathing thing you do when you're stressed out," Lucy said, with her head cocked to the side as she examined me from her spot lounging on my bed. My oat-colored comforter was bunched up under her stomach. "Is it because of Ryan?"

"Well, Luce, I'm not exactly thrilled he's going to be there," I muttered, even though I was nervous about so much more than Ryan.

I twirled around in front of my full-length mirror, smoothing the black silky material with my shaking hands.

"I hope it doesn't ruin the fancy dinner for you. I know

you've been excited about it. But, hey, at least Victor will be there." Lucy crossed her ankles in the air behind her. "Honestly, him showing up as your date will probably make it things just as awkward for Ryan. So you won't be the only person suffering tonight."

"Making it awkward for Ryan wasn't really my intention, you know," I said, turning to Lucy. "I just wanted to have my person there."

She had her thinking face on. Her nose was all scrunched up. "Victor's your person?"

"Well, yeah, but I didn't mean my person *like that*." I crossed my arms. "Not like how Adam is your person."

"How did you mean 'your person,' then?" Lucy sat up on the bed, serious about this conversation.

My nerves were already on edge. I didn't have the emotional bandwidth to be grilled about my feelings for Victor by one of my sisters again. "He's become one of my closest friends. It's as simple as that."

"Well, he's a good person to have," Lucy said. Victor hadn't just won me over this summer. He'd made fans out of the whole Rhodes clan. "Is knowing he's going to be there helping you feel better about tonight at all?"

I turned to her and let out a big exhale. "Not the way I'd hoped."

"I can tell." She gave me a sympathetic pout.

The room was getting darker, aglow with only a couple of lamps.

"The last time my colleagues saw Ryan and me in the same room, we were *Ryan and Olivia*, the golden couple of the history department." I twisted my auburn hair into a low knot at the base of my neck. "After he left, I wasn't half of a couple anymore. I became poor Olivia, left behind by Ryan."

I paused, catching eyes with Lucy in the reflection of the mirror.

"I worked hard to finally become *just Olivia*. To rebuild my identity at the school outside of him. And now, I'm afraid of what will be going through everyone's heads tonight. What if Ryan's presence reminds them how I was pathetically dumped? One day, we were together, popping in and out of each other's offices, and then abruptly, it was just me alone in my office. Everyone would poke their head in with this pitying little look."

I still remembered that look—the awkward shrug and down-cast eyes. The bone-deep embarrassment I'd feel every time I saw it, wishing I could hide under my desk.

"No one will feel sorry for you, Olivia. That department knows—and has seen—what a strong, capable woman you are. They've had front row tickets to see how you've bloomed out of his shade," Lucy said, then with a conspiratorial grin added, "Plus, you're going to have a hot date on your arm. No one will feel bad for *you*."

I laughed despite my heart knotting up in my chest and trying to crawl out of my throat.

"I had my worries about letting everyone think Victor is your boyfriend, but I'm actually really glad he's going with you tonight. I hope you can loosen up and forget Ryan's even there. Your department is big—you might not even see him, you know?"

"Can I tell you?" I said, turning back to my mirror. "I'm a little nervous to see how Victor interacts with my colleagues. I've never seen the man in a serious setting, much less a dinner with the head of my department."

Lucy chuckled. "I mean, what's the worst that could happen?"

I had a few ideas. "I could see this little plan of ours going awry. Maybe I feel sick and should stay home?" I stopped combing back my flyaways.

"You look too hot to stay in." Lucy slid off the bed, coming over to stand behind me in front of the mirror. "But you do need big hoops with this hairdo."

Lucy's messy red hair was pouring out of her own claw clip. She started digging through my jewelry. I looked in the mirror, remembering how Ryan used to complain that I "never let my hair down." He'd sometimes pull it out of its ponytail when we were out, without even asking me, no matter how many times I'd explained how I liked my hair out of my face while I worked.

And I like how it looked. Lucy and Gracie always said I had my Olivia Power Pony. It was an Olivia trademark.

I looked at my sleek auburn bun. Ryan would hate it. And I loved it, smiling in the mirror at my reflection and the sprinkling of freckles across my nose.

Victor had his hands on the doorframe when I opened the front door, leaning over me in his navy button-down and slacks.

"Well, hello." I shook my head. He couldn't just stand on my front porch in a normal way. The porch swing rocked in the breeze.

"Hello to you, too." His eyes lit up as they tripped down my body in the silky black dress. As he brought his eyes back up to meet mine, my stomach fluttered.

*That's just the Victor effect*, I reminded myself. The pitfalls of having such a charming and disarmingly attractive friend.

"How're you feeling about tonight?" He stepped back, bringing his arms down to his sides, fixing his sleeves. Wavy dark hair tamed, he looked good—too good.

I hated how possessive it made me feel, how it made me anxious about all the other baristas that may be in his life that I didn't know about.

"I'm feeling optimistic," I said, turning to lock my front door. "How are you feeling?"

"Lucky, honestly," he said, his voice soft around the edges.

I turned back to him, meeting his gaze.

"Look at you. And I get to be the one by your side all night."

I felt my cheeks go pink. "Such a flirt."

"No, no." He shook his head. "Not flirting. Just being honest. I mean, *come on,* Olivia." His eyes were wide on me.

I hopped down the front steps toward his truck. "You clean up pretty well yourself."

A smile broke across his face, his eyes crinkling. "You think?"

I giggled. "Why do you make everything *a thing*? Can't I just say you look nice tonight?"

"Says the woman who branded me a flirt for saying she looked nice tonight." Victor opened the truck door for me. "Why you gotta always make everything a thing, Liv?"

I shoved his shoulder before sliding into the front seat. His car smelled like him—sawdust, mint, and that spicy cologne of his.

He started his car seconds later, and "She's My Kind of Rain" filled the car. "A classic," Victor said, humming along.

Sitting in the passenger seat in Victor's truck while the two of us bickered and laughed was one of my favorite places in the world, whether we were heading for a late-night Taco Bell or heading to a dinner party. It made my blood pressure lower, as if something in Victor's DNA was a natural repellent for my anxious thoughts.

He looked at me from the corner of his eye, reaching across the console and brushing his fingertips against my bare neck, goose bumps scattering at his touch. "I love when you wear your hair like this."

My mouth went dry, my heart skittering in my chest. "Like what?"

"Pulled up?" He searched for the words. "Pulled back? I just like seeing your whole face. And your neck."

I laughed nervously, trying to gather my feelings into something small I could tuck away. "You like my neck?"

His eyes went a little darker. The truck hit a pothole. "I *do* like your neck."

Sometimes, he made my blood pressure lower. Sometimes, he made my heart rate spike. "See, you *are* a flirt. That was a flirty comment."

"I'm simply answering a question." He smiled crookedly, with his eyes flickering between me and the road.

"You have a nice neck, too," I conceded, as we exited on the highway that took us from Sweet River to the school.

He chuckled as I pulled on the collar near his neck. As my fingers brushed against his warm, tan skin, his breath caught.

I felt an urge to run my fingers higher up until they tangled into his inky hair, to make his breathing go rough.

I yanked my hand down and nestled deeper into my seat, swallowing back those thoughts.

"How're you doing, Liv?" Victor assessed me for a second before glancing back toward the road. "How's this week been with Ryan running around campus?"

"It's been ..." I let my voice trail off as I thought about my last week on campus. Ryan hadn't really been part of it.

"What's going on up there?" He tapped a finger lightly against my temple.

"A lot is going on in my head, honestly."

"Always."

"You know what it's been like, having Ryan there? Annoying. It's not been heartbreaking or sad, even. It's been irritating, knowing he's around. I think like six months ago, maybe it would've been harder. But I've come a lot further than I realized."

"Maybe seeing him is a good thing, then? It can show you how far you've come. Sometimes, you undersell yourself."

"You think?" That was funny. I always thought Victor was the one underselling *himself*.

"I do think so. You undersell yourself at your job. You don't need to be scouring old classes to imitate. I think you could come up with a class all on your own, and it would be amazing. You undersell yourself with your house. You always think you owe so much to my help, but I feel like I'm just following your lead most of the time." He couldn't keep his eyes on the road, glancing back at me every few seconds, hand waving in the air for emphasis. "Even with this. You were freaked out about having Ryan back on campus, but I knew you could handle it like a boss. You barely ever need me for half the stuff I try to help you with." Victor said this with a tone of awe.

He meant it as a compliment, but my heart felt defensive of his role in my life.

"I do need you, Victor," I said, an embarrassingly vulnerable tone to my voice. I didn't want him wandering out of my life, thinking I didn't need him around.

"Oh, don't worry. I don't trust you with a chainsaw or anything. I'll still be there to build your bookshelves and whatever you need. I'm just saying ..." He drummed his fingers against the steering wheel. "I'm just saying you don't realize how amazing you are in a multitude of ways."

I chewed on my lip, with a new country song crooning through the truck.

"Anyway," Victor said before I could respond. "What's our game plan tonight?"

"I don't think we go in with a game plan. I like what you said earlier. We'll just let people call it whatever they want," I offered, my heart racing at the reminder of our ruse.

"So, no making out on your desk again?" he joked.

I choked on air. "No, there'll be no need for that," I said, my face hot. I even touched my cheeks.

His eyes twinkled. "If that changes, I'm here."

"Victor." I closed my eyes, shaking my head.

Texas fall was moody. Some days, it was crisp and cool, and then by the afternoon, it was sticky and humid.

Tonight, as we strolled across the dimly lit campus, there was a light chill in the air. I rubbed my bare arms. Victor's eyes tracked the movement.

He had slipped on a dark sports coat after he parked his truck. Noting my cold arms, he immediately shrugged it off and wrapped it around my shoulders.

It was warm and smelled like him. I tugged it tighter around me as we walked up the cement steps toward the wide glass doors of the history building.

"You know," he whispered, leaning closer to my ear, eyeing his jacket around my shoulders, "you *do* look like my girlfriend right now."

I grinned as he pulled the door open for me.

"Olivia!" Gabby raced over to me, her long, velvety, plum dress swaying at her ankles. "I—" But then she stopped, her gaze stopping on Victor. "Wait, you brought Victor?"

"Duh." Victor slung an arm around me, his fingertips pressing into my shoulder.

"Yeah, the invitation said we could bring a plus-one," I said.

"Are you wearing his jacket?" Gabby crossed her arms, eyes assessing the two of us.

"I was cold." I shimmied the jacket off my shoulders.

Victor's face fell.

I immediately missed the warmth. "What's up?"

Gabby chewed on her lip, as if she were considering asking something else. "Okay, this whole situation distracted me. I came over to tell you that the bar has fall-themed cocktails, and they're actually good. So, come along." She grabbed my hand to drag me through the sea of fellow professors, department aids, and staff. The scent of warm perfumes and cheesy appetizers wafted by my nose.

I glanced behind me to make sure I hadn't lost Victor. His eyes were on me, smirking amusedly at this other version of me. The one who wore silky dresses, attended events with open bars, and had work friends who definitely knew about him.

I asked the bartender for a spiced apple fizz, and Victor got a maple old fashioned. The hard apple cider and honey were warm on my tongue. A couple of my work friends joined us by the bar, eager to meet *my date*, Victor.

Victor fit naturally into my evening, into this other part of my life. He asked thoughtful questions, eager to learn everything he could about Professor Olivia. His arm was always around me, which hadn't been part of our game plan, but I guess we didn't have one. There was no label, no rules, letting how we fit together say it all. His presence felt steady, comforting, and frighteningly addictive.

I was taking the last crisp sip of my drink, deep in conversation with the head of my department, Dean Oates, about the coming semester, when Victor chimed in.

"I've loved hearing about Olivia's romance book club with the students," he said, beaming.

My heart stopped. The book club was ninety percent accidental, and I hadn't ever run it by the department. It honestly felt separate, like a vacation, from the school. I wasn't sure how my bosses would react.

I glanced nervously toward Victor for help, but he was the one who'd randomly dropped the conversation dynamite.

Dean Oates raised an eyebrow, her glossy lips pursed. "Romance book club?"

"Yeah, it was honestly just a few friends reading romance books together, and a few students joined in ..." I put the empty glass to my mouth and took a fake sip, my mouth suddenly dry. "It's very unofficial."

"You know, I've heard some rumblings about this book club here and there, now that you mention it." She tucked a strand of her chestnut hair behind her ear. "I've heard the students really love it."

"You should see a couple of the emails students have sent her thanking her for including them," Victor chimed in. He gave my arm an encouraging squeeze.

"I'm not surprised. I know I'd love to be part of something like that. Nothing like decompressing with a romcom," Dean Oates said.

I tried to imagine professional, academic Dean Oates curled up with one of my favorite romcoms.

"Honestly, some of the kids have actually drawn some parallels toward what we're studying and learning with some of the romances we're reading. It's been fun to hear it pop up in our book club chats." I felt myself talking quicker in that way I did when someone got me started on something I was passionate about.

"I love that, Dr. Rhodes. It's been fun to see some of the ways academia is starting to utilize and embrace popular culture. Here it is popping up naturally on campus." She smiled, then someone across the room caught her eye. She raised a hand to them. "It's been nice to chat and nice to meet you." She smiled at Victor. "I have someone over there I need to talk to."

She hurried away in her heels.

I spun to Victor. "I'm so relieved she loved the idea of our book club." I laughed breathlessly. "I would go down swinging for that club."

"See? You totally undersell yourself," he said, shaking my shoulders in faux frustration, grinning down at me. "Olivia Rhodes, you have such good ideas. Such good instincts."

"Like bringing you as my date?" The words tumbled out. Stupid fizz.

He chuckled. "Like your passion about this book club. Follow your passion, Liv. It ends up bringing good things into your life."

Like it brought me to this school. And to my book club. And to my historical house.

And to Victor.

"Passion has always scared me," I confessed, my voice soft, as if I couldn't quite commit to sharing this with him. The room was loud around us.

"Your dad?"

Victor knew. He'd heard my stories. Most of my life, *passion* had sounded impulsive and reckless to me, like when I was eight years old and my dad packed up one night and left my mom and sisters. Mom had always described Dad as *passionate*. She'd said he was just too passionate. He couldn't be tied down.

So, I didn't have any use for passion or recklessness while growing up. Better yet, I had an aversion to it.

I'd spent most of my life searching for the opposite of my father. Where he had been reckless, I sought structure. While he'd left my family, I stayed.

I looked for what had put the pieces of our family back together after he broke us—and my mom. She rebuilt a life for us through long night shifts, raising three girls on a nurse's salary, and sheer willpower. Her steady presence, fierce commitment, and fastidious work ethic—that was my blueprint.

I found comfort in my mirrored work ethic. My own planner

was clutched tight. My to-do lists and routine were something I could rely on.

I liked that my job didn't rely on whims or feelings. It revolved around things you could rely on, like research, facts, and best of all, *history*. History stayed still. It wasn't going anywhere. Most of my colleagues and I had committed our entire work lives to a specific era. We were a committed bunch—no flights of fancy. No changing our minds.

Victor cleared his throat, waking me from my thoughts. "It surprises me. You're obviously passionate about history, you know." His voice was as soft, gentle as mine had been. I leaned in closer to hear him.

"I guess that's one way to describe it." The room was warm, crowded. Someone bumped into me with an apologetic wince.

"Maybe your dad was passionate. He was also selfish. And dumb. Those were probably his worst problems."

"Immature, too," I added. That was another way my mom had always described him.

"Plus, your mom is always passionate."

My brows furrowed. I wasn't sure I agreed. I also wasn't sure this party was the place for our conversation.

"About you and your sisters—she's the *most* passionate. All of you Rhodes women are." He took a sip of his drink, giving me a beat to process.

I chewed on my lip, Victor's tender gaze on me. "I guess I just like to do my research first."

"Yeah, yeah. I love my little bookworm. But don't mistake stagnation for preparation, Liv."

His words sliced through, a knife between my ribs. I looked up, mouth agape.

"I want to see you—" But before he could finish his thought, we were interrupted.

"Well, hello," Ryan said, his eyes on me, his back toward Victor. He followed my eyes past his shoulder toward Victor. "Oh. Hi."

"Hey, man." Victor lifted his chin, hands in his pockets.

"I thought I'd check in," he said apologetically, shoulders rising with each word.

"On?" I asked.

"How you're ... doing?" It felt like he'd wanted to say "holding up" but stopped himself.

"She's great. Dean Oates was just talking about how excited she is for Liv to start putting together the curriculum for her own class next semester," Victor said, stepping beside me, slinging an arm around my shoulder.

Ryan's eyes went wide. "Wow, Olivia, that's a big step for you."

I burrowed deeper into Victor's arm, his fingers brushing my shoulder. "I've been doing my research, compiling ideas."

"If you need advice, I'm here the next few weeks!" Ryan chuckled.

Victor's smile fell flat.

"Sure," I said. *Please, someone, say cocktail hour is over.*

"Man, I'm trying to remember when I started designing my own classes." Ryan squinted, eyes upward.

"I'm sure it's been a while. Honestly, you should be asking Liv for advice now. She is so good at knowing what her students need. She even has a book club with her students that's been a huge hit." Victor's eyes were on me the entire time he spoke, like he was really saying all of this as a reminder to me.

"Oh, a book club?" Ryan asked.

"Yeah, a romance book club." Victor beamed.

Ryan smirked. "I forgot about your little guilty pleasure."

"Guilty pleasure?" Victor asked, tugging me closer.

"That's what Ryan always called my love of reading romance. My 'little guilty pleasure,'" I said, monotone. I'd always cringed at the scene he'd make at the bookstore when I grabbed anything that wasn't critically acclaimed, or the way he'd roll his eyes when I'd carry a love story around in my tote bag with us.

"Why?" Victor was confused because Victor didn't have a condescending bone in his body.

"It embarrassed Ryan that someone he dated would read romance." I shrugged.

"It's not that. I just personally can't read books like that—the characters are always so immature—"

"Oh, sure," Victor said with a grin. "Because people in love are known for acting rationally and maturely?"

Ryan cleared his throat. "It's not just that. Those books tend to be overly sweet, like sweet as sugar—"

Victor slipped his arm around my waist. "Well then, better steer clear of me. When I fall for a girl, I'm a total sap. I'll give that girl a toothache." Victor looked down at me playfully. "Ain't that right, baby girl?"

I tried to bite back the laugh that bubbled up.

Ryan took a long gulp from his drink, eyes flicking between us. "I have a few more people to check in with." He paused, then turned to leave. "Good luck with your book club."

After he'd disappeared into the crowd, I turned to Victor, shaking my head with laughter. *"Ain't that right, baby girl?"* I said, mimicking his voice through a grin.

A proud smile spread across Victor's face. "That was pretty good, huh? He couldn't stand me." He beamed as if that was the greatest achievement.


A farm-style oak dining table. A headboard built from a refurbished barn door. Mahogany bookshelves with ivy etched into the side. I was sliding through a folder in my phone titled *Victor's AMAZING Creations* with an older professor named Charles with gray hair and thick black glasses. "Okay, okay, but see, I love this coffee table." I zoomed in closer to tiny ornamental carvings of leaves on the table legs. "Look at this detailing!"

Victor was blushing beside me. He grinned down at his plate.

Our meal was being catered by a restaurant, the Vintage Table. Their famous fall dish was roasted mini pumpkins stuffed with an herby wild rice blend.

I'd devoured mine, and Victor had been telling me on the drive over how he hoped and prayed they would serve those "life-alteringly good little pumpkins," but instead had only nibbled on his.

Probably because showing off my Victor Fan Girl album was one of the only moments in the evening that he hadn't been the life of the party.

I'd sat beside him, starry-eyed. He'd told the best history puns (*had he googled these beforehand?*), asked the right questions that led to fun dinner party conversations, started one heated debate about the Sea People, and somehow, using his Olivia-whisperer skills, he'd pulled me, the department's resident introvert, into all of it.

I'd worked at this school for years, and yet tonight was one of the first times I'd felt my department had seen the real me. How I snorted when I laugh. Funny tidbits about me that Victor brought up. All these little pieces of me were tightly tucked behind my polished Dr. Rhodes persona.

I closed my phone screen. "See? He's underselling his talent."

"Well, Victor, you got the president of your fan club, right here," Charles said, pointing to me.

A small votive flickered in the middle of the table.

"I am a fan. Deservedly so." I gave Victor's shoulder a squeeze.

Victor leaned closer, lowering his head near mine, whispering, "You're doing it again." His breath was hot against my ear. "You sound like my ... you know." *Girlfriend.*

A nervous laugh escaped me, but that was the goal, right? Then why did it feel dangerous? Like a secret I was accidentally sharing with my table of coworkers?

"Okay, you two," June, my colleague and friend, interrupted Victor and me, patting both her hands on the table. "How did you meet? I know you were friends for a while." Her gaze bounced between us. "What's the story here?"

The table is long, and our conversations had mostly been confined to my end of it. But after June's question, we caught a few new listeners from the other end. Ryan's ears even perked up.

I swallowed, my mouth instantly dry. I'd been okay letting people believe what they wanted to believe and play into it a bit, but I didn't want to outright lie. Should I speak up now? Tell them the truth? Set everyone straight?

I glanced up at Victor, who looked calm, unfazed as he'd been all night.

He cleared his throat before beginning. "It's a good story, actually. See, her sister was working with *my* boss. It was a ... well, let's say, *tenuous* working relationship at first, so my boss had asked me to show up to one of their coffee meet-ups to help smooth things over."

"And I showed up to be nosy," I added, following Victor's lead. "I wanted to check out who my sister had been griping about." The table chuckled in response.

Now, Victor's eyes were on me. "But the minute she walked in the door with ..." He waved a hand in front of me. "*This face.* These freckles. She had on a tank top and jeans. I still remember the paint she had on her arms. I think I stopped breathing when I saw her." He shivered, as if the memory affected him.

The table laughed. But his voice was serious, eyes still on me. "I completely abandoned my boss, Adam. He asked me later where I went, but I had gotten in line with Olivia, pretending I couldn't decide on what milk alternative I wanted just to keep her talking."

I'd forgotten about the first oat milk versus almond milk chat. Now the memory came back to me—how we'd discussed that whole latte he ordered, oat versus almond, vanilla versus caramel, foam or no foam, all of it.

"That entire milk debate was fake?" I asked, narrowing my eyes. *Was he being honest, or was this for the charade?*

"Olivia, have I ever used oat milk again?"

I hadn't ever noticed that it'd always been whole milk since then. But the debate had been fun. Discussing anything with Victor was fun.

"I even looked up articles—"

"Yes, you did. It was adorable. Your knack for research kept you in line with me longer. I loved it. Still use that tactic to keep you with me longer."

*How many pretend research assignments had I been on?*

"We wound up talking about that old house of hers. I was intrigued by this smart, stunning woman covered in paint, saying she was going to knock out a bunch of walls. I liked her, liked knocking out walls, so I couldn't resist weaseling my way into more of her life."

"I'm grateful. I definitely needed help with those walls." I held up my hands as if in defeat.

"I harbored a crush, but she was obviously way out of my league—"

"Don't say that." I shook my head. Victor was in a league of his own.

"It's true, though. It's why I didn't push it. Somehow, so easily, we became best friends. We talked about everything. We built things together. She's basically a stepmother to my dog, Watson."

"When did you two ... become more?" June asked.

The table hushed, leaning in to hear Victor. Even I was enraptured, waiting to hear what he'd say next.

He took a deep breath, dark eyes locking on mine. "We kissed. It was a good kiss. The kind of kiss that made me think: *hey, maybe I'm not the only one that feels that there's something here.* Now ... here we are."

Someone whooped. There was a ripple of "oohs" and "ahhs" around the table. My heart skipped like a record, stuck on the fact that this story didn't sound fake at all. Every part was real, except maybe how he felt after our kiss.

I wasn't sure if he was enhancing the story for our ridiculous charade, or if our kiss had messed with his mind like it had messed with mine.

If our kiss left him with aftershocks. If he relived it in the space between dream and sleep. Because I did. Eyes closed, blankets over my head, Victor's lips stained on mine.

*Ten*

D inner was over before I was ready. I'd happily take Victor by my side at every future work dinner, even if we were only pretending. We walked out the door together, with my arm hooked in his, after saying goodbye to people, when I noticed him glance down at his watch.

"Hey, can I show you something funny on campus?" I felt a desperate urge to keep the night going just a little longer. Similarly to how I tried to keep him working at my house a little longer. As Lucy called it, my Victor habit.

"Of course, anything for my baby girl." He winked.

I shoved him playfully, then grabbed his hand and led him a little ways down the sidewalk.

We stopped in front of a tall, worn bulletin board.

"Am I looking at this for any specific reason? A specific ad? Some other ridiculously hot redhead desperately in need of renovation help?"

"Victor!" I chastised him. It was as if a filter had broken loose. I almost told him to stop calling me hot, but I didn't. I hated how much I liked his filter being off. "Look closer." I pointed toward the bulletin board where people were supposed to post announcements and ads, but instead, there were tons of handwritten notes.

"About a year ago, students started using this board to post anonymous love notes."

He squinted and stepped closer, reading them aloud.

*Anna, you always apologize for rambling during Lit 101, but I hang on your every word.*

*Guy With the Dreads and Converse, I get to class late just so I can see where you're sitting and sit beside you.*

*Leeanne, I used to hate my student work job until you started working with me. Now I'm taking extra hours cause it's become the best part of my week.*

Victor smiled warmly, hand on his chest over his heart. "These aren't mere love notes. These are love *confessions*."

"I like to read them. Sometimes, people will post responses right beside the originals. It's quite sweet," I said. "I come out here almost every day. It's like a little pick-me-up."

"Romance book clubs and anonymous love confessions. What's going on at your school?"

"We're straight out of a Hallmark, huh?" The dark blue sky glimmered with stars overhead. A breeze bustled through the trees.

"Should we post our own?" He patted his pockets. "Man, I don't have any paper."

"I don't even know what I'd write," I lied. I could see my confession in my mind already: *I want to kiss you again.*

"I'd write: I lied about the oat milk to get you talking to me." He leaned a shoulder against the board, thinking. "Or I offered to help you build a back deck ..." His voice trailed off for a beat. "'Cause I get shamefully greedy for time with you."

I walked over to him, placing a hand on his chest. His suit jacket was rough under my palm. "You had a crush when we first met?"

His breath caught at my touch. He placed his hands tentatively on my waist, rubbing the material of my silk dress between his fingers. "Something like that," he said, his voice rough.

This closeness felt new and breathtaking, like standing in the first beams of light at sunrise.

My voice, my breath, my feelings knotted together in my chest.

My hands spread wide against his chest. I stole a glance up at him. He looked down at me with serious eyes. I swallowed. Memories of our kiss flashed through my mind, making my mouth nearly water.

Squeals erupted down the sidewalk. A group of students stole our attention. We looked around, trying to find where their voices were coming from.

"CHRISTOPHER! DO NOT LEAVE ME UP HERE!" someone screamed.

"I have your other shoe!" another shouted.

"Jessica! You can jump down barefoot. It's okay! Come on!"

"Guys, we have to get out of here before security comes sniffing around. I can't get another fine!" someone scolded the group.

We slowly realized the shouting group of students was climbing down the roof of the theater building behind the bulletin board.

"The students like to climb on the roofs," I whispered. "They also like to pull fire alarms."

"Pull fire alarms?" Victor echoed.

"Yeah, pulling fire alarms. It's been a campus drama lately." I nodded, rolling my eyes. "Fire alarms going off randomly, day or night."

The group finally jumped down. Then they raced past us in a rush of giggles and heavy, nervous breathing.

After they left, I turned back to Victor. My hands were still on his chest. His hands were still around my waist. *Where were we?*

Serious and focused as before, he said, "I think we should climb up on that roof."

Climbing onto the roof wasn't as easy as the students made it seem, for me anyway. Victor seemed to be a natural. He hoisted me up onto the roof and then basically leaped up after me with ease.

While I was nervously scrambling on all fours to find a place to sit, he strolled around the roof, taking in the view. I was pretty certain I'd pulled something in my lower back but didn't feel like mentioning it to the twenty-four-year-old guy with perfect balance.

"This is like a much cooler tree house. I see why kids like to climb up here," he said, with his hands tucked into his jacket pockets. He turned back to glance at me.

I was sitting with my knees folded to my chest. The breeze pulled a few strands of my ruby hair out of my bun, and they were flying around my face, around my neck.

"Hey." He plopped down beside me.

"Hey." I rested my head on his shoulder. "It's been fun having you here tonight."

"I had a great time. I liked seeing the faces and voices to match the work stories you tell me." He gestured at the dark campus below. "I'm finally getting to see the place you run around every day."

It was really fun to share these pieces of myself with him. I relished it in a way I hadn't anticipated. "Does it match what you imagined?"

"Yes and no." He tapped his knee thoughtfully. "I thought you'd be a little more freaked out, honestly. With ..." He rolls his eyes while he says his name. "*Ryan*, there."

"I honestly kept forgetting he was there. Forgetting why I had my copilot enlisted for support."

"You started thinking you just had me there as your hot young buck or something?"

"Please, don't ever say that again." I covered my face with my hands. But to a degree, maybe he was right. I'd started thinking Victor was there just for fun.

He pulled my hands from my face. "I'm kidding. I'm kidding. But speaking of Ryan, he did interrupt a conversation."

I nodded. The one about passion. A conversation we'd started at absolutely the wrong time and place. "You were making some good points about passion. I'll admit."

"I think your dad has given it a bad rap when you don't need to be so afraid of it."

"I know it isn't *passion* I'm actually afraid of ... it's ..." I looked out at the tops of oak trees veiled in night, thinking.

*I was afraid of a loss of control.* Of loosening my tight grip on things like my heart, my time, my future.

"I like to feel sure of something before I take a chance on it," I finally said.

Victor sat quietly beside me, taking his time with his response. "But are you really taking a chance then?"

A couple strolled by hand in hand on the sidewalk down below, their voices a distant murmur.

Victor continued, "You can't always be sure of everything. I know you know that."

"Of course, logically I know that." But that didn't stop me from trying. Logic was no match for my feelings, my heart. Sometimes, it felt like my heart was racing ahead of me, trying to come up with a safety plan while my mind was still only learning about the mere existence of a situation.

"Some of the best stuff in life is the stuff you didn't see coming. The stuff that God knows you're ready for, even if you don't yet, you know? Like Watson."

"Watson?" I instantly thought of Victor's furry, playful

golden retriever bounding to me when they came over. How had I never asked Watson's origin story? I'd just taken the two of them as a package deal, no questions asked.

"Watson's first owner got sick, really sick. She was an old family friend and couldn't take care of him anymore. When she reached out to me, I impulsively took him in. I didn't research golden retrievers. I didn't have a dog bed or leash. I didn't even know if my townhouse was cool with pets. I didn't think about how inconvenient a dog might be. I just took him in. I took care of that other stuff later." He leaned back on his elbows, stretching his legs out in front of him. "What if I'd waited to take him in and she'd called someone else? Could you imagine life without Watson?"

"No." I shook my head.

Victor was passionate and impulsive, but in a way I trusted because he wasn't carried by whims or desires. He was carried by his care and his values. His passion was an arrow pointed at whatever he cared about most.

Watson needed a home, so he gave him one.

I needed a copilot at a history department dinner, so he was my date.

"I don't know if that helps. Or makes any sense." He ran a hand down his face, questioning himself.

"It helps." I stretched my legs out beside his, my freckled knees blue under the moonlight.

He tapped the toe of his dress shoe against my bare feet.

I'd left my high heels on the ground below. "You always help, Victor."

He smiled to himself, unable to hide the pleasure he took in my comment.

Some students squealed from dorm rooms across the way.

Victor turned his head toward me suddenly, a curious gleam in his eyes. "Should we talk about the kiss?"

"We should talk about the kiss," I complied. My heart sped

up, remembering how it felt to have his lips against mine only days ago.

"I've got to admit. I have a few questions." Our arms brushed with every minor movement, his heat warming me.

"Shoot."

"Well ..." He swallowed. "Was that kiss more about him ... or me?"

"That kiss ..." I licked my lips, searching for the right words. "Was about a lot of things. It was about *me*. And you. And, yeah, he'd been gasoline on the fire. But, in the moment, I wasn't really thinking. He'd belittled you, and I think wanted to make him eat his words ... and then ..."

"And then it was a really good kiss," Victor said.

I nodded. "I got a little caught up in the, uh ..." Words escaped me. I had barely talked about this with myself.

"In the chemistry?" Victor breathed, his voice low.

"Yeah. But the whole little charade I was putting on when you came back into the office was an impulsive move," I said. One of those rare moments I acted without thinking. Yet, it'd been with one of my safest people, so it hadn't *felt* like a dangerous move. "But you saw, I even started second-guessing it right before the ... kiss."

As Victor pinned me with his gaze, I had to admit how reckless it was. I'd been playing with fire.

"Do you think it was a big deal? It kind of felt like a big deal *to me*. You seem to have brushed past it. I've had trouble getting a read on what you think," he said.

I almost laughed. If the man could hear how fast my heart started beating every time I thought about the kiss, the way my mind had been playing the memory on a loop, he wouldn't be asking.

"It wasn't a small deal," I said quietly. "By any means."

His shoulders eased. "Okay, okay," he said, then paused, before way too casually asking, "Do you think it'll happen again?"

I turned my face toward him in surprise. "Happen again?" I whispered.

His eyes dropped to my lips. My stomach turned syrupy, my mind fuzzy.

*It'd be so easy to bring our lips together right now. I'd barely have to lean. And we'd be right back where the lines between us turned soft and blurry.*

The night was quiet, just the sound of the two of us breathing. My breathing grew rapid in my chest. A part of me ached to be closer, just a little bit closer.

I wanted Victor in more parts of my life, I'd thought earlier ... but really, I just wanted more Victor.

A siren blared below us, making us jump, jolting us from the moment.

Victor stood up and peered over the side of the roof. "Security," he said with a low laugh, as if this was hilarious.

My eyes widened. *They had sirens?* I started scrambling toward the edge of the roof farthest from the security guards on my hands and knees.

"Woah, woah, slow down, Dr. Rhodes. You look like you're about to topple off the roof!" Victor jogged over, with his annoyingly perfect balance, to meet me. He leaped to the ground, landing on his feet in a squat.

"Please, get down from the roof," the security team was saying into their speaker. "Students are not allowed on the roof. This is against camp—"

"Hey, you're not a student," Victor offered up.

I was still panicking. I kicked my feet over the edge and began to shimmy down, when his two big hands wrapped around my waist and gently pulled me down to the ground, to safety.

Footsteps on the concrete shuffled closer to us. "You are not allowed—" a deep voice was saying as he stepped toward where we'd been scrambling off the roof.

I took off, weaving behind the campus buildings toward the

parking lot. After years, I knew the shortcuts. Victor was close behind me, jogging to keep up.

"Dang, for such small legs, you're fast," he said, breathless.

I'd run track all through high school. I was a sprinter.

It wasn't until we made it, panting and sweaty, to Victor's truck that I realized my feet were still bare. My black slingbacks were tossed in the grass behind the theater.

I hit my palm to my forehead. "My shoes."

"I'll go back." Victor spun on his heels.

I grabbed his arm and pointed toward security, riding toward us on their golf cart.

"There's no time. We've got to go." I tried opening the front door, but it was locked. "Come on, Victor. I'll check lost and found later."

His brows furrowed as if he didn't completely agree with me as he clicked his truck unlocked. I nearly threw myself inside as he slid calmly into the driver's side.

As we cruised out of the parking lot, I kept glancing out the back windshield.

"Liv, do you really think the campus security would be chasing us through the parking lot?" Victor asked through a half-compressed chuckle.

I settled into my seat. "Maybe."

Victor shook his head amusedly as he turned onto the main street. "You always made it home a good fifteen minutes before curfew in high school, didn't you?"

"Well, no reason to make my mom worry," I said defensively. I tightened my seatbelt.

"And you always tiptoed around during the dorm quiet hours," he mused.

"I was considerate, yes."

"Never snuck candy into the theater—"

"Okay, okay. I get it. You think I was a Goody Two-Shoes." I crossed my arms.

Victor laughed. "I know you're a Goody Two-Shoes. You're

scary strict about following every code and rule for your historical house. I also have to show up to things nearly fifteen minutes early when we go together. We always stop to read every instruction a couple of times through when we're playing a game."

"Some of those are just normal things, Victor." I turned on the truck's heaters even though it was only in the sixties outside. "Let me guess, you were one of those students who had a secret pet in their dorm."

His eyes widened in surprise. "Well, it wasn't *my* pet. It was the whole dorm floor's hamster. How do you know that story?"

"Your mom. She said it was a crazy fine you guys paid when the RA found the hamster."

"Poor Rufus." Victor sighed sadly.

"So, that wasn't your first time being chased by campus security?" I twisted in my seat, so I was facing him.

"We weren't being chased." He hit the blinker. "I think to you, Miss Rule Stickler, simply being corrected felt like being chased."

"They had a siren!"

"That was barely a siren."

"You've climbed roofs before then?" I felt a little sad that this new, risky experience we'd shared was maybe old news to him. A bubble burst in my chest.

"Nah, that was the first time I'd climbed onto a roof, actually." He grinned at me, eyes studying me briefly before looking back at the road.

"Same."

"But not the first time I've been called out over a speaker," he said with a gleam in his eyes. "I can say, I've never seen someone nearly fling themselves off a roof to avoid a security guard in a golf cart."

"I was about to fling myself off that roof, wasn't I?"

We both burst out laughing. Tears pooled in my eyes, I was laughing so hard.

Victor was shaking. "*You abandoned your favorite shoes, Liv.*"

Eleven

LUCY

SO how did tonight go?

ME

It actually turned out to be a really good night

definitely in large part due to Victor being there

LUCY

And was Victor a good BF???

ME

*fake* BF

he was the best!

LUCY

Did this make you think about what he'd be like as a boyfriend in real life?

I took out my earrings, rolling my eyes at Lucy's text. Victor Hernandez was a magnetic force of a man. Of course I'd wondered what he'd be like as a boyfriend. He'd be a great boyfriend, just like he's a great best friend, but he was not ready to be a *serious* boyfriend to a woman about to enter her thirties, which was the type of boyfriend I needed. My heart could not handle any other kind of boyfriend right now.

As I showered and brushed my teeth before bed, a memory from late July kept playing over and over in my mind, like a wave to the shore.

*It was a late evening, after eight p.m. Victor was a volunteer at the Church of Sweet River's VBS at the request of his nieces and nephews, and earlier that day, he'd called me to see if I could pick him up that night after work. His truck's starter was having some troubles, so he'd taken it over to Roger's Auto Shop, and they'd have it for a couple days.*

*I wandered into the church that night, walking through the same old wooden door that had once felt so heavy to my tiny girl hands. Wandering down the same aisles where I'd dropped petals as a flower girl at weddings.*

*And there, snoring across an old wooden pew, lay Victor Hernandez. I'd grown up seeing him out of the corner of my eye and in passing at this very church on Sunday mornings, but his circles had never overlapped with my circles. Different grades, different friends, never officially meeting.*

*Until that day in the coffee shop.*

*My forehead crinkled as my gaze settled on him. Victor's dark brown hair was streaked with blue and green paint. His face was drawn all over with colorful face paint. As I studied him closer, I realized it was on his arms and hands in messy, colorful circles. I grabbed his sneaker and shook it.*

*He popped up, blinking. "Liv?"*

*"Hey, sleepyhead."*

*"Those rugrats can really wear you out." He rubbed his eyes.*

*"I'm loving the look." I bit back a laugh.*

*"Oh, yeah, I'm covered in paint." He glanced down at his arms. "VBS has an Under the Sea theme. The pre-K group tried to turn me into a mermaid—or, merman, I guess."*

*"Oh." I looked at the circles on his arms again. "Those are supposed to be scales. I can kind of see it now."*

*"Hey, for a preschooler, these scales are pretty darn good." Victor flexed his biceps. I tried to resist the urge to ogle. He was on a pew, after all.*

*"How was it? Besides being turned into a merman?" I asked.*

*A few kids whose parents were talking in the lobby were squealing and racing around. Their sandals slapped against the tiled floor.*

*"Loud, high energy. So much fun, I required a nap after. I remember coming to VBS as a kid. It's cool to see it from the other side now." Victor stood up from the pew, running his fingers through his messy, colorful hair, accidentally spreading the paint.*

*"My sisters and I used to be the kids painting the volunteers." I bumped my shoulder into his.*

*"By the way, my mom is requesting my presence at family dinner, if you don't mind dropping me off at my parents' place instead of my place?"*

*"Sure, that's no problem," I said as we headed toward the lobby.*

*"She also extended the invitation to you, if you want to join. My dad is out back flipping burgers on the grill."*

*There was a surge of butterflies in my stomach. I shouldn't care so much what his family thought of me, but I did. I'd adeptly avoided meeting his parents. His eyes were on me, though, big and hopeful.*

*"Sure," I said. "I can stop by for a few minutes, at least."*

The gravel crunched underneath my tires from the country roads as I drove up to the Hernandez house. Victor's family grew up on acres of grassy land on the edge of Sweet River. I could *imagine a young Victor running barefoot across this property he called his backyard.*

*I was so nervous, I barely responded to Victor's excited chatter, telling me how that old tree was where a big tire swing used to hang that he and his brothers broke a couple years ago when they all piled on it one night after a couple of beers. And that shed over there was where he tried to start a band when he was fifteen that was a complete failure from the first practice. And if we walked far enough down their property, beyond all those pecan trees, there was a stream that he loved to sit by and think.*

*I kept nodding along to his chatter as we walked up the steps of the sprawling farmhouse. He turned the doorknob, all excitement and joy, and I swallowed the big, dry lump in my throat.*

*No, I didn't want to examine why I cared so gigantically much about what his family thought of me.*

*"Mom," he shouted as the door shut behind us.*

*I resisted the urge to grab hold of his arm, or hand, for comfort, following him across the hardwood floors.*

*I glanced around, mentally wishing I could pin the open-concept home to my Pinterest boards. If we walked toward the right, we'd be in the formal dining room done in reds and creams, but if we turned left, which, as I followed behind Victor, we did, we entered the big living room with walls covered in family photos and comfy couches and armchairs.*

*"Victor, you're finally back!" his mom, Linda, said. Her jet-black hair was pulled back in a loose clip. Her eyes peeked up at us from behind the kitchen sink. "Is this the famous Olivia?" She didn't bat an eye at Victor's face paint.*

*"Hi." I hurried ahead, reaching out a hand.*

*She turned off the faucet and shook my hand. "I'm so glad you're here. David, Victor's dad, is out on the patio grilling burgers. But we've got chips and freshly made guacamole out there—"*

*"And salsa?" Victor checked.*

*"Yes, and my salsa. The kids love my salsa. I have to have it out*

*every time we eat." Linda laughed. She made her way around the long, granite kitchen island. "How're you doing, dear?"*

*"I'm pretty good," I said. "I had a long day. I'm a professor. I'm not sure if Victor has mentioned that? I usually teach summer classes, but I took this summer off. I've been filling my days up with home renovations—"*

*"You bought that old fixer-upper downtown, right off Main Street and Perrin Avenue, right? Victor's shown me so many pictures," Linda said, leading us toward the sliding doors that opened to the back patio.*

*"Yes, that's the one. It's coming along beautifully, thanks to Victor," I said.*

*Victor and I exchanged a smile.*

*"Victor, man, come grab a beer!" Victor's younger brother, Ricky, called as we stepped onto the patio. The sky beyond the backyard was flaming pinks and purples as the sun set over the grassy hills. "Oh, Liv is here!"*

*I'd met Ricky a few times over the summer. He'd tag along with Victor to grab pizza or help us work on installing new cabinets.*

*"You good if I go talk with Ricky?" Victor checked with me before he ran over to his brother.*

*"I'm fine." I chuckled. Victor's attentiveness still surprised me, and it made Linda smirk.*

*He turned to leave but then spun on his heels. "You want anything to drink?"*

*"I've got it covered, Victor," Linda said, shooing him away. "Olivia, we've got beer, wine, water, and I made a big pitcher of sweet iced tea."*

*"I'll have a glass of iced tea," I said.*

*Linda and I settled on patio chairs around a round table with our iced tea. The air was warm and humid. She was asking me about my sisters and mom. "You know, I've known your mom for years through church. Right when you walked in, I had flashbacks to you and your sister running down the aisles between pews back when you were still girls. I feel like I know you without actually ever meeting you."*

*I shook the ice in my glass. "Same. I've grown up hearing about the Hernandez boys and Mom's friend, Linda, who made the best salsa, without ever officially meeting you—until now."*

*Linda laughed. "Small-town life."*

*My gaze settled on Victor playing with his squealing kid nephew and nieces. He was chasing them around the patio, growling. They were soaking wet in swimsuits, leaving behind a trail of watery footprints.*

*"You're a history professor, Victor says? Is that what you always wanted to be?" Linda asked.*

*"Mom, don't grill her!" Ricky walked over, resting his hands on the back of his mom's chair. "Is she grilling you?"*

*"I'm just getting to know the girl! Can't a mom ask a few questions?" Linda shook her head.*

*"It was sounding like a literal job interview when I walked up." Ricky raised a dark eyebrow. His skin was the same caramel as his brother's.*

*"Mom," the kids shouted to Victor's oldest sister through fits of laughter.*

*The game had taken to the grassy backyard lawn beyond the patio. Victor was getting soaked and didn't seem to care a bit.*

*His sister was laughing as she walked over to our small patio table, a glass of white wine in her hand. "Hi, you must be Olivia. I'm the big sister, Tanya, mom to two of the screaming children out there." She had a baby against her chest. Her hair was in a messy bun on her head.*

*"I'm the dad to the other two screaming kids out there. I'm Luis." One of Victor's older brothers sat down with us.*

*Tanya was the super mom who worked as a nurse on the weekends and sent Victor silly videos of her kids that we'd watch together on my back deck. Luis was the big brother working his way up at a law firm a town over. Victor wrestled between wanting to call him for brotherly advice and trying to prove that he didn't need it.*

These two older siblings I'd heard Victor speak about with such admiration and reverence were now sitting beside me, sweaty and laughing about their kids.

"Is Katie coming?" Tanya asked the group.

"She and Terrence are on their way. They were closing up Coffees and Commas first," Linda explained.

"And of course, Emma and Gabriel are out of town, I'm assuming?" Ricky said.

"Yeah, haven't you seen Em's latest Instagram post? They're in Colorado!" Linda said, grabbing for her phone.

Even I'd seen the post.

"Why are they in Colorado?" Luis asked, before taking a sip of his beer.

"She's writing about some marathon there, and then Gabriel has a book signing that weekend. They'll be back here afterward," Linda said, sounding like the family manager.

"It looks like a blast," I added in. "And much cooler than here."

"Not hard to be cooler than a sweltering Sweet River July," Tanya said, fanning herself.

Linda broke into a story, telling me about the hot Fourth of July party they threw last summer.

I thought about Gabriel, Victor's older brother by a couple years. A successful writer and photographer, happily engaged to the family's longtime friend, Emma, also an ambitious writer. Victor spoke as if his family wished he were more like Gabe.

But I sat with his family, laughing while we watched him run around barefoot in his backyard, tirelessly playing with his nieces and nephews, and I couldn't think of any other kind of man I'd want to spend my time with than Victor. No other man I'd call my closest friend.

So, as nervous as I was, I let them grill me over burgers and way too much salsa and chips (Linda's salsa definitely lived up to the hype).

The sun set. But it was Texas in July, so the air stayed hot and *sticky. Victor and I wound up with our feet in the pool after his older siblings had to take their kids home for bedtime.*

*Linda was back inside, having told me she didn't need my help cleaning up. "You kids enjoy yourself," she said.*

*The sky glittered overhead, blanketed in stars. "I forgot how many stars you can see out here in the country," I said, looking upward.*

*"I know. I love it. I grew up with this. To me, it's how a night sky is supposed to look."*

*I swayed my feet back and forth. "It was nice to finally meet your family. You and Ricky are basically twins."*

*"I know. Everyone came—that's rare for a family dinner lately."*

*"Yeah, everyone except Gabriel and Emma. I saw they're off in Colorado."*

*Victor watched his feet in the deep blue water. "Yeah, he's always doing something cool."*

*I narrowed my eyes. "Your whole family is cool. You know that? You've got the nurse telling crazy stories about the ER, a lawyer you can call up if you ever break the law—"*

*"He's actually a financial attorney," Victor interrupted me.*

*"—two writers, a coffee shop owner, and her entrepreneur husband—"*

*"Are you two talking about me?" Terrence asked from the patio chairs where he was talking with Victor's dad.*

*"I'm telling Victor how cool you guys are," I said.*

*"Well, thanks." Terrence shot me a big, cheesy smile before returning to his conversation with David.*

*"Then"—I grabbed his shoulder, his warm bicep in my hand—"there's you. Your family told story after story about you all night—"*

*"Because you're my friend." Victor chuckled.*

*"No, not because I'm your friend. Because they love you. And stories about you make everyone laugh. You light their faces up,*

*Victor. They can count on you to show up. To play with their absolutely adorable kids. To build them coffee tables. To be pretty much everyone in Sweet River's friend. I mean, you've got an in everywhere." I squeezed his arm. "You're the coolest one at like, every party. How can you not see that?"*

*His cheeks were a warm pink.*

*"You're always worried about making 'em proud, but all I saw tonight was a proud family."*

*It was quiet for a beat, just the cool water swirling around our feet.*

*"The kids do love me." He grinned that sideways grin of his.*

*"Yeah, it was pretty cute." I tucked a strand of hair behind my ear. "They absolutely soaked you, though."*

*He pulled on the front of his wet T-shirt. All the VBS face paint was smeared now. "This isn't soaked. This is a light splashing."*

*"Oh really?" I crossed my arms.*

*He quickly splashed me, a spray of cold water hitting my chest. I squealed.*

*"See, that's a splash."*

*My mouth hung open as I looked down at my wet tank top. "This is what I get for hanging out with the fun uncle."*

*"And this," he continued, jumping into the water with his clothes still on, "is getting soaked." He snaked his hands toward my hips.*

*I squealed but didn't put up much of a fight. The water felt good on my skin, and Victor's rough hands felt even better.*

*We splashed each other, shaking with laughter. David and Terrence drank their beers and stepped away, unfazed by our childish, giggly pool fight.*

*Later, I ran inside, with a towel wrapped around my dripping self, looking for the bathroom. As I turned a corner, I stopped, finding Linda and Katie were talking in what looked like an office.*

*I opened my mouth to say something, maybe ask for help finding the bathroom, but then I stopped when I heard them say my name.*

*"Olivia's pretty cute, huh?" Linda said quietly.*

*"Oh, she's so cute. She's sweet, too," Katie said. "And smart. You know she's a professor?"*

*They were talking about me. I leaned in closer, water dripping from my clothes onto the hardwood floor.*

*"How could I not know? Victor brings it up all the time. Mom, she knows Latin. Mom, she studies Greek texts. Mom, she's oh so brilliant," Linda said, through laughter. "He's so impressed."*

*"It's honestly so precious to see Victor proud of her like that." Katie leaned against the big mahogany desk in the center of the room.*

*"He is proud, huh?" Linda smiled thoughtfully. "You know, he told me he's never been able to talk to someone the way he does with her."*

*My heart tugged. Victor had said that?*

*Katie put a hand to her chest. "Well, he told me that they're hanging out almost every day. He makes it sound like he's just working on her house, but it's more than that. They're eating dinners together, hanging out late talking, and meeting up with friends and her sisters."*

*"Do you think he's lying to us that they're only friends?" Linda sounded hurt.*

*"No, I think they're lying to themselves, maybe." Katie huffed. "I think they're playing it really safe with the age gap. She's like thirty, you know."*

*"Do you think she's leading him on?"*

*I felt all the blood drain from my face. I wasn't trying to lead Victor on, though my feelings for him were confusing and complicated.*

*"No, no." Katie swatted that idea away with her hand. "You can tell she really cares about him. I think they're genuinely best friends ... for now."*

*"Victor's never settled down," Linda said, setting down what-*

*ever book was in her hand. "I've never seen him like this. I don't think there's ever been a girl he wants to spend this much time with. He's usually bored and moving on to the next thing, the next project."*

*"Yeah, he told me he's never even said the word 'love' to a girl before," Katie said, her voice nearly a whisper. I had to strain to hear. "Our Victor's never fallen in love."*

*A breath caught in my throat. Victor was younger than me, sure, but I'd never imagined he'd never even said the word love before. Never been in a serious relationship. I felt my guard going up.*

*"Yet," Linda said, louder, stronger. "He seems different with this Olivia. I've never seen him look at someone the way he looks at her."*

*"I saw it, too," Katie said.*

*I took a few steps back, then ran back into the living room, colliding with Victor.*

*"I was looking for you. Could you find the bathroom?" he asked.*

I crawled into my bed, pulling the thick duvet under my chin as I recalled that overheard conversation. I'd played it in my mind so many times since that July night. *Victor had never been in love.* He'd never been in a long-term relationship. He'd been jumping from girl to girl. That scared me.

I remembered my first love, at sixteen, and I also remembered how it went up in flames and how that first scar had become just another lesson learned, another stepping stone into the woman I was now.

Becoming Victor's first serious girlfriend, with the likelihood of being just a stepping stone for him, sounded like a real demotion from a best friend who would be in his life for years to come.

The best friend role came with longevity, while the girlfriend role came with risk.

He'd so quickly become someone I didn't want to lose.

So, it scared me, not enough to run away, but enough to pump the brakes on our relationship and keep us coasting as friends. Enough to put my guard up.

# Twelve

good morning to the rule-breaking-roof-climbing Olivia Rhodes ;)

now go check your doorstep.

I slipped on my house shoes, and while still rubbing the sleep from my eyes, I shuffled over to my front door.

When I opened the door, my eyes dropped to my black slingbacks neatly placed on the welcome mat. Alongside them was a paper bag and a to-go coffee cup from my favorite spot.

I scooped everything up in my arms, a slow smile spreading across my face.

*Of course he did.* Because Victor always found the seemingly small, but most intentional ways to help.

I called him after I brought the items inside.

"You get your delivery?" Hearing Victor's deep, raspy voice made my heart swell, even over the phone.

I rested my hip against the kitchen island, with my phone in one hand and the coffee cup in the other. "When did you go back to get my shoes?"

"After I dropped you off last night. Those are your favorite shoes."

I wore those shoes pretty much anytime I dressed up, and he'd *noticed*.

"Victor, you didn't have to do that. You added an extra, what, hour to your night by driving there and back?" The paper cup was warm in my hand, smelling of clove and cinnamon. I took a sip.

"Don't worry about it. I wanted to make sure they didn't get lost or stolen." He yawned into the phone. It was still early. He'd made sure to drop it all off before I left for work, too. This way, I could have my chai latte and, I peeked into the bag, an apple butter scone from Coffees and Commas before I left for work.

"I appreciate you saving my favorite shoes. And for bringing me breakfast."

"I do have an in with the owner," he said, referring to his older sister Katie, who owned Coffees and Commas, the café bookshop downtown. "She knows your favorites."

*You're my favorite*, bubbled up to the top of my mind, surprising me. I swallowed it back. "Katie wasn't the one who stayed up late on the shoe rescue mission," I said. "That was you. *So* you."

"Well ..." He sighed. I could nearly see him rubbing a hand over his chin scruff. "You're my best friend. There's nothing I wouldn't do for you."

"You're my best friend, too." I took a soft, warm bite of buttery scone. "You bring me shoes and scones. No better friend than you," I said through a mouthful.

I t was the first day of October, and the school was kicking it off with a big fall festival. They were setting up booths and tables as I walked down the campus sidewalk under a heavy, gray sky. The air smelled of wet leaves.

I made it into the office to drop off my bags before my first class of the day, Introduction to Roman History.

"Will we be seeing Victor this afternoon?" Sonny, the department secretary, raised a curious brow as I attempted to rush by her desk.

I'd told Victor he didn't have to try and fit this into his busy day. I could handle this small festival myself. Honestly, I was realizing I could handle the presence of Ryan way easier than I'd expected. But Victor had firmly told me, *I'll be there*.

"Yeah, he'll be here." I adjusted my bag strap.

"He sure was a hoot at the dinner last night." She leaned back in her leather desk chair until it creaked. "I like him."

"I like him, too."

"He likes you, but you know that, right?" she said, her expression serious. But then her voice softened in a way that she reserved for moments when she was imparting random bouts of wisdom. "You don't always get one that sweet on you."

"I don't know. It's pretty casual." My bag was growing heavy on my shoulder.

"You sure about that? The way he looked at you didn't seem all that casual." She crossed her arms. "The man followed you around like a lovesick puppy."

"Early days and all," I muttered, glancing toward my office door. "We were, you know, friends first. We're taking it slow."

"Well, I'm just going to say it again: you don't always get one as crazy about you as he seems to be. Not everyone has it in 'em to love like that."

I chuckled, because whatever façade we'd put on last night, Victor *does* love well, even if it's just how he loves his best friends or his family. "You're right. He's pretty special."

Sonny hummed. "I like him," she said again as I hurried out of the office.

I shook my head. *The Victor Effect.*

. . .

I was typing at my computer, catching up on emails, when a light tap on my door caught my attention. I glanced at the doorway to find Dean Oates popping her head into my office, short dark hair curling to her chin.

"Hi, Dr. Rhodes."

"Come in." I waved her inside.

"How're you today?" she asked as she took a seat across from my desk.

"I'm doing well. Yourself?"

"Well, I'd intended to talk with you more at the party, but the night got away from me. I know you're working on pitching your own syllabus for the spring semester. I wanted to check in and see how you're feeling about that. I'm available if you want to bounce any ideas off me." She smiled encouragingly.

I crossed my legs behind my desk. "Well ..." I had several ideas. Questions brimmed at the top of my mind. I loved Dean Oates and valued her input. "I have a few ideas I'm sifting through."

"Anything in particular?"

I'd recently read about courses being offered that used elements of popular culture to enhance a course or even use it as a means to study a specific topic. I opened my mouth to ask her, but then, I thought, *who am I to start something like that here?*

I'm one of the youngest professors. This is my first time putting together my own course. People are expecting me to do it a certain way.

I'd sound silly.

So, I bit my tongue. "Not yet," I said, giving a halfhearted half smile.

"You know, I have a few ideas I can float by you," Dr. Oates said. She shared a few courses she knew the department had been considering implementing, even the course Dr. Lewis was pushing for me to take on.

These ideas were great, although not at all what I'd been envisioning. It was so kind of her to take the time to share them with me, so I nodded along. Though everything she said only confirmed my suspicion that there was definitely a direction the department was expecting me to take. Any fresh or trendy class ideas might take people aback.

We shook hands as she left, and my heart sank a little. I knew she probably walked back to her office feeling good about our conversation and would report back to the rest of the department that I was on the right track. But I felt like I'd let myself down, biting my tongue when I should've spoken up.

I found myself glancing at my watch and the clock on my computer, over and over, counting the hours and minutes until I got to escape to the fall festival down on the campus grounds. *Until I got to see my best friend.*

Pumpkins and bales of hay were scattered across the campus. Fall had arrived at our little college. I skipped down the steps outside the history building and was hit with the scent of fresh apples, cinnamon, and the pre-rain smell in the air. The air wasn't necessarily cold today, but it was cooler under the haze of gray and muted sunlight.

I'd worn a long red button-down open over a white tank top. My hair was in a low bun.

Victor gave the bun a light tug in greeting. "Hey, baby girl." He winked as I turned to him. He had his leather jacket on over his white T-shirt.

"Hey there, it's my hero." I slid an arm around him for a hug, which he turned into a full embrace and lifted me off my feet, making me giggle. But I could feel a few eyes on us.

*There's Olivia and her hot, new boyfriend.*

He set me back on my feet, with his arms still around my

waist, mine around his, smiling up at each other, easily selling the idea that we were something more than friends.

"Pie walk? Pumpkin carving? Candied apples? What's up first?" he asked.

"Pumpkin carving. The last few years, the pumpkins ran out fast." I snaked my hand into his and led him toward the pumpkin carving tent.

We got in line, but we didn't drop our hands. His warm fingers were still tangled in mine. *It's just the charade*, I reminded myself, an attempt to calm my excitedly beating heart. *He's just trying to make the Ryan fiasco easier on me.*

Even though Ryan wasn't even in sight.

I introduced him to a couple of my students as we slowly moved up in line. When one of the students called me his favorite professor, Victor gave my hand a little squeeze and shot me one of his proud smiles.

It was finally our turn in the pumpkin carving tent. We walked up to the long table lined with pumpkins for us to choose one and carry it over to the carving stations, which were set up at smaller tables with backless stools.

"I like this one." Victor pointed at a big orange pumpkin with a bit of a slant. "He looks like one we could turn into a vampire or something."

"Okay." I cocked my head to the side. "I think I see the vision."

Victor scooped up the pumpkin and carried it over to an empty carving station. A student working the booth had just set out a fresh knife, spoon, and a couple of thick black markers. We sat side by side at the plastic table, arms touching.

I picked up the marker. "So, a vampire?"

"A vampire." Victor rubbed his hands together excitedly. His eyes were eager on me as I drew the two triangular eyes and then added fangs to the mouth.

I dropped the marker when I was done, feeling pretty proud of my work.

Victor examined the pumpkin skeptically, then cleared his throat. "The fangs are good, but his eyes look too friendly for a vampire."

"Too friendly?"

"Yeah, I think a vampire needs menacing eyes."

I chewed on my lip, trying to figure out how to make triangle pumpkin eyes ... more menacing. After a couple of minutes, I picked the marker back up and made the eyes more angled, thicker. "Menacing enough?"

Victor tapped his chin. "He needs eyebrows."

I squinted at our pumpkin. He could use eyebrows.

Once we'd finished the outline, Victor glanced down at the knife, then back up at me. "You want to carve?"

I nodded eagerly. "My family never carved pumpkins. I'm not sure if Mom wanted to avoid the mess or, since she worked as a nurse, maybe wanted to steer clear of knives, but we only ever painted our pumpkins."

Victor chuckled in his quiet way, eyes crinkling as he grinned. "Oh, why does that sound just like Mama Rhodes?"

I shrugged. "Now, here I am, nearly thirty, and a first-time pumpkin carver."

"Well, you know my mom. She handed me a knife to carve when I was, like, two. She was too busy chasing my siblings. I'm an old pro." He stood up from his seat.

I imagined Victor with his five siblings, as one of the youngest, wielding a knife as a toddler.

"Victor, please tell me you're kidding. I love your mom, but —" I realized he'd pulled up a stool behind me. "Why are you over here?"

He scooted his stool right up against me, sliding his arms around me to grab the knife, then set it in my hand and kept his hand on top of mine. "I want to show you my perfect carving technique," he said so close to my ear.

Goose bumps trailed down my arms, my shoulders.

"Want me to move?" He turned his head a little, his breath hitting right below my ear.

I shook my head. I preferred trying things for the first time on my own. I'd never been a fan of hands-on teaching. Group projects irritated me. Give me thick books to read over an interactive lesson.

But Victor always had a way around my defenses. With him, I never felt prickly about his help. He was my hands-on exception.

I leaned against his chest, feeling his warmth and breathing in that familiar mix of sawdust and that musky cologne.

"See, the key is to cut the top out at an angle," Victor said, his words a rumble against my back, as we pushed the knife into the soft pumpkin, cutting a circle at the top around the stem. "So, the top doesn't drop when we set it back on."

I hummed in agreement.

"Now here's the messy part," he warned.

I turned my head to him, my eyelashes against his rough jawline. "What's the messy part?"

He leaned forward, guiding my hands into the pumpkin. "We've got to clean the pumpkin out, so our candle has somewhere to go."

Together, we scooped up a handful of soggy pumpkin seeds.

A giggle escaped me. "I appreciate how you're walking me through this experience."

We wiped our hands off with a paper towel, then got back to work. Now, it was time to carve.

Victor's eyes narrowed, serious as we sliced into my little Sharpie drawings. "First, we make the rough, big cuts," he said, warm against my ear. "We can come back and clean the edges later."

His chest was solid behind me—strong from carving things from lumber and wielding hammers—but I couldn't take my eyes off how he took our silly jack o'lantern just as seriously as his carpentry work.

Victor was playful and easygoing, but he had the things he

handled with precision and a humble intensity—the things he took seriously. Like the things he made with his hands.

I'd seen that intent focus before, how he'd mindlessly lick his lips and narrow his eyes as he sanded down a plank of wood or wrapped a present for his brother's birthday, smoothing down the tape with the same focus he gave his sliding saw.

If it was under his care—be it carving a jack o'lantern or fortifying a wall—he did it with his whole heart.

His chin brushed against my forehead as he moved. "Here we go," he murmured, guiding our hands together to angle the cut.

I wasn't watching our hands. I was watching him—how he bit his lip in concentration. *Why did Victor's lips have such an effect on my stomach?*

I felt eyes on me. I glanced across the tables to find Gabby. She sat across the table, surrounded by students and some very messy pumpkins. She arched an eyebrow like she knew exactly what I was thinking.

Last time she'd seen me, I was wearing his jacket. Now here I was, enveloped in his arms and gazing at his mouth.

Victor didn't notice. He announced we were done, pulling his hands from mine. I felt like I was being jolted awake from a sleepy stupor—a Victor stupor.

I blinked a few times at our pumpkin vampire. It was truly perfect.

"Victor, wow." I picked it up to inspect it. "It's adorable." Each shape was cut precisely. My silly drawings came through adorably. The eyebrows were adorable. I spun it around to show Gabby across the way, who was still guffawing at us.

"Not fair. He's a literal carpenter," she said, shaking her head.

"It's not a contest," Victor said with the cocky grin of a winner.

# Thirteen

Sometimes, like when we were talking with my work friends, Victor's arms slipped around my waist. He'd rest his wrist on my hip, like my body was his own personal comfort spot. I'd lean into him when he told a joke, in a way I usually stopped myself from doing.

This charade felt less like pretending and more like surrendering. Some mental and physical muscles I'd been controlling around Victor suddenly released, a part of me I hadn't realized was waiting to let go.

The closeness felt like a hit of caffeine straight into my bloodstream. I was giggly, and I wanted more.

"Hey, Katie told me she had a Coffees and Commas cart set up on campus," Victor said as we strolled by a couple of students clinking cans of apple cider. "Want to go find her?"

"Of course," I said. My tongue was salty and sweet from the caramel popcorn we'd just shared.

The sun was getting lower in the cloudy sky. The Texas heat was cooling. We weaved through the center of campus where the festival took place to find a metal and wood coffee stand with a big *Coffees and Commas* sign.

Katie poked her head out of the window. Her brown messy bun was lopsided on her head. "Victor, Olivia! Hi!"

I set both my hands on the bar opening of the window. "I love this traveling coffee shop. You've got the coffee. Now you just need the books. Victor should build you a bookshelf to set up with it to really complete the picture."

"I'd have to be a redhead with the name Olivia to get Victor to start building me things off the cuff." Katie leaned on her elbows, with her chin resting on her hands.

"Hey now, who built most of the new shelves in Coffee and Commas?" Victor defended himself with a hand on his chest.

"Well, I know I'm not the highest priority sibling at the moment—what with Gabe and Emma basically booking you up for their wedding," Katie said. "Did he tell you, Liv?"

I shook my head.

"They just asked," Victor said. "I'm building them a wedding arbor. We're going to cover it in vines and flowers, maybe even throw a canopy over it. I've been working on the design," Victor said, his voice rising in excitement. He was beaming. "I can't believe they asked *me*."

"Of course they asked you." I placed a hand on his shoulder and gave it a reassuring squeeze. "It's going to be beautiful."

"There's no one else they would've asked, but you," Katie said before looking over at me. "You're coming to the wedding, right, Liv?"

I had the invitation hanging on my fridge. "Yeah, for sure."

"Are you coming to the other wedding things with Victor, too? The rehearsal dinner? I think you get a date," Katie said, tapping the coffee bar.

She might've meant it innocently and intended I'd be tagging along as Victor's pal, but my cheeks still went pink.

She smirked while Victor scratched his head. "I haven't thought much about who I'd be taking."

I felt the pink spread to my shoulders. "Maybe I'll go? We haven't discussed it?" I said, my voice high.

"Honestly, I think we've all assumed you'd be at everything," Katie said with her back turned as she started up the espresso machine behind her. "You two are a package deal lately."

"Well, I'd be honored to be at any of the wedding celebrations," I said, my eyes on Victor.

His eyes softened on me.

"I love Emma and Gabe."

"Really? You'd be my date?" Victor said. His voice was a lull under the sound of whirring latte foam.

"Get her the details," Katie said, setting two lattes in front of us. She pushed a cup toward me. "A chai with pumpkin seasoning on top." Then she handed one to Victor. "Maple latte."

A couple of professors stepped in line behind us, so we quickly thanked Katie while we grabbed our drinks and left.

T he festival was dwindling. Students had mostly left and gone on with their evening classes or off to the cafeteria for dinner. But I didn't want this bubble where Victor and I held hands or linked arms, where we wandered around in the gray, where I knew I'd go home with his scent on my clothes, to burst.

"Hey, we haven't done the pie walk!" I said, sounding like I was straight out of a holiday movie.

"Oh yeah." Victor nodded. "Lead the way."

We made it over to the pie walk area. They were folding up the chairs and knocking down the table. I felt my heart sink.

"Oh, we missed it," Victor said, pulling me to his side in a consolatory hug. "Want to go find pie somewhere else?"

"You guys want some pie?" a woman with tight gray curls, who'd eyed us as we walked up, said from her spot, wrapping up a tablecloth. "We have two slices of pecan pie left."

Victor tilted his head in question.

"We'll take 'em!" I said.

•   •   •

We walked over to my favorite tree, nestled under the shade, and dug our forks into our slices of pie.

"I feel like pecan pie is so underrated. It tastes so autumnal," I said around a mouthful of gooey, nutty goodness.

Victor nodded, with a soft smile tugging at his lips. "Mom used to always have us go outside and pick up a bag of pecans and then shell them every fall so she could make a pecan pie for Thanksgiving." His tone was warm, nostalgic.

The golden hour glow made everything feel softer around the edges. The evening stretched before us.

I shifted slightly, turning my head toward him. "Hey, I wanted to ask—" But before I could finish my sentence, my paper plate wobbled where it rested on my knee before flipping over.

We both stared at it lying dramatically face down on the grass.

My mouth hung open. Victor's eyes were wide.

"My pie," I gasped.

"Your pie!" he shouted in shock, slapping a palm over his mouth. "Liv, I'm so sorry."

I shook my head, a laugh deep in my chest bubbling up. "My poor pie."

He held out his plate. "Take mine."

"I'm not stealing your slice," I said with an arched brow. But then, with a grin, I grabbed his fork, scooping a big bite. "But I will share it."

We passed the fork back and forth, sitting shoulder to shoulder under the shade of the tree. This closeness felt so easy. The sun was almost completely set, leaving the sky purple and pink and the October air crisp.

"What were you saying before you lost your pie?" Victor asked as I chewed a bite.

"Oh ..." I handed him the fork. "I was going to ask you how your business plans are going. You were supposed to show them to me. You know, the arch at the wedding and the shelves at Coffees and Commas would be great in your portfolio." The oak shelves at Coffees and Commas, with their intricate ivy detailing along the edges, were stunning. Almost every time I waited in line for coffee, someone pointed them out and commented on how beautiful and unique they were.

Victor swallowed his bite. "I know. I've been planning to show them to you, but then I keep putting it off. I mean, you're the only person I can imagine showing right now, but also … I really don't want you to look them over and then laugh at me."

"Victor Hernandez, do you really think I would ever laugh at you?" I leaned across him, my arm brushing across his denimed knee, and grabbed the fork. I peered up at him through my auburn hair, dangling in my eyes.

He narrowed his eyes. "You laugh at me daily."

"Maybe. But I'd never laugh at someone making the brave choice, taking a chance on themselves. There's nothing funny about that." I kept my arm against his leg, and my body leaned toward him.

His eyes were hooked on mine.

"I can't wait for you to get this business started—to see your work popping up all over Sweet River."

He put his hand on my wrist where it rested on his knee. "You don't think …" He took a beat. "You don't think there's a chance people will think that I'm delusional and my pieces are not really as great as I think they are—or hope they are?"

I shook my head vehemently. "Not a single chance."

He gave my wrist a squeeze before removing his hand.

I scooped up the fork, and his eyes followed it to my lips. My stomach dipped.

"Well, I'm finishing up the plans, and then they'll be in your inbox. That way, you can force me to actually take the steps." He leaned his head against the tree.

"I'm good at the whole pushing people thing. I'm a Rhodes woman, after all." I set the fork back down on the plate. "And hey, I better remain your priority customer, even after you get popular."

"Well, I don't know how good you'll be for my business. Most of the stuff I do for you, I've done for free or discounted just cause you're really cute."

I fought back a grin. "Victor." I gave him a playful shove. "I try to pay you, and you refuse! I don't want to hurt your business."

Victor would've been worth every penny, because Victor's work *was* really good. But there were other factors in why I kept wanting more and more Victor creations. More than I could ever afford.

Partially, it was because I just wanted more and more *Victor*.

I wanted him in my kitchen or my backyard when I got home from work.

I wanted to look at my kitchen table and think of him, his hands, and his heart.

I loved that when I walked across my back porch in the mornings barefoot, I saw the wood he picked out and sanded down. I could still hear the old rock he blared as he worked, singing along, and feel his hands on mine as he taught me proper sanding technique while we built it.

Everything he built me carried that instant peace I felt in his presence, like he was my own personal remedy.

It was the Victor in all of it that I loved.

"Want the last bite?" Victor asked, waking me from my thoughts.

I reached for the fork, and he snatched it away, holding it up over us out of reach.

"Not so fast, Freckles!"

"Hey." I twisted around him to grab the fork. We started wrestling over the fork, breathless and laughing. His warm body was against mine again, still sending my heart racing, when the plate fell off his lap.

Our last bite was in the grass.

"You have some kind of pie curse," Victor said from our place, all twisted up, both with a grip on the fork.

"That time was definitely your fault," I argued.

I let go of the fork, opting instead to rest my head on his shoulder. The sun was completely set, and the lamp posts around campus flickered on.

I had papers to grade, syllabi to work on, a lecture to write, and dishes in my sink, but I just kept trying for more time here with Victor.

VICTOR

*sends close-up photo of Watson; mostly just his nose and left eye are shown*

I got up to grab something from the kitchen and left a bowl of fruity pebbles on the coffee table and this dog ate my last few bites

which isn't the exact same as knocking it to the ground (…like you did), but I still had the last bite of my dessert ruined again

ME

Fruity pebbles are a dessert to you?

VICTOR

sugary nighttime cereals are one of the best desserts imo

ME

I suppose Watson agrees

VICTOR

proud and disappointed

I guess that's being a parent

. . .

"Adam visited my class yesterday," Lucy said from her spot at my kitchen island.

She and Adam had stopped by my house after a dinner date to pick up the dress I'd borrowed and drop off a purse of mine she'd borrowed, but somehow, it turned into the three of us sitting around my kitchen island, breaking into the to-go boxes.

"It was career day."

Adam shook his head and let out a sigh. "Kindergarteners are scarier than you realize."

I narrowed my eyes. "Scary? What happened at career day?"

Lucy and Adam exchanged a glance.

Lucy cleared her throat. "Adam came to talk about the city management offices. He brought all these fun mementos from the summer festival, plus some of the snacks we'd had at the festival to pass around. Popcorn and funnel cakes. The kids got pretend tickets. That part went really well."

"Okay." I stabbed a piece of ravioli from the Styrofoam container with my fork and took a bite.

"It went awry after the presentation part was done. I went over to tell Adam goodbye. We were standing by the classroom door, and mind you, he isn't around large groups of kids much. So he's totally out of his element," Lucy said.

"I'm around large groups of kids a regular amount for a non-teacher," Adam said, picking at a roll from the other Styrofoam container.

"Fine, but the point is he was completely out of his element. I'm trying for a quick and chaste goodbye, and instead, Adam grabs me by the waist and gives me a big kiss goodbye right on the mouth," Lucy said through a fit of laughter.

"Oh, I've seen those goodbye kisses." I rolled my eyes, stabbing at another bite. "I can't imagine how a mob of five-year-olds reacted to it."

"Hey, I wasn't warned to avoid kissing in front of the

students!" Adam defended himself, with his thick glasses sliding down his nose.

"I didn't think I had to!" Lucy said, catching her breath after her laughter.

"I also think you should consider your audience more. I've seen you smack a big kiss on her at church, too." I tsked judgmentally.

"I'm set in my ways." Adam shrugged.

Lucy pushed me away from the takeout box to get her own bite. "Now, when the kids saw the kiss, it was full-on chaos. They were pointing and shouting, "look at Lucy and Mr. Lucy.'"

"Mr. Lucy?" I snorted.

"That's what they've taken to calling him. Then they all started singing 'K-I-S-S-I-N-G' at the top of their lungs. It was so much commotion. I was trying to calm them down."

"Lucy and Mr. Lucy sitting in a tree, K-I-S-S-I-N-G," Adam sang in imitation, head hanging down.

"Adam was beet red. I was trying to usher him out the door, since he'd now become a total source of mania to the kids. I mean, they were singing so loud I had neighboring teachers coming over to check on our classroom, asking 'Miss Rhodes, we heard a lot of commotion, is everything okay?'"

Adam's head was in his hands. "One. Small. Kiss."

"Small to you, but huge and full of cooties to a five-year-old," I said.

"That's all it takes for kindergartners. It was a scandal. I checked my inbox a bit ago, and emails were already rolling in with questions from parents about what their kids were saying about class today. *I was told Miss Lucy was kissing a boy in class today. Is it true you were teaching the kids how to sing K-I-S-S-I-N-G in class today? Did you have a date at class today?*" Lucy was grinning from ear to ear, though. It was never boring with Lucy and Adam.

Adam's phone rang. "Oh," he said, checking the caller ID. "That's my brother. I'm going to take this really quick."

Adam stepped out of the kitchen, and Lucy spun toward me. The light over my kitchen island made her green eyes glow. "I've been dying to ask how the dinner was with your *pretend date*?"

*Better than I'd hoped. Way too fun; way too confusing.* "It went fine." I tucked a strand of hair behind my ear. "We were convincing. Victor was actually amazing the entire time. Everyone adored him."

"He is easy to adore," Lucy said.

"It's the Victor Effect," I said with a small shrug, tearing a piece off Adam's roll. "He came to the festival today. He's dedicated to being a buffer at all of the events."

"How'd today go?" Lucy asked, her eyes searching mine.

"It was fine," I said.

"Fine?" Lucy repeated.

"It was great, actually," I said, feeling my guard lower a little. Victor was making my work life, which I already loved, somehow even better when he was there.

"Did you see Ryan?"

"We spoke briefly at the dinner last night, and then today, I saw him in the distance at the fall festival. He's basically just an annoying background presence at these things, now, like a fly buzzing around. I can mostly forget about him if he keeps his distance," I said, feeling only mildly guilty to compare him to a bug.

Lucy patted her chin thoughtfully with the plastic fork. "What happens if everyone finds out about this scheme?"

I took a beat to think. My eyes settled on Adam in the living room across the way, laughing into the phone. "We're just taking advantage of the assumptions everyone had already jumped to," I said, trying not to think too much about when Victor told our couple origin story last night at dinner.

"Or maybe you two will start dating and—" Lucy said.

"No, no, no. Let's not go there!" I said, holding up a hand. I felt like I'd gotten into the habit of saying the same thing over and over to my own heart: *no, no, no, let's not go there.*

Adam walked back into the kitchen, where Lucy was closing the takeout boxes. "You ready to head out, Luce?"

She nodded to Adam, but placed her hand on my arm, looking at me with serious eyes. "I'm calling you tomorrow, and I need *actual details* about the past couple of days, okay? *Details, Olivia.*"

# Fifteen



**LUCY**

*sends multiple screenshots from their mom's LoveLocal inbox of her accepting date offers*

mom is just accepting almost every date offer!

some of these guys look like creeps. Especially the first one I sent.

I think we need to intervene.

**GRACIE**

I just got mom to stop snooping around my love life, I do not need to start snooping in hers

"It feels like my uterine lining is clawing its way out," I groaned into my phone's speaker, sending a voice message to Lucy. I was burrito-wrapped in my thick white comforter on Saturday morning.

Lucy was calling again. She was adamant we sisters needed to investigate Mom's new suitors. Meanwhile, I was curled up in a ball on my bed, hanging onto my heating pad for dear life. I had no energy to investigate.

I patted around my bed for my remote so I could put on something light and fluffy to distract me from my period pain. I turned on *Friends*.

Rachel and Chandler were eating cheesecake off the floor when my phone vibrated again. I slid the call open without checking the screen. "Lucy, call Adam or something," I groaned into the phone.

"I talk to Adam more than enough, actually." Victor laughed. "I tend to avoid my boss on the weekend."

"Sorry," I said, my voice muffled by my pillow. "Didn't check who was calling. Lucy has been trying me all morning." I glanced at the clock on my phone. It was eleven a.m., and I still hadn't gone downstairs for coffee. My stomach growled, too.

"You doing okay, Liv? You sound down." Victor's voice softened as he checked on me.

I paused the show. "I'm cramping pretty bad, actually," I admitted. Over the summer, Victor had become familiar with how bad my menstrual cramps could be after seeing me clinging to my heating pad multiple times.

"Ah, Menstruella is here?" Victor, after learning this about me, had also nicknamed my period.

I shook my head at the name.

I buried my face under my pillow. No one but my sisters and mother had ever known me so well. *How had the goofy younger guy from the coffee shop with a crush become someone I shared this much of my life with?*

Maybe because only the goofy younger guy had ever made me feel safe enough to share it all. He had tenderly taken care of each piece of me I gave him until there was nothing left to share now. He could even tell when my period was here.

"Yes," I admitted.

"You still in bed?"

I just laughed.

"You need another coffee delivery?"

I could imagine him standing in his kitchen with his lazy weekend hair, pouring himself a second cup of coffee. He'd smell like minty toothpaste and fresh laundry.

"No, no. Enjoy your weekend. Go be young and carefree." I snuggled deeper into my bed. "I'll eventually leave my bed for supplies."

"You have painkillers?"

"I keep them in my nightstand."

"Okay, okay." He still sounded concerned.

"I'm fine, Victor. I've had *Menstruella* visit monthly for over a decade. I know how to handle her." Said the woman in the fetal position, ignoring her stomach growling for food.

"I'm sure you can handle her. You're Olivia Rhodes. You can handle just about anything. You just don't always *have* to handle everything," Victor said, his voice bordering on chastising, but still soft around the edges.

"I have Chandler and Rachel. I'm good. It's the cheesecake episode."

He chuckled. "Okay, Olivia. Promise me you'll eat?"

"Stop worrying. Girls have periods all the time. I'm lucky it's a Saturday, and I can mope and don't have to teach class through the cramps."

"None of that makes me worry less." I heard a door close, and a lock turn on his end of the call.

We hung up, and I forced myself to brush my teeth and shower.

The way Victor knew all these personal little details about me was more intimate than any other guy friend I'd ever had. The way he checked on me—the concern in his voice—blurred the lines for me.

Our phone call didn't feel like a conversation I'd have with my best guy friend. It felt like something hazier, closer. Something I wasn't sure I was ready to name.

I was padding around my kitchen, about to start my coffee maker, when the doorbell rang.

I could see his shadow through the window on my door. I had to fight my grin.

"Victor Hernandez," I said in a tone of disbelief as I found him on my front porch with his arms full and a coffee cup in his hand.

He waltzed into my house, heading to my kitchen.

I trailed behind him in my baggy gray sweatpants. "I told you to go have fun."

He set the load down on the kitchen table. "I think I've made it pretty obvious by now that I don't find anything more fun than hanging out with you." He turned to me. "You haven't even had a cup of coffee yet, have you?"

"Okay, no, but I have showered." I pointed to my wet hair.

He placed the warm cup in my hand. I could smell the spicy sweetness of a dirty chai latte. My whole body responded as I took a sip.

He patted a takeout bag. "I got you a big breakfast sandwich. Google said you need iron."

My stomach growled in response. I glanced at a box on the table. "Chocolates?"

"Growing up, my dad always got my mom a box of her favorite chocolates when it was her time of the month."

I smiled. That sounded like Linda and David. I could imagine little Victor watching his dad pick out his mom's favorite chocolate at the grocery store.

I chuckled when I spotted tampons and pads. He followed my gaze.

"I wasn't sure what you like or need." He shrugged. "I also got a bottle of Midol. Google recommended that, too."

I set my cup down, rubbed the soft fuzzy socks from the bag, and looked through the pile of my favorite snacks.

An image of Victor throwing everything into his grocery

basket, hurrying through the store to get here quickly so I didn't get too hungry, popped into my mind.

I felt my heart tug in my chest. I threw my arms around his neck. He held me tight against him. With his big hands against my back, I could feel his heart beating through his white T-shirt.

"You're too good to be true sometimes," I said into his chest. I felt tears spring to my eyes at the truth of it. He was so good. Sometimes, it scared me. Like if I relaxed into it too much or held onto it too tight, it'd burst. I'd lose it just like that.

"Nah, you deserve someone to get you food when you're hungry and don't feel good. Simple as that, Liv." He reached over for the takeout bag and plopped it into my hands.

Victor retrieved my heating pad from upstairs, and we set up a cozy spot in the living room. I'd nestled under one of my favorite throw blankets when he said, "Wait," and ran back to the kitchen. He came back with the fuzzy orange socks.

"Do those have pumpkins on them?" I asked.

He nodded. "I thought they were festive." He grabbed my feet, slipping them on me.

"I can put my own socks on." I giggled.

"Again, I know you're a fully capable woman. I just like to help you."

"Help me put socks on?"

"Help with anything." He shrugged a shoulder.

He was already making me feel better. "I am getting a big preview of what an overprotective dad you're going to be."

He grinned at that comment, his eyes crinkling in that way that made my stomach flip.

We bickered over movie choices like we always did. Victor thought we should watch something new, but I wanted an old comforting favorite. I won. We watched *Titanic*, and I sobbed into the tissue box in my lap, while Victor ranted for a good ten minutes about how they could've shared the door.

I shared my chocolate with Victor. We ordered Chinese for

dinner and ate straight out of the containers, side by side on the couch.

His jacket was thrown over my dining table. His sneakers were on the ground by the door. His arm was slung behind me on the couch. Victor invaded all of my spaces.

How had our lives become so intertwined?

My heart felt that familiar tug. A tug I never felt brave enough to examine, even though I knew I should. If I was giving advice to my younger sisters, I would ask them, *and what do you think that feeling means?*

But in moments like this, I didn't want to mess any of it up. It felt delicate, like when someone falls asleep on your shoulder and you try to stay perfectly still to not ruin the moment. For months now, I'd been holding still in every way that mattered, trying to keep my feelings still, my thoughts still. I didn't want to ruin *this*. I didn't want to wake up.

*And why would you think that would ruin it?* I'd press my younger sisters. *Stupid big-sister brain.*

I pushed the pushy-big-sister thought away.

"You look like something's going on up there." Victor gave my foot a squeeze. His eyes were on me.

"Always." I ran a hand through my hair, pulling my feet closer to me.

"Work stuff or life stuff?" he asked.

*Us stuff,* I thought quietly.

"I don't know." I looked down at my hands, knotted up in my lap. "I was thinking how our friendship feels so easy. It feels so easy to let you into my life. It's never felt like that with anyone else. What is it about you?"

"Maybe it's because I show up at your door even when you tell me you don't need any help," he said in a self-deprecating tone, mostly jokingly.

But the words cut straight to my heart.

Most people walked out my door without notice, but Victor was the opposite. He would *show up* without notice.

Dad had slipped out the door even though I cried for him to stay. For so long, I cried for him to stay.

Ryan had packed his bags and left, even though I wasn't going with him. Even though he'd told me he would stay.

But Victor always showed up.

He was over here even when I told him I was perfectly fine without any help. If he knew I was in pain, he'd show up with a bag of supplies. If he knew I was sad, he was hanging birdhouses in my backyard.

I didn't have to ask, or hint, or hope for him to care. He just did it.

"You're joking, but it's true. You do show up. I know I can count on you to show up." I curled my body to face his against the sofa cushion.

His eyes softened on me.

"You make my heart feel safe."

It sounded cheesy, but it felt true. One of my favorite things about Victor was also one of the scariest things about him.

When we were together, I felt like I let my shoulders drop and my mask slip. I'd forget I was Put Together Olivia. I didn't have to be the smartest one in the room, big sister, mother number two, and instead, I could just be the same Olivia I was as a little girl.

"Your heart deserves to feel safe, Liv." Victor's eyes were narrowed fiercely. "I hate you've had idiots let you down. You should've always been treated with care."

Hearing Victor talk about my heart felt like we were letting the lines between us get even blurrier.

"Yeah, sometimes I hate it, too. But I don't regret the person I am and the life I have for a second. I've learned something from every relationship I've had." I sighed. "Plus, who knows if I'd appreciate what a great friend I have in you if I hadn't gone through some of it?"

"I think you would," he said. "I'm pretty dang amazing, you know." He pumped his brows.

I let my head fall back laughing.

He yanked on my feet to get my attention again. "Okay, okay. I wanted to ask you something. Do you remember Katie asking about the rehearsal dinner and stuff yesterday?"

"Yes. She asked if I'd be your date."

He swallowed. "You said you wanted to be my date. Is that true?"

His shoulders straightened. His jaw tightened. My response mattered to him.

"I'd be honored," I said in a playful tone, trying to ease the tension. "Plus, I owe you. You've been my date a couple of times now and counting. It's only fair."

A smile flickered across his face, but something in his eyes dimmed. He looked disappointed at my response, like maybe he'd hoped I might say something different. "It's settled then. *You owe me.* I'll get you the info."

There was a beat of silence between us. It felt unusually awkward, heavy with things unsaid.

"I'm going to head out," Victor finally said, patting the couch cushion before he stood up. "I have an early morning tomorrow."

"Oh, okay." My feet hit the ground as he got up. I felt like I'd accidentally popped whatever cozy bubble we'd been in.

"Don't forget, you're due for Midol in a couple hours," he said as he walked over toward his sneakers.

I wanted to tease him for playing Dr. Victor, like I'd been doing all day, but his eyes were still downcast.

I stood up and walked over toward him.

"Go sit back down. You're supposed to be resting," he said, finishing slipping his shoes on.

"I'm okay to walk a few steps, Victor." I'd been feeling much better this evening anyway, in no small part thanks to him. I stood in front of him. I wanted to chase the disappointment I'd seen in his eyes away. "Thank you for coming over."

His eyes creased, a small half smile. "It was selfish. I like hanging out with you."

I shook my head. "You don't see how kind you are." I pointed toward the table in the dining room, still covered in his shopping trip finds. "That's not selfish."

He dragged a hand through his hair. He sighed. I was still saying the wrong thing.

"I didn't do all of that because I'm such a nice friend," he said, his voice low. "*I care about you.*"

"But you *are* the closest friend I've ever had. Don't you see, your friendship ..." I put a hand to my chest, over my heart, where I felt that tug, that pull.

He nodded slowly, taking a step back. "Your friendship means a lot to me, too." His disappointment was thick in the air like humidity.

Frustration that I wasn't getting my point across—how much he meant to me—was sharp under my skin.

I grabbed his shoulders tight, fabric curling up my fingers. "You don't get it," I said forcefully.

His eyes widened.

"You mean ..." I tried to find the words. My breathing was heavy at the proximity.

Victor's eyes dropped to my lips. He licked his.

My heart was a fire alarm in my chest.

"I don't get it?" he asked, breathless.

I shook my head. I couldn't even remember why I'd chased him down and grabbed his shoulders. I just knew that I wanted him closer. Our charade had broken that physical barrier, and I couldn't get it back up.

Couldn't get how good it felt to be close—lip to lip—out of my head.

My hands clutched his broad shoulders. His eyes searched mine. Our breath hitched between us.

Then I pulled him to me, feeling reckless, desperate, and our mouths collided.

He immediately responded, arms sliding around my waist, pulling me against him until I was up on my toes. I slid my hands over his shoulders, his neck, fingers tangling in his hair.

"Olivia," he rasped, like he'd been waiting for this.

The sound flooded my body with goose bumps.

A push and pull between us, we moved together until we hit the doorframe between my living room and dining room.

His hands were up in my hair. His breath was hot against my chin as he kissed his way down to my neck. My body lit up like a forest fire.

"What are we …" I stepped away. "What am I …" *I couldn't finish a complete thought.*

Victor let out a long, slow breath, like he was trying to calm himself.

I covered my mouth with my hand. "I'm sorry," I whimpered.

His eyes twinkled. "Don't be."

"That was an accident," I said through my hands.

"Yeah?" he said, almost laughing. "The way you literally grabbed my face felt pretty intentional to me."

My face went red. "Okay, it might not have been accidental, but it was definitely not thought through."

"Like when you kissed me in your office?" Victor's hair was messy from where I'd pulled it.

I bet my neck and cheeks were pink from his five o'clock shadow.

"These accidents that involve *my mouth* just keep happening around you." He was enjoying watching me squirm. "You know how people say they *accidentally* ate chocolate? But really, they just can't help themselves …"

I shook my head, knowing where this was going.

"It's like maybe you can't … help yourself around me?"

"Victor." I turned my back to him, burying my face in my hands.

"I mean, actually, please help yourself around me anytime." He grabbed my shoulders and twirled me around to face him again.

"The kisses are good. I think that's the problem." I gestured helplessly.

"I don't know if *problem* is the word I'd use."

"It's making everything too confusing. We shouldn't have ever gone there!"

He leaned against the doorway he'd just pushed me up against. "That kiss has been on your mind, huh?"

"Has it not been on yours?"

"Every single second," he rasped.

I hated that the way he said this made my toes curl in my socks.

"I think the wisest thing would be for us to have better boundaries," I said, everything in me screaming against this idea. "All this hand holding and arms around each other, and you breathing into my ear while carving a pumpkin—"

"You liked that, huh?" Victor's eyes looked like trouble.

"I'm saying it muddled things up! Pretending we're dating has confused us. We've taken it too far."

"I thought how good we are at kissing each other is what confused us?" He crossed his arms.

My living room was dark, with only a couple of lamps turned on. I sighed. "How good all of it feels isn't the problem—it's that we now *know* how good it feels. That's the problem."

He grinned. "*All of it*, huh?"

"You are missing my point on purpose, Victor Hernandez." I walked over to my couch and sat down.

He stayed leaning against the doorframe that I'd never be able to look at the same way again.

"We need to have boundaries. Let's keep some distance, okay? I know we've been pretending we're a couple at my campus ... but let's cool it. No more touching, no more sitting so close, and absolutely no more kissing."

Victor's jaw ticked, like he was really mulling this over.

"Don't you think it's confusing?" I asked.

He parted his lips like he was about to say something but stopped himself, like he'd swallowed back the words. His forehead wrinkled. "You and I ..." he started, then hesitated again.

I waited.

"Are you sure this is what you want?" he asked.

"I'm sure," I said quickly, before I could even stop and think through his question or why he asked it.

"I don't think *any* of this is a problem. And I'm not confused about what I feel for you, Liv." His tone wasn't joking at all anymore. "But if you think we need those boundaries, then I'll do whatever you need."

I nodded. *Okay. Problem solved,* I lied to myself.

*Sixteen*



Since Gracie was back home in Sweet River for fall break from school, Lucy decided to host a dinner party with Adam at her house on Sunday night. She'd enlisted me to provide appetizers, but I was not much of a cook. I made a mean grilled cheese and loved a salad kit and frozen lasagnas. The local restaurants around town knew my regular takeout orders by heart. I didn't even have to say anything when I called anymore, except *takeout for Olivia Rhodes.*

So when Lucy asked if I'd bring an appetizer, I headed straight to our local market downtown. The ceiling was hung with flimsy paper pumpkins and turkeys, streamers in browns and yellows strung about. Our small-town market was always decked out for the season. I strolled through the aisles, pressing my cell phone against my ear.

"Hey, Liv," Lucy answered my call.

"Hey, I'm at the store shopping for an appetizer, but I wanted to double-check who is coming tonight."

"We have me, you, Adam, Gracie, Mom, and she is bringing a date—"

"Mom is bringing a date? Who?" I set the box of muffins I was studying back on the shelf.

"One of the guys she's been messaging with on LoveLocal. Jeff. He seems nice. He's a banker or something like that. He has a few kids, all around our ages," Lucy said before yawning. "Him coming tonight means we can vet him, I guess."

"Is this their first date?"

"Yeah, this'll be their first date," Lucy said. I could almost see her shrugging. *Mom on a date.*

"How do you already know so much about, what'd you call him, Jeff?"

"It's called talking to Mom, Olivia. I asked her about him."

"I forget Mom even has a love life now to ask about." I pushed the cart through the chip aisle. "Is this more of a chip and dip situation, or a cheese board situation?"

"Cheese board. Definitely," Lucy said decisively. "Oh, by the way, Adam invited Victor."

"What?" I stopped pushing my cart, frozen in the middle of the aisle.

My stomach fluttered. Flashes of our kiss raced through my mind—my hands on his chest, his lips on mine, my back against the doorway.

"Why do you sound so surprised? You're close to him. Adam's close to him. Of course he's invited." Lucy's chuckle was muffled on her end of the line, like she was holding her phone between her ear and shoulder. "What? You afraid you'll kiss for a second time?"

*A second time? Try a third time.* I swallowed.

"Have you talked to Gracie since our last margarita night when she FaceTimed?" Lucy asked.

"Uh, just a few text messages back and forth. Have you?"

"One phone call. And I asked about her message from Austin, and she really dodged it."

My heart sank. "What is it about Austin?"

Lucy groaned on her end of the line. "Seriously."

I perused the premade cheese trays. Did I want simple or elaborate? I picked up an elaborate one.

"Maybe we're jumping to conclusions. Maybe she just doesn't want to talk about him anymore, like he's a sore subject," Lucy said optimistically.

I dropped the tray in my cart. "Doubtful. I know our little sister. If she's avoiding a topic, it's because she's hiding it."

"Huh, I know someone else who hides from topics, too," Lucy said in a sing-songy voice, oozing with insinuation.

"I don't hide from any topics," I said. A '90s love song crooned from the market's stereo system in the background.

"Really. How's Victor?"

"He's great. Brought me over Midol and breakfast yesterday for first day cramps," I said smugly. *Did leaving out a few details count as hiding?*

Our conversation continued, but the back of my mind snagged on what Lucy said. Did I hide from certain sensitive topics, like the topic of Victor?

I'd remained quiet about the kiss.

And the feelings I'd been wrestling with.

I'd never felt like I hid, but I definitely wasn't sharing it. *Because,* I thought to myself later while buckling the cheese tray into the front seat of my car, *why involve others in my own messy thoughts until I cleaned them up?*

I knew Lucy. She'd just try to clean it up for me. Or with me.

And then there was a thought I wrestled with the whole drive to Lucy's, in my big-sister voice: *and what's so wrong with someone helping sort out the mess alongside me?*

Lucy's house smelled like tomato sauce and garlic. My mouth watered at the bubbling, gooey lasagna she and Adam had made for dinner.

She was tossing the garden salad at the kitchen counter while Adam told Mom and Jeff about how he'd seasoned the lasagna meat. Lucy's own art hung on the walls around us.

I leaned over Lucy's shoulder. Her wild red hair was back in a messy clip. "What do you think of Jeff?"

Gracie suddenly appeared by my side. "You guys whispering about Jeff?"

I shot a glance at Mom. She was completely immersed in the lasagna conversation as Adam used his hands to emphatically describe something about the recipe.

"He's nice. He brought a great bottle of red wine." Lucy shrugged, adding a few more croutons to the salad.

"He seems friendly," Gracie mused, stealing a crouton from the opened bag.

"I think he really likes Mom," I said.

So far, he'd found multiple reasons to make physical contact and looked at her like he was taken aback by her beauty, her shaggy auburn bob, and her big, brown eyes.

"I noticed that, too. He seems flustered," Gracie agreed, reaching for another crouton.

Lucy swatted her hand away from the salad toppings. There was a knock at the door. "That's probably Victor. Will you go answer, Liv?"

I wanted to protest, but that would garner suspicion, so I swallowed back my nerves. We hadn't seen each other since our second accidental kiss.

*He's just my old pal Victor,* I reminded myself.

I pulled open the door to find Victor standing there in a hunter green sweater that made his mocha eyes pop. My heart swirled in my chest. "Hey," I said, trying to sound casual.

"Hey," he said almost tentatively. He shifted like he was going in for a hug, but then stopped himself, hands returning to his sides.

It was my own rules, so I tried not to feel disappointed.

"Come on in." I stepped to the side, and he trailed into Lucy's house.

We all piled around Lucy's long, wooden dining table for dinner. Everyone caught Jeff, the newcomer, up to speed.

"So, how'd you two meet?" Jeff asked Lucy and Adam.

I grinned. They loved to answer this question.

"She stormed into my office to yell at me." Adam chuckled.

Jeff's brows raised in surprise.

"It's true."

"I didn't yell at him. I did confront him. Do you know the Sweet River Summer Festival?" Lucy said. The candle in the center of the table flickered.

"Of course. I take my family every year," Jeff said.

"Well, it was my late grandmother's brainchild, so I'd started running it in her memory. Adam moved to town and immediately tried to take it out from under me. That was how we met."

Adam shook his head. "I was going to let her volunteer."

"Selling hot dogs."

Adam burst out laughing. "We wound up working together after she confronted me, and I was honestly impressed by her passion."

"And her hotness," Gracie whispered behind her glass of iced tea, but loud enough to make the whole table laugh.

"You guys ran it this past summer? It was incredible, and that's even with the storms," Jeff said through a big bite of salad.

Lucy shimmied her shoulders with pride. "We made a good team."

"Okay," Jeff said, turning to me and Victor, who sat beside me. "How did you two meet?"

"Oh, uh ..." I stumbled over my words, a forkful of lasagna hanging in midair on the way to my mouth. "We met at a coffee shop. Actually, we both had shown up that day to act as moral support for Adam and Lucy. But we're not a couple."

"Try as I might, I still haven't won this one over," Victor joked, in the way he always had, but his voice rasped at the end.

I gave his shoulders a playful shove in the way I always had, but the giggle felt stuck in my throat. "Be serious."

"I got her talking about the old house she'd been renovating. Those green eyes lit up, the way they do when she's talking about something she loves. Our conversation flowed so easy. It always does with us." Our eyes were on each other's as he spoke. The rest of the table faded into the background. "We were fast friends."

"Fast friends," I repeated. I felt an urge to squeeze his hand or press my shoulder into his, but I resisted.

"The best friendships are the ones where you can talk for hours on end," Jeff said, breaking my attention from Victor.

I turned to him to listen.

"My late wife, Angela ... She and I were friends from childhood. I used to call her my safe zone."

"Safe zone," Victor repeated. "I like that."

"Angela was always my safe zone from grade school and beyond. I could talk to her about the important things, the ridiculous things, even the commercial we'd just watched on TV—all of it. Those types of relationships are a treasure." Jeff gave a small smile.

My mom rubbed his shoulder gently. "Angela sounds like a treasure."

I glanced across the table and saw Lucy mouth to Adam that he was her safe zone. I quickly looked away. The moment felt like an intrusion. The moment wasn't mine, but it cracked something open in me.

I could feel Victor's gaze on me heavy as a touch, but I didn't dare look back at him.

I was trying to handle everything between us delicately, carefully. I didn't want to risk losing my safe zone.

•  •  •

When you got Lucy and Adam together, a board game always found its way onto the table, or a dart board got hung on the wall, or a deck of cards got pulled out of Adam's pocket. This time, after dinner was finished, it was a game of charades.

We settled into Lucy's living room, piling onto her couch and armchair. The sky was dark outside. A few lamps switched on around her house. Some of us had carried our glasses of wine along with us.

Adam's City of Sweet River hat was filled with tiny pieces of torn paper with phrases written on them.

First, Lucy and Adam went. Lucy was acting, and Adam was guessing. Lucy mimed singing.

Adam said, "Song title?"

She nodded.

First, she shook her head, as if to say *no*.

He asked, "No?"

That wasn't right, so she tried again, this time wagging her finger.

"Don't?" he guessed correctly this time.

She nodded excitedly.

Then he correctly guessed, "Go," after she mimed pointing toward the door.

Quickly after that, she made a heart with her hands and then broke them apart.

"Don't go breaking my heart?" He shouted his guess with his words running together.

The two high-fived at their victory. I chuckled into my big glass of wine.

Next, it was Jeff and my mom's turn. My mom offered to act and Jeff guess. Jeff correctly guessed it was a *person* after my mom stood with her hands on her hips. Mom set her hands in front of her in the air and twinkled her fingers for mere seconds.

After only a beat, maybe half a beat, Jeff shouted, "Kenny G!"

Mom whooped.

"That was so fast. I didn't even have time to register what she was doing," Victor said from his spot on the floor beside my legs, his back resting on the couch I sat on.

"How?" Lucy gaped from the couch.

"I love jazz." Jeff shrugged bashfully. "I recognized she was miming a saxophone right away."

"If you think of a saxophone, you've got to think of Kenny!" Mom said, thoroughly impressed. She was a huge Kenny G fan. At Christmas, his albums played on a loop.

"He's the king!" Jeff said, waving his arms emphatically.

"I've seen him live several times," Mom said as the two returned to their seats on the couch. The two of them were lost to their own chit-chat.

"You girls go ahead," Victor said to me, and I assumed Gracie, since we'd decided to be a team.

As I glanced around the living room, she was nowhere to be seen. "Gracie?" I asked.

A few of us looked around. She poked her head around the corner from the doorway of Lucy's makeshift art room, her cell phone pressed to her ear. She pointed at it and mouthed, *On the phone, you go ahead.*

My only non-Victor option was gone. I felt my feeble attempt to get some clarity drifting away.

I turned to him. "I guess it's you and me."

Victor stood up from the ground as I got up from the couch, the rug fuzzy under my bare feet. I told myself I was being dramatic. Charades didn't involve any touching, and that was really what I was avoiding with Victor.

"You're a good guesser. I think you should guess, and I should act," Victor said, rubbing his hands together.

"Agreed," I said.

Lucy handed a scrap of paper to Victor from the hat as we strategized.

He read the paper and took in a sharp inhale, thinking for a few beats. He ran his fingers through his messy black hair. I watched his wheels turn. He turned to me and made quotations in the air with his fingers.

"A phrase," I said.

He nodded in response. He held two fingers at his elbow.

"Two syllables," I said.

He nodded again, walking over to me, so close that my jaw dropped a little. His feet bumped into mine, and he grabbed my hip with one hand, then pressed the other warm against my upper back through my sweater. My breath caught in my throat as he slid his hand around my upper back over to my shoulder, pulling on it until I dipped low. My stomach was fizzy as his arms cradled me. My hair fell into the air around us.

"Victor," I gasped, my voice lilting in question.

His gaze was heavy as it met mine, and he slowly brought his mouth closer to mine. His jaw was tight as our lips held a breath apart. My heart was skyrocketing as his mouth hovered over mine. His warm hands held me tight, my arm dangling by my side.

I looked straight into Victor's caramel eyes. His bore right back into mine. *How on earth was I supposed to think clearly enough to make a guess when he was dipping me like this? If he moved his mouth half an inch closer, he could kiss me.* My mouth pursed at the idea. His eyes dropped to my lips at the movement. He swallowed.

Lucy was oohing from her spot on the couch. My mom whispered conspiratorially to her that I looked like a bride.

Then, he twirled me right back to standing, taking a step back, putting distance between us.

I sorted my thoughts. Our pose mimicked wedding photos I'd seen. I looked like a bride being dipped. He looked like he was going to kiss me, like a groom at the altar.

"A dip and a kiss? A dip kiss?" I said shakily. My palms were sweaty, and my cheeks were pink.

"That's right," Victor said with a smile, raising his hand for a high five.

Our hands made contact.

"Team Volivia!"

I laughed as I fell back onto the couch, like it was a hilarious shenanigan, but my heart fluttered like a leaf in the wind.

Mom and Jeff kept guessing within seconds the rest of the night: *Murder She Wrote*, the Bible, and Ina Garten. They wound up winning the whole game. Lucy and Adam seemed oddly smug about how the game went, even though they lost.

Like maybe somehow they'd still won.

Lucy kept grabbing the phrases out of the hat for everyone. *She wouldn't have rigged it, would she?*

Giving Mom and Jeff phrases that helped them get to know each other better.

Giving Victor and me a near kiss?

"Rematch?" she pleaded with Mom playfully, the two side by side on the couch.

I shook the thought from my head. "It's getting late. I need to get home," I announced, although Gracie still hadn't emerged from the other room. I wondered who this lengthy phone call could be with.

"I know, you have work in the morning. Thanks for coming, anyway," Lucy said as she wrapped her arms around me for a hug.

"It was so great to meet you," Jeff said after Lucy released me from her arms.

"You, too," I said.

He was still sitting on the couch with Mom. The two of them had been chatting like old friends. Mom looked at me with a question in her eyes, and I gave her a little nod of approval.

"Drive safe, honey," Mom said as I made my way toward the door.

I was retrieving my purse from the coat stand by the doorway when Victor walked up behind me.

"Can I walk you out?"

"Of course," I said, trying to sound normal. Another charade. Nothing felt normal between us.

As Lucy's front door shut behind us, the crisp night air blew through my hair. I rubbed my arms for warmth as we paced down the front steps.

"Sorry if I crossed the boundaries during charades," Victor said, his voice low and sincere. "On the spot like that, I couldn't think of another way to act it out, but then I saw how it shook you up. I was sitting there the rest of the game, realizing all these other ways I could've acted it out that didn't involve holding you in my arms."

I stopped walking in the middle of the sidewalk and grabbed his elbow. "You don't need to be sorry. You didn't cross any boundaries. If anyone did, it was Lucy Rhodes for putting that phrase in the hat."

"She probably hoped it would be her and Adam who got it." Victor chuckled. The night sky twinkled with stars overhead.

"Whatever her intention, I know yours. We were just playing a game." I tucked the cuffs of my sweater sleeves over my fingers. "You always handle me with care, Vic."

We started walking again. My car was parked a few paces down the sidewalk.

"I wanted to make sure you were feeling okay, Liv."

I couldn't hide from Victor. It was like seeing me was a secret talent of his, the way some people immediately understand the keys of a piano. He knew something was off with me all night.

"I *am* feeling okay. How are you feeling?" I said, wanting to make sure he was doing okay through all this confusion.

Victor messed with the zipper on his leather jacket. "I'm great. I got to hang out with you and your family. Watch Mama Rhodes make a love connection in there."

That made me laugh. Leave it to Victor to find a way to break the tension a little. "They were really clicking, huh? When he mimed the Bible, I swear she had hearts popping out of her eyes," I said.

"I think she was smitten the minute he said Kenny G."

"Yeah. Tonight was pretty fun," I said.

The two of us stopped in front of my Prius parked along the pavement. I should walk to my driver's side door, say goodbye, and wave at him like I would any other friend. But one thing was completely clear in the midst of all my muddled thoughts and feelings: Victor Hernandez was not just any other friend.

I looked down at my ankle boots. *Do we hug goodbye? Is that too much? Should I try for an awkward side hug?* We always hugged goodbye.

Going in for a hug felt weird. *Not* going in for a hug felt weird.

Victor sighed resignedly, slipping his hands into his pockets. A car sped down the street, headlights streaking through the dark.

I glanced up to find him already looking down at me. His eyes were creased in that familiar, thoughtful way of his. He was reading me like a favorite book, pages he knew, passages underlined and highlighted.

There was something heavy in the air between us. It felt like there was more to say, but I didn't know how to say any of it.

"Olivia," he said, his voice surprisingly commanding. "Good night. Drive safely."

I bit my lip, pulling open my car door. "Good night. Thanks for being my charades partner."

"Honestly, I might think twice before being your partner again. We were in dead-last place," he said as I slid into my driver's seat.

"It takes two to suck that bad," I argued, sliding my buckle into place.

He leaned over my driver's side door. His scent was woodsy and warm through the open window.

He pulled away, taking a step back onto the sidewalk. He closed the car door firmly. "Goodbye, Liv," he said, raising his voice since the door was closed, giving the hood of my car a pat as he walked away.

I stared at my steering wheel. I knew he was respecting my wishes and honoring my no-more-touching rule ... but I couldn't put the keys in the ignition. I was hoping he'd come back and knock on my door.

Suddenly, a tap at my window jolted me from my thoughts.

It was Adam holding up my phone. I'd been so distracted tonight. I was going to drive home without my phone.

"This was sitting on the kitchen counter," he said after I rolled down my window.

"I can't believe I forgot my phone. Thank you for running it out to me."

He handed it to me. "Living up to the absentminded professor stereotype, huh?" Adam chuckled.

"I guess so." I shrugged. "I think I got distracted by everything going on." Mom had a date, Gracie was on a dramatic call, and I was trying to keep my distance from Victor even as he dipped me and smelled warm and woodsy.

"It was one of the more dramatic games of charades I've ever played," Adam admitted.

"No chance Lucy rigged it?" I tipped my chin curiously.

A smile cracked across Adam's face. "I can't say! Really, I don't know!" He raised his hands up in surrender. "But I wouldn't put it past her."

I shook my head. "I bet she did."

"Just the game bothering you?" Adam asked, sounding almost brotherly. He'd taken to checking on Gracie and me sometimes. A nice new member to our crew.

"It was mostly the game," I said, twisting my phone in my lap. "But I have had a lot on my mind."

"Funny enough, Victor said the same thing to me earlier tonight."

I could just imagine Adam and Lucy both talking about me and Victor tonight as they cleaned up after dinner. The two of them were conniving together.

"I know Lucy told you about mine and Victor's charade at work—letting everyone think we were dating."

"She did." He nodded, crossing his arms. "You having some regrets?"

I went to answer that of course I did. Things had been so confusing since it started ... but I realized, I didn't. I didn't regret a second of it. I'd loved all of it. "No. Not one."

"Then what's the problem?"

"The whole charade got us a little confused. I think we're both having trouble going back to normal." Or maybe it was mostly me. I was the one who'd pulled his lips against mine last night.

"I've seen how important your friendship is to both of you. I know it's not romantic or anything between the two of you, but it does remind me of when I first met Lucy," he said, the light from the streetlamps glinting off his glasses. "Our relationship quickly felt like the home I'd always wished for as a kid. Safe, welcoming, warm. All of it." His face turned toward Lucy's house, steps away. "I know neither of you would do anything to lose what you have in each other."

As I drove home that evening, headlights and streetlamps lighting my path in my small town, I thought about what Adam said.

Since I was a little girl, I'd wanted stability, reliability, so deeply that I found a way to give it to myself, so I'd never rely on it from anyone else.

But this relationship with Victor had somehow become a home for my heart. A place I could rely on. A stable ground beneath my feet. A birdhouse hanging in my trees.

I turned onto my street. I wasn't just looking for clarity. I was trying to find the safest way to keep what we had.

The next morning, I was running late to work after tossing and turning all night. My thoughts were a tangled mess over Victor and me. I drove under a sheet of rain to the school, running across the campus, trying to avoid puddles with my jacket over my head.

"Long morning?" Sylvie asked as I passed her desk, feeling like a soggy mop.

"Long *night*," I moaned, running my fingers through my damp hair as I headed toward my office.

I collapsed into my office chair, dropping my tote bag on the ground beside me while taking a few deep breaths in and out. I chuckled a little because it reminded me of Victor. Back when we first started spending time together, I had just moved into my house. The early stages of renovations were chaotic and stressful, and he saw firsthand how tightly wound I could get.

I remembered the first time he gently reminded me to breathe.

*"Your shoulders are by your ears," he said, eyes squinting at me. He placed a heavy, warm hand on my shoulder, pressing it down gently.*

*"I'm stressed." I was sitting on my hardwood floor among a scattered pile of plans for my house that felt daunting. "I store my stress in my body. It winds up my neck and shoulders."*

*"Liv." Victor's usual playful voice took on a soft tone. It immediately settled my thoughts like someone turning the radio from static to silence. "Don't worry about all of this." He patted the pile of papers. "Just worry about this." He picked up one of the first plans we'd agreed upon. "This is the only thing we worry about right now. We're doing this one step at a time."*

*I took the paper from his hands and looked at it. This one we were ready to tackle. All the kinks were sorted. I liked the idea of letting the others patiently wait to be worried over.*

*"And if you start trying to carry your worries around on your shoulders again"—he gave my shoulder another squeeze, his rough fingertips against my soft skin—"breathe in and out, in and out."*

*We took a deep breath together, over and over, until it felt silly, and we were laughing there on my living room floor, my stress burned off at the edges.*

It became a consistent ritual between the two of us. Anytime

I'd start getting stressed, my shoulders drawing up toward my ears, Victor would step in.

Wherever we were—my house, the pizza place downtown, the hardware shop—he would look me in the eyes and say, in that steady, warm voice that felt like an embrace, *breathe in and out, in and out.*

Somehow, something so simple felt like a balm to my raw nerves. Something about it always worked. I wasn't sure if it was the breathing. Or Victor. Probably both.

Yet, even now, on a stressful day with rain running down my neck, alone in my office, Victor still found a way to settle my nerves, without even being here.

I turned on my computer to begin responding to emails when a student knocked on my door. I waved her in.

Chloe, a student in my Ancient Greek History class, sat down in the chair opposite my desk. "Hi, Dr. Rhodes. I saw you had office hours today. I wanted to pop by for a second."

"That's great. I love when my students pop by." I leaned back in my chair.

"I heard about your romance book club. My friend Ashley is in it, and she's always raving about how fun it is. I've been too busy this semester to attend any of the meet-ups, but the other day, I grabbed one of the books you guys are reading for October," she said, as I reached for my coffee cup to steal a sip. "It's set in Ancient Greece. I was meaning to just flip through it for fun, but I wound up devouring it over the weekend."

"Sometimes, a book will sneak up on you like that. You won't expect it, but it'll hook you. I've missed a lot of sleep thanks to some good books."

"The interesting thing is that I've really struggled to wrap my mind around your Ancient Greece course. We're supposed to be learning about their daily lives and customs, and my mind has trouble grasping onto it in a concrete way. But this book"—she pulled it out of her bag and waved it around—"has really helped.

It made what we're studying come alive and really grounded it in my mind."

I couldn't contain my smile as Chloe went on about specific details from the book that helped her understand key concepts from our class. This was exactly what I loved about teaching. We wound up talking for nearly forty minutes.

"I'm telling you, Dr. Rhodes," Chloe said, swinging her backpack over her shoulder before she left. "You should include a book like this in your syllabus."

"That'd be fun," I said, half laughing, as Chloe walked out the door. I spun in my chair back toward my computer, but what Chloe said was stuck in my head like a new song.

It *would* be fun to include romance books set or even written during a specific time to a history class to make the details come alive and add depth and dimension to the facts and concepts. I imagined discussing the corresponding details like I'd just done with Chloe, her excitement palpable, with an entire class.

It felt like a dream.

There was another knock at my door. I glanced up to discover Victor leaning against the doorway, his dark hair swooped down over his eyes. His gray sweater was tight over his shoulders, and his hands were in his jeans pockets.

My eyebrows knit in confusion. "Hey, what are you doing here?"

"The lecture is in half an hour, right?" He glanced down at his watch.

"Yeah, but ..." I stood up from my desk, frazzled. I didn't remember inviting Victor to the seminar. "I didn't know you were coming to the lecture?"

"Well, when we decided I'd be your copilot to the Fall Seminar events, I went and screenshotted the schedule the school posted to their Instagram," Victor said, still leaning against the doorframe.

"You follow the school on Instagram?"

"You don't?"

I crossed my arms. "So, I have a date to the classics lecture by Dr. Shannon Hadaway?" Dr. Shannon Hadaway was notoriously long-winded and boring, some might say.

"You've got a date to anything you want, baby girl." He walked into my office toward my desk.

I shook my head. "You know, my pretend boyfriend showing up to a dinner or a festival makes sense. My pretend boyfriend showing up to a lecture by a guest professor might look kind of weird."

"Not that weird. Clingy, maybe? But I'm a clingy pretend boyfriend," Victor said. "Plus, what if Ryan winds up sitting next to you or something and you need backup?"

"Doubtful." I started packing up my tote before heading over to the auditorium for the lecture. "But you're here already—might as well tag along."

We wove across campus under the sprinkling rain and trees the shades of copper and amber. Victor carried my tote bag so I could hold my blazer over my head to protect myself from the downpour. As he told me about his workday, making me laugh, I accidentally bumped into his shoulder and caught the scent off his sweater. The smell of him mingled with the fresh rainfall. I felt giddy to have him back on campus with me. We didn't have that much longer to this fall series.

My stomach sank at the thought that the school's Fall Seminar was ending soon. This was one of the last events before we headed into finals and holidays.

I stole a glance at Victor as we walked into the auditorium. His eyes crinkled at something I'd said. I was amazed that something I'd dreaded—these fall events with my ex-boyfriend—had somehow become something I was sad to see end, like the days of a long-awaited vacation drawing closer to the flight back home. Closer to reality.

We slid into our seats, chatting as the auditorium slowly started to fill up, until one of the only seats left was the seat right in front of me. Ryan rushed in and plopped down before it was taken.

Victor bumped his arm into mine. "I told you," he whispered, not above gloating.

I didn't remember the back of Ryan's head being so irritating, but it was now. *Did he always use that much hair gel?* I squinted. *Did he color his hair?*

He was hunched forward, his posture nervous.

"He keeps glancing back," Victor whispered low, leaning toward me. "He knows you're behind him with your hot young buck."

I snorted. A couple of people, Ryan included, glanced my way. "My *hot young buck*?" I whispered slowly, emphasizing each word.

"I know what I am, Liv." Victor stretched his arms, folding them behind his head. His feet stretched in front of him, crossed at the ankles.

"A hot young buck?" I pulled his arms down, setting them politely at his sides. We didn't need to make a scene at this lecture.

"*Your* hot young buck." Victor's voice was syrupy, warm.

I should hate that sentence, but something about Victor made everything adorable and, well, kind of hot.

I shook my head disapprovingly, crossing my legs. The lights dimmed. I could see Dr. Hadaway walking toward the podium. "It's starting," I murmured.

Dr. Hadaway introduced herself, but I couldn't hear a thing she said after that. Victor and I, without any planning or acting, both scooted closer toward one another over the shared armrest. His body heat mingled with mine in a reassuring, disarming way.

My heart pounded loudly in my ears.

I remembered how my sisters and I would spot a happy older couple, or a couple chasing their kids at the park, and we would swoon over the natural way those couples moved throughout the world together: hands reaching for hands reflexively; shoulders playfully, instinctively bumping into one another; eyes catching across dinner tables and crowded rooms; a hand brushing a loose strand out of an eye; a hand sweeping across a shoulder as the other walked by. It was that simple but rhythmic way two people would lean into each other. Two halves never quite close enough, always reaching, always leaning, to get a little closer.

No measly armrest was enough to keep them apart.

I swallowed, my mouth dry. The crowd was laughing at something. Victor chuckled, and his eyes snagged on my gaze. He searched my eyes. I pretended to laugh, but his eyes narrowed, noting it was fake.

I looked ahead at the stage.

I was on high alert, so I noticed when Victor's left hand reached for my right hand resting between us, hovering for a moment with our skin barely grazing. Then, as if he realized what he was doing, he quickly snatched it back to himself.

He scratched at his chin. I tried not to think about how that chin felt against my own skin—a diabolically perfect amount of stubble.

Colleagues around me were nodding to the lecture, taking notes, and murmuring thoughts to people beside them. I was thinking about Victor's shaving habits and wondering if I could come up with a good enough reason to break our new no-contact rule.

Victor leaned down and pulled a pen out of my tote. I chuckled inwardly that he knew me and my routines so well that he could casually reach into my pen pocket without looking.

He wrote a note on the back of a bulletin we were handed when we walked in and slipped it into my hand.

*You okay?*

He'd written in thick, blunt handwriting.

I glanced up at him. His eyes were full of care as they rested on me attentively. I nodded.

He grabbed the sheet again and wrote furiously before setting it on my lap.

*I'm sorry I showed up unannounced. I got excited.*
*I think I have too much fun being your boyfriend.*

I turned my head and shook my head at him, reaching across his chest to steal the pen.
I wrote,

*I'm not upset. I like that you're here.*

He wrote back,

*Is it because of...?*

He nodded his head toward Ryan.
I bit my lip. I wasn't too bothered by Ryan's presence. I'd gotten fully distracted by Victor's presence.

*I think I'm tired!*

I wrote a measly excuse.

*Your hot young buck keeping you up too late?*

Victor wrote in big, thick letters with a winky face.
This made me snort again. I covered my mouth. When suddenly, a shrill beep started ringing across the auditorium. In a matter of seconds, the audience was scrambling, and the lights were back on. People raced for exits—no one following the fire alarm protocol we'd practiced during drills or training as staff.

Victor and I jumped up, turning toward the aisle to exit our row. He reached his hand for mine, pulling me behind him. I bumped into Ryan, who was trying to race past us, causing me to drop my armload of things.

Ryan sputtered to a stop, dropping to his knees to hurriedly grab the notebook, pen, and papers I'd dropped when he slammed into me. "I'm sorry, I'm sorry," he said anxiously.

Victor bent down to help, and Ryan waved him off as he stacked my fallen papers.

Ryan set the bulletin that was in the pile on top of the stack, his eyes stopping on the big, thick letters about too many late nights with my young buck. He shoved the papers into my arms, his cheeks blazing red.

Victor held back a pleased smile. Ryan hurried ahead of us.

I slowed my pace, falling in step with Victor as we weaved through the crowd.

"I suspect the alarm might be a prank," I said, my voice raised over the chatter.

"You think?"

"There's been quite a few alarms pulls across campus this semester. I'm wondering if it's some frat initiation thing or a freshman dare."

"Some annoying guy who thinks it's hilarious."

"Some young buck," I murmured. We stepped out onto campus, sunlight hitting our eyes.

"You gotta watch out for 'em, I tell ya." Victor shook his head.

Victor and I kept our eyes on each other, an unspoken thing hanging in the air between us, thick like smoke, always pulling me under.

We stood at the entrance, an announcement sounding over the speakers that it was a false alarm and that they'd resume the lecture shortly.

Victor's eyes fell on mine, and he opened his mouth to speak.

"Well, hey, you two," Gabby said, skipping up the steps. The sky was still gray, and the cool damp of rain hung in the air. "I didn't see you in there."

"We were in the middle rows," I said, trying to collect myself after the whirlwind of the past few minutes.

"I was up front. I can't believe someone pulled the stupid alarm again. I'm getting tired of this prank. It's been interrupting too many classes." Gabby pinched the bridge of her nose.

"I heard someone woke up a whole dorm the other night," I added. "All these students stuck outside in their pajamas for an hour."

"Well, maybe they finally found the culprit?" Victor offered hopefully.

"Doubtful. There's been so many cases, I'm wondering if they're connected somehow." Gabby tapped her chin like she was a detective on the case. Then, like she'd just been awoken from her own thoughts, she said, "I can't believe you're sitting in this super long lecture about classics, Victor. Are you even interested in classical antiquity?"

"I'm barely grasping what *classical antiquity* means," Victor admitted. "But the professors are *super* hot."

My cheeks flamed.

Gabby chuckled, unsurprised. "Or something like that got you attending boring lectures, huh?"

"Okay, okay, let's head back in. This is your last chance to bail, Victor, if you so choose. We're not even halfway through the lecture," I said, as people flowed around us back into the building.

Victor slid his arm around me, his warm fingertips pressing into my shoulder through my button-down. "I'm in it for the long haul."

At that, Gabby shot me a knowing glance, and I quickly marched ahead toward our seats.

I'd always been a good student who paid full attention during classes, but I missed most of this lecture because Victor and I passed notes the entire time.

Should I change my ringtone to Hot for Teacher?

I need to ban you from this campus from now on. You are a distraction.

As your hot young bf I'm just fulfilling my duties.

what are these hot young bf duties?

duty number 1 is to make your day easier
duty number 2 is to make you laugh
duty number 3 is to be a good copilot
duty number 4 is to distract you with my charm and good looks

You mean distract me with your goofball antics?

goofball antics and good looks

we probably look like highschoolers passing notes right now!

Hey, Dr. Rhodes needs a distraction every now and then.

*Eighteen*

ME

I'll be there to pick up Watson in an hour

VICTOR

I think you've walked him more in the past six
months than I have in his whole life

ME

that's sad, Victor

he needed me

VICTOR

we both needed you

W atson and I had our walking routine down. I would pick
him up a couple times a week. He'd jump in my car, his
furry golden tail wagging against the leather seat. We'd drive to the
walking trail along the river with the windows down.

We had our favorite stops with the doggy water fountains. We
walked slowly, so he could peruse the path and sniff everything his
heart desired. I'd take those moments as reminders to slow down

my breathing, to look up at the sky, and notice the sun on my skin. These walks were easy to skip before I had a walking buddy in Watson. Now, when I considered pushing it off my schedule, I thought of how excited Watson would be to see me walk in the door with a leash in hand.

Sometimes, Victor joined us and he'd stop to look at things—the ducks in the river, the weird thing in the sky, the cooing baby in the stroller—nearly as often as Watson.

Other times, Lucy joined me. We took no time to notice the sun on our skin, instead talking a mile a minute. This time, Lucy *and* Gracie met us there.

"Mom has another date," Lucy said, almost like an announcement. She looked at Gracie and me expectantly, her wavy red hair piled atop her head in a bun.

"When?" I asked.

Gracie asked, "Who with?"

"Jeff, probably," I said, moving out of the way of a mom chasing two toddlers, my black hoodie falling from my shoulder.

"No, not Jeff," Lucy corrected me. "Some new guy."

"What?" I frowned. "I liked Jeff for her."

"She said she's not putting all of her eggs in Jeff's basket," Lucy said.

"I mean, I get it." Gracie shrugged, tugging on her pink sweatshirt with a dance studio's name embroidered across the front.

"When's the date?" I asked.

"Tomorrow night," Lucy said.

"I wish we could check him out like we got to check out Jeff." I chewed on my lip, stopping so Watson could sniff some grass by the river. The rushing water was a soft murmur.

"Me too," Lucy said. "Could you imagine—the three of us accidentally bumping into them at dinner?"

Gracie chuckled. "Fancy meeting you here, while we scoot into their booth."

"No, no. We'd have to spy from afar, hiding behind big

menus," I joked. Watson's leash was rough in my hands, yanking me ahead.

"I feel like we'd actually be good at it," Lucy said, something flashing in her eyes. "We could pull it off. They're not even going to a restaurant. They're playing mini golf. We could easily hide around the course to hear what they're saying."

"*Easily hide around the course?*" I asked, brows furrowed. "Lucy Rhodes, you're not suggesting we spy on Mom's date for real!"

"Not for the whole date. Merely pop in for like half an hour and check the guy out. It's not that crazy. I'm sure it happens more than we realize," Lucy said.

"I've never heard of anyone spying on someone else's date, except for on sitcoms," I said.

"Liv, they get those ideas from somewhere." Lucy crossed her arms.

"I don't think it's necessarily a bad idea," Gracie said, slowly offering up each word, her blonde hair bouncing as she walked.

"You both don't think it's a bad idea to spy on our mom's date?" I stopped in the middle of the sidewalk. "Seriously? You want to do this?"

I could think of several reasons it was a bad idea. Namely, Mom's reaction if she caught us. *Also,* her date's reaction if he caught us.

"I think I do." Lucy grinned. "I want to check out Jeff's competition."

"I mean, we can bail if something goes wrong." Gracie's eyes were lighting up in the way they did when she was scheming.

I closed my eyes and took a breath. "Fine. I'm in." I couldn't let the two of them go without me, that was for sure. "But both of you have to work on your whispers."

"Work on our whispers, how?" Lucy asked as we all started walking again at Watson's behest.

"You both 'whisper' super loud," I said, making air quotations with my fingers around the word *whisper.*

Lucy shook her head as if this just wasn't true.

"We do not." Gracie rolled her eyes. "You'll see."

"Let's wear all black," Lucy said excitedly.

"What time is the date?" I asked.

"Six. Let's get there like fifteen minutes beforehand, so we can spot them when they walk in and can follow them," Lucy said.

"Yeah, we can lurk around the lobby—" Gracie began.

"Lurk? Follow them? This sounds so—" I tried covering my face with my hands as best as I could with a chunky leash in my hand.

"Olivia, it's not creepy," Lucy said.

"I didn't even say *creepy*." I raised my eyebrows. "You used that word all by yourself."

"I'm saying, it's not creepy because we don't have creepy motives. It's sweet because we're watching out for Mom," Lucy said, stopping to take a sip of water from her yellow bottle.

"Plus, it'll be pretty funny." Gracie grinned. She was always in it for the laughs.

"Well, I'll be there," I said. "This guy better be another sweet one like Jeff."

"So, how'd Jeff seem during charades? Was he fun? I feel like I missed a big chunk of the night," Gracie said, her eyes on the sidewalk.

"Yeah, that seemed like a long phone call. Is everything okay?" Lucy said, pulling her hoodie tighter around her waist.

"Yeah, it wasn't an emergency or anything," Gracie said. She licked her lips, squinting as if she were weighing something in her mind. Maybe her next words. "It was Austin."

*Austin.* That answered all my questions. Austin and Gracie talking might not be an emergency, but it was always a big, miserable mess. Every single time.

"Are you two ..." I let the sentence trail off. I thought part of me didn't even want to say his name out loud.

"Sort of," she said, shoulders up to her ears. "We're talking again. Tentatively."

Lucy was being uncharacteristically quiet. I shot her a glance.

"Tentatively is probably good." I nodded. "Last time ..." Last time, Gracie had called me in tears. Last time, Austin had called it off after disappearing on her for two weeks. Last time, she'd said she wouldn't let him treat her like that ever again.

"Last time, he was in a weird place. He wasn't prepared for a real commitment. He was busy with school and wanted to enjoy his freedom," Gracie said.

"Enjoy his freedom? Being with you, Gracie Rhodes, is the real joy. The biggest, brightest joy, and he's dumber than I thought if he thinks there's anything more fun than being with you!" Lucy burst out.

Gracie half smiled, half groaned—touched but frustrated, that unique emotion sisters tended to bring out.

"What makes you think he's out of that weird place?" I asked.

"We're almost done with school, so I think the freedom thing isn't such an issue ..." she said, her voice growing smaller with every word. "Plus, he said he was tired of fighting his feelings. What the two of us have ... we can't turn it off."

The sun hid behind a cloud, offering a respite of shade overhead.

Lucy asked, "What do you feel for each other?"

Gracie sighed. "Drawn to each other. I think about him all the time. He said he can't get me out of his head. I mean, it feels impossible not to answer my phone when he calls, even after everything."

I chewed on my lip. "I get that you can't turn feelings off."

"So, you have feelings for each other. And those feelings probably feel good sometimes," Lucy started.

"And sometimes feel like agony." Gracie laughed.

"But how does *he* make you feel? Not how do your feelings for him feel, but how does Austin make you feel?" Lucy asked.

It was quiet, except for our footsteps hitting the cement and the river streaming beside us. No one else was on the sidewalk for a few moments, just the three of us mulling over Lucy's question.

"It's hard to answer that question, you know?" Gracie mumbled. "He's made me feel a lot of things. Our history has made me feel good and bad and crazy and sad and high."

"But do the good feelings outweigh the bad?" I asked.

"Because relationships aren't solely about what you feel for the person," Lucy said.

"It's also about how the person makes you feel, especially about yourself. How your relationship with them makes you feel. Adam has made me feel a lot of things, but primarily good things. He makes me feel hilarious, beautiful, worth sticking around for, interesting, smart, strong. Our relationship makes me feel braver, safer. Sure, sometimes Adam makes me feel pissed off. But, primarily, like Olivia asked, the good outweighs the bad."

Gracie swallowed. "Is this some intervention or something? Did y'all plan this?" Her voice was shaky.

"No, no." I grabbed her hand. "This was super unplanned."

She pushed out her bottom lip. "I hate that you asked me this," she said, her head turning to Lucy. "Because mostly, if I think about it, Austin makes me feel like I'm lucky to have his attention, lucky if he calls me back, and if I don't do enough, if I can't *be* enough, I could lose it in an instant."

I tugged Gracie into a hug, and Lucy threw her arms around both of us while Watson circled our huddle, slowly wrapping the leash around us.

For the rest of the walk, Lucy's question echoed in my mind. *How did Victor make me feel about myself?* Many of the words she used were true for me, too. He made me feel interesting, strong, and smart. Our friendship made me feel brave. It made me feel safe.

But there was more, too. Victor made me feel silly and carefree, like the goofball kiddo I'd decided to tuck away when my dad left, so I could be the mature eldest daughter my mom needed. She was let loose in his presence. She finally got her time.

And he made me feel good about things I'd been taught to

apologize for. With Victor, my know-it-all self wasn't something to tone down. He always treated it like an impressive asset.

The good our relationship brought far and away outweighed the bad.

But the bad was a giant neon sign flashing one word: terrified. I was *terrified* of ruining all this good with my new, confusing feelings.

I was stuck in my head while Gracie and Lucy discussed some celebrity gossip I knew nothing about. Their voices were background noise. Watson veered off the sidewalk, nose twitching as he sniffed something in a bush. He pawed at something hidden in the leaves; his ears perked at attention before he jumped back with a loud whimper.

"Watson?" I jogged toward him.

My sisters crowded around him, too.

He couldn't step on his right front paw, whimpering when he tried to stand on it.

"What do I do?" My mouth went dry. I scrambled for my phone. I tried Victor, but he didn't answer.

Lucy tried Adam in case they were together, but he was driving back from a meeting and not around Victor.

I tried Victor again—nothing. I glanced at poor Watson, who kept his paw curled up in pain.

"I know where Watson's vet office is," I said to my sisters.

Both were kneeling down, stroking Watson's golden fur. He looked up at me with his big, amber eyes.

"I think I should just take him myself."

# Nineteen

ME

> Victor, I took Watson to the vet! I think something bit his paw. Meet me there when you can.

Watson was limping along in the parking lot of Pawsitively Perfect Veterinary Clinic, trying to avoid using his right front paw, which he had curled close to his chest. We were not going to make much progress, both of us walking. I finally slung my purse over my back and scooped him into my arms.

He was a big, heavy golden retriever, even for only around a year old. I wobbled into the office, out of breath after fighting with the door.

"Oh, hi there," the front desk receptionist greeted me with a sympathetic head tilt. "Is everything okay?"

"No," I said, as Watson placed his paws on either of my shoulders. "His name is Watson. He's a patient here. We were on a walk only half an hour ago, and he was sniffing in the grass and pawing at something, then jolted back. Now he can't stand on his right paw." I reached for the paw to hold it up. "See?"

The clerk stepped out from behind the front desk to examine Watson's paw.

I glanced around the clinic. It was a slow day, only one woman with tight blonde curls in the waiting room, with a sleeping cat on her lap.

"I'm Joanne, by the way," the receptionist said as she walked back toward the office. "Watson, here, seems to have been bitten, but it looks manageable. Dr. Sanders can see him right away and get him all fixed up." She started clicking on her computer keyboard. "And what's your name and address?"

*Oh. She probably thinks I'm his owner.* My palms began to sweat. What if they wouldn't see Watson without his owner present? What if they took him back there but wouldn't let me go with him? He'd be so scared.

I was one of his favorite people now.

"He's probably registered here under Victor Hernandez's name and address on Cherry Avenue. Victor's the one who always brings him to his appointments." I swallowed. I knew the next words out of my mouth were ridiculous, but I said them anyway. "But I'm Watson's co-owner. I'm engaged to Watson's dad, Victor, so I'm basically his mom."

If this was an odd way to put it, Joanne wasn't fazed. She brushed a strand of her dark brown hair behind her ear. "Yes, I see your fiancé's information here."

*My fiancé.* I could hear Victor howling with laughter in the back of my mind.

My ring finger felt cold and bare as we wrapped up Watson's intake form.

*Why did I tell a lie that could be so easily disproven by one glance at my finger?* I followed the nurse to an exam room, chastising myself for being dishonest.

But, as I rubbed behind Watson's furry golden ear while he nervously nuzzled his nose against me, I did feel like his dog mom.

And I felt like more than Victor's best friend.

I felt this even stronger while I discussed Watson with the vet and comforted him during the exam. I was so much more than Victor's pal or renovation buddy. I discovered I knew more about their little life than I'd realized as I answered the vet's questions.

We were about to discuss his recovery plans when there was a knock at the door. Quickly, it swung open.

"Mr. Hernandez, here's your fiancée and Watson with Dr. Sanders," Joanna said, her polka-dot scrubs rustling as she gestured toward us.

"My fiancée." Victor's eyebrow shot up, a grin spreading. Then his eyes fell on Watson. He hurried over to him as he said, "And my poor injured boy!"

"It looks like he found a garter snake by the river that bit him. It's non-venomous, but I've cleaned it up and was talking through antibiotic cream options to ensure it doesn't get infected," Dr. Sanderson said from his spot on the silver rolling chair, his glasses sliding down his nose as he looked up at Victor.

Victor ran a hand through his messy curls. He had on his construction work clothes—a white T-shirt and baggy, torn jeans. "Is there anything we should look out for over the next few days?"

The *we* instead of *I* wasn't lost on me.

"Yeah, I shared a list there in Miss Rhodes's hands." He gestured to the typed list I was holding. "Monitor any swelling, redness, limping. You two can call us if you have any questions at all."

"Can we still walk him or play with him? Does he need to rest?" he asked.

"Let him rest today and then watch him over the next couple days. You can let him take the lead. I gave him a painkiller that might make him drowsy tonight," Dr. Sanderson said. "If you'd like, I can order a prescription for you to give him if he starts to show signs of pain again over the next couple days?"

Victor looked at me, his brow furrowed, head cocked. "What do you think, Liv?"

I'd expected to be brushed aside once Victor arrived, but instead, it appeared we were making these decisions together.

I glanced down at Watson. His paw was still up against his chest as he sat on the exam bed, nervously panting. "He did seem to be in a lot of pain. Couldn't hurt to have them on hand just in case. If he's fine, we just won't use them."

Victor nodded. "Yeah, that's the right idea. We don't want you in pain, do we, bud?"

I reached my hand toward Victor's shoulder, giving it a small squeeze, but then I remembered I was trying to refrain from touching. My hand dropped back to my side.

I tried to focus back on the appointment as we wrapped up, but the way my heart pulled to Victor like he was a crackling fire and I was just so dang cold without him was all too apparent with these new boundaries in place.

The door swung closed behind us as we exited the veterinary clinic with a sleepy, drugged Watson in Victor's arms.

"Well, *fiancée*, you may have taken this charade a bit far now."

"I did have Joanne add my information to Watson's account," I admitted with a wince. The parking lot was still pretty empty and quiet. The air was cool with the sky darkening.

"I mean, it's not a bad idea," he said.

We exchanged a glance before bursting out laughing as we approached his truck. He tucked Watson into the backseat of his truck.

"How've you been, Rhodes?" Victor asked.

A couple days had passed since our last check-in. I felt filled to the brim with things to share with him.

"Give me the work update?"

"Well, I'm still stuck on my new class. I've been daydreaming about basing it around something a student said to me during office hours—about the romance book club."

"A hit with the kids."

"Says the young buck." I chuckled. "It would be fun to explore history through the lenses of romantic literature through the ages. My mind's been running away with ideas since that meeting."

"If your mind is running with it, that's a sign, Liv." Victor leaned his shoulder against his driver's side door, tan arms crossed over his chest.

I shook my head. "It's not at all how I envisioned this next step in my career going. It's a little risky. I'm not sure what the department chatt—"

Victor broke through my storm clouds like a warm ray of sunshine. "Remember why you're doing this?"

I blinked.

"Your students. Not your career expectations or timelines, or even your department—it's about the students. That's who you spend ninety percent of your time talking about when we talk about work."

I could still see how Chloe's face lit up when she let the literature infuse the history lesson. How it got her an A.

"I say, run with the daydream." Victor shrugged casually, but his voice was rough with emotion.

"Speaking of daydreams." I walked closer to him. Watson was snoring loudly inches away in the truck's backseat. "I need to see a picture of the wedding arch. I was told you would send me a picture, and you still haven't."

He closed his eyes and let out a breath. "It's not ready."

"Not ready?" I cocked my head to the side. "Is this like an artist thing? Can't-show-it-until-it's-done thing?"

He set his eyes on me. My arms felt nearly bare where he'd usually have grabbed them in playful annoyance.

"It's more of a terrified-to-show-my-work thing."

"But it's me." I pressed a hand to my heart.

He chewed on his lip. "Yes, it's *you*. I probably care the most what you think."

A breath hitched in my throat. I tucked a strand of hair behind my ear. "It's *me*, the girl who loves everything you make."

Victor ran a hand through his mess of waves. I reached up,

grabbing his wrist without thinking, and pulled him a step toward me.

"I don't have to see it to know it's going to be one of Emma and Gabriel's favorite parts of their wedding—because everything you make is my new favorite thing ever. Victor Hernandez is the most talented carpenter. Everything he makes is magic."

"Magic." He fought a grin.

"Magic."

He took a deep breath in and out, then pulled his hand from mine to pull out his cell phone. "Man, your speeches always work on me."

"Yay." I clapped my hands eagerly.

He held his phone in front of me, open to a photo of the wedding arch. Two teakwood triangles overlapped one another. The smaller, wider triangle and the narrower triangle both shared a space in the center, both together, both separate. Breathless, I zoomed in to see how he'd already begun his trademark engraving details—little vines of ivy.

I glanced up to find his eyes warm on me, studying my face as if my words were critical to him. A remedy he'd been waiting for.

"Like I said, magic," I said, my voice tender at the core.

He sighed deeply. His relief was palpable.

"Get ready, buddy. Your inbox is going to be flooded with requests after the wedding guests see this. It's ..." I looked at the picture again. "It's truly beautiful."

A car rolled past us in the parking lot. Watson's tail wagged in his sleep. He cleared his throat. "Thank you. But there's still some work to be done."

"I'd use it at my own wedding as is."

The air went still. *My wedding.* I tried to imagine asking Victor to build an arch for my wedding to another man. The idea made me sick.

I tried to imagine him at my wedding just as a guest. Him sitting in the pew, that familiar smile on his face as I stood hand in hand with someone else. My heart collapsed in my chest.

Everything between us had grown so gray, muddled, and murky.

"Whatever you need, Liv," Victor said, sliding his hands into his pockets.

"For you, too, you know?" I gave his shoulder a gentle shove. Because apparently, I couldn't keep my hands off this man.

"I know," he said, eyes twinkling. "You're my biggest fan."

I wanted to ask him about his job with city management. I wanted to ask about the hectic Hernandez wedding planning. I wanted to hear if he'd watched the latest episode of our favorite show and hear all his controversial opinions.

But the sun was disappearing from the sky far too quickly.

My stomach growled loudly.

Victor glanced at me with a knowing smirk. "You're hungry, Liv," he said. "You should head home."

I wanted to ask him to come over and order a pizza with me. Put on one of our shows. Fall back into our usual rhythm. But our rhythm was lost in that muddled gray.

I was sure pizza and late-night chats were not within our new boundaries.

"I'm okay," I lied.

"Nah, you should go eat some food. I should go pick up Watson's prescriptions, anyway. Thanks again for being such a good fake fiancée and dog mom today. You rushed him straight to care, didn't hesitate at all. I really appreciate it."

"I love him."

"He loves you, too," he said, sliding into his driver's seat.

I slowly dragged my feet over to my own car, the weight of unspoken things weighing heavily on me. Victor didn't start his own engine until after I'd started mine and pulled out of the parking space, waiting for me like he always did.

I was confused about a lot when it came to Victor Hernandez, but a couple of things were achingly clear. How much I hated saying goodbye to him. And if I got him alone anytime soon, I'd probably kiss him again.

*Twenty*



I arrived home the next day after a whirlwind of meetings and classes, kicking off my shoes and grabbing a bottle of my favorite red wine blend. A warm bubble bath was in my near future.

I heard the click of a key in my front door. There were only three people with keys to my place: Victor, Mom, and Lucy.

Victor had his tux fitting tonight. Mom had her date.

*Oh yeah.* My tired heart sank. *Mom had her date. There goes my bubble bath.*

The door swung open, and in walked Lucy and Gracie, giggling and wearing head-to-toe black. I squinted at Lucy's leather pants.

"I hadn't heard from either of you today. I hoped that meant yesterday's idea to crash Mom's date was a big joke." I pointed at them with the bottle of wine in my hand.

"Not crash her date—*check on* her date," Lucy clarified.

"I was being nice with *crash*. Let's be real, your idea is to *spy* on her date," I said. I grabbed a glass and poured myself a big cup full. "I still think it's a bad idea."

I looked around for Gracie. I'd seen her walk in, but she was now suspiciously missing.

"Olivia, we're doing this with or without you," Lucy said, also grabbing a glass from my shelf and pouring herself some wine. She took a sip. "Do you want to miss out?"

"Luce, have you ever heard of JOMO? The joy of missing out?" I took a sip of the earthy, berry tones.

"Doesn't apply here. I know you, big sis. You have SOMO. The stress of missing out. You'd be stressed out not being there to wrangle Gracie and me in. Worried about the bad choices we might make without you there to put your foot down—"

"I'm *trying* to put my foot down right now. Look how well that does me." I took a gulp this time.

Down the stairs stomped Gracie with a big black hoodie and black leggings for me to wear in her hands. She wore a black cap over her long banana-peel blonde hair.

"You were going through my closet?"

"What else is new?" She shrugged, tossing me the hoodie.

"That is giant," Lucy said as I slid it over my head. It hung nearly to my knees, and my hands were lost in the sleeves. "Where did it come from?"

"It's Victor's," I explained.

Lucy and Gracie exchanged a glance with raised brows. I ignored them.

I finished changing my clothes and then took another big swig of wine before I looked at my sisters and said, "I guess we're doing this."

.   .   .

Sweet River took its mini golf seriously. Mini Golf But Big Fun was expansive with an eighteen-hole course, a loud, colorful arcade off the lobby, and various snack stations to keep your energy up as you played.

"I guess we're doing this," I said again, to myself, as we walked into the noisy lobby full of teenagers. I bought our tickets from the freckle-faced teenage receptionist as Gracie and Lucy scoped the place, searching for Mom around the lobby and trying to find a view of the golf course.

After I paid, they raced over to me, nearly crashing into each other to breathlessly tell me that it seemed Mom had already arrived. She and her date were already on the course.

"We'd planned to be here early. Now we've missed all the introductory conversations," Lucy groaned, speedwalking toward the courses. "If only all of us had taken the mission seriously."

"I'm here, aren't I? That's as good as it's going to get," I grumbled, following after them. I looked out into the abyss of bright green golf grass, tiny pastel-colored windmills, and bridges.

Gracie and Lucy were stomping around, completely noticeable. Honestly, the head-to-toe black attire made them stick out even more. I grabbed them both by the arm and pulled them behind the bushes.

"Okay, if we're really doing this, we can't be marching around the place. We need to be discreet, and we need a real plan," I whisper-shouted. "We can't follow them around—it looks like they're at hole two right now, and three and four are out in the open. I think there are bushes over by hole five, though. Let's *discreetly* head over there and check them out."

Lucy and Gracie nodded in agreement.

We scurried behind the bushes and snack bars, crouched low. By the time we reached hole five, the three of us huddled behind a thick green bush, Mom and her date were already strolling over for their turn.

I placed a finger to my mouth, giving my sisters a serious glare to hush them. They stifled their giggles, and together, we peered over the hedge to check in on Mom's date.

"Mom looks great," Lucy whispered in awe.

"She's in my dress." I snorted.

Mom's auburn hair was twisted at the nape of her neck, and she had one of my favorite old red wrap dresses with a cream cardigan. I'd lent her that dress over a year ago.

"Well, Ernie, this is actually my first time in ..." Mom's voice got cut off by a group of girls squealing at the neighboring hole.

"Ernie," Gracie repeated to us, drawing out his name. "Jeff versus *Ernie*."

"See, it's all in twist," Ernie said in an attempt to show Mom how to swing.

"Ernie looks like a bit of a bad boy in that jacket," Gracie said.

Ernie had on a leather jacket and scuffed-up cowboy boots. His hair was dark, and so were his eyes.

Mom laughed, all twirly and flirty at something he said. *Had she laughed like that with Jeff? Or was she nervous tonight?*

She tucked her hair behind her ear while she waited for her turn to play.

"He seems fine, guys. She doesn't seem as comfortable as she did with Jeff, maybe, but the night's still young," I said. "We've seen. Let's go." I had a hammering fear that we were on the verge of getting caught.

"I've barely heard anything from him," Lucy said, facing her ear in their direction. Early 2000s pop was pumping through this golf course. All we could hear was Michelle Branch.

There was a lull between songs, and we all leaned forward.

"Oh, yeah, I don't watch much TV. I spend most of my free time on my bike," Ernie explained.

"I've never been on a motorcycle. Did you ride yours here?" Mom asked.

"I did. We could take a spin after we finish up here," he said.

Lucy looked at me with wide, worried eyes and nostrils flaring. She popped right up.

"No!" I squealed.

Gracie yanked on Lucy's sweater. "Get down!"

A sharp pop of a golf ball ricocheting off a windmill's metal blade filled my ears. I barely had time to react as I watched it soar in the air before it smacked Lucy in the face, sending her tumbling backward.

Gracie and I screamed in unison, scrambling to the ground where Lucy lay, clutching her head. While people ran toward us, feet pounding across the turf, my eyes locked with Mom's across the way. Confusion wrinkled her forehead before it gave way to wide-eyed panic as she ran toward us.

The hospital room was bright with fluorescent lighting. Lucy crinkled the paper on the bed as she twisted on the exam table, adjusting the ice pack she held to the right side of her forehead over her eye. Mom was standing beside her, rubbing Lucy's back in the way she used to when we were young girls sick at home.

"Well, Miss Rhodes, your pupils and reflexes appear normal. Your memory, as well. With a hit to the head like this, our main concern is concussion, but you seem to be in the clear," the doctor said, his blond hair swooping into his eyes as he read the charts. "Bruising is expected with swelling and a knot like you've attained. I'd recommend you keep icing it for the next twelve hours. I have some paperwork here for you to take home that lists the signs of concussion to watch for, as well as some instructions on treating pain and swelling."

"Okay, thank you," Lucy said, taking the paperwork he handed her.

After the doctor left, my sisters and I started to grab our purses and stand up to leave.

Mom held out her hands, saying, "Wait, a minute, girls."

We froze. The sounds of people shuffling around the hallway and voices murmuring at the nurses' station filled the room. Mom crossed her arms, her signal she had something to say and it was serious.

"I know that I never dated while you three grew up. I honestly just didn't have the time, or after a long day on my feet here"—she gestured toward the Sweet River ER around us, where she nursed for decades—"I didn't have the energy. But now, I think I want some fun. Some romance. And you are going to have to deal with it. I don't need you spying, or snooping, or *worrying*."

"We want you to date, Mom!" Gracie interjected. "You deserve some fun."

"It's not that we don't want you to date—" I spoke up, before she cut me off.

"I know you girls are excited for me. I don't question that. The problem is you need to cut the apron strings," Mom said, making a pair of scissors with her fingers.

*Cut the apron strings.* A couple beats of silence.

"As your mom, so many pieces of me and my life have been communal. I've shared it all. My food is your food. My workplace, your second home. My bed? You still crawl in it when you're scared. I get it," Mom said, taking a deep breath, lips pressed together. "But this part of my life is just for me, okay? I'll share it over margaritas, like you girls do. Wait to hear about my date until then. No more hiding in the bushes."

I chewed on my lip. "I tried to stop them."

Lucy and Gracie immediately gasped in response.

"Olivia Marie!" Lucy shouted through laughter. "You Goody Two-Shoes!"

"Mom, she was hiding in the bushes right along with us!" Gracie pointed at me.

We all started to laugh.

"You've always been our world, Mama," I said softly, trying to hold back the tears. "You've given us so much, like you said—your food, your time, your paycheck, your *everything*. If we can save you any bit of hurt, make your life any bit easier now, we'll do it. Even if it's something dumb like snooping on your dates."

"The dating world is ridiculous out there. I didn't want any jerks creeping around my mom." Lucy shrugged. "I know I get carried away. But it came from a place of love."

"I thought it was fun to wear all black and pretend I'm a spy. Okay?" Gracie admitted, making us chuckle.

Lucy gave her a shove.

"Listen, I know my daughters. I'm sure it came from the best place. But if I could step back and let you three make some very questionable relationship choices, you can step back and trust your mom can handle a few dates."

"Um, questionable choices? Those two, maybe. I'm with Adam," Lucy said, glancing at her watch.

"Lucy, I had to let go while you pretended this man who was just perfect for you was some cartoonish villain and let you figure it out," Mom said.

Lucy smiled. Even just the brief mention of Adam had her grinning from ear to ear.

"On one hand, it's hard to keep tight-lipped about the walking red flags you girls might date, but it's equally hard to keep a tight lip when I watch my girls pushing away chances at something real and true. Pushing away their own potential for happiness," Mom said, her eyes catching with mine. "You know what, though? I trust you three. I trust God. I know the women you're becoming, or have become, so I can let go and know you will figure it out. You'll end up in the pages of whatever beautiful story God's writing for you. Even if you keep throwing in ridiculous plot twists."

A nurse popped her head into the room. "Do you ladies need anything else?"

"We were just heading out, thanks," Lucy said, chuckling.

We Rhodes women had a habit of staying places way too late and then apologetically scurrying out.

We were laughing, hurrying down the fifth-floor hallway toward the elevator.

"I thought we would probably get caught by Mom, because,

well, she's Mom and we always get caught, but I didn't expect to wind up in the ER," I said, lacing my arm through Lucy's.

"Yeah, getting hit by a golf ball surprised me a little, too," Lucy said dryly.

"Oh, think how I felt! I was on a date with this handsome man when I heard all this commotion and glanced over to see what was going on to find Lucy lying on the ground behind the bushes!" Mom said as we arrived in front of the elevator doors.

"I'm sorry we ruined your date with the handsome man." Gracie turned to Mom, shoes squeaking on the shiny linoleum floor.

"Oh, he thought it was funny. He said he was surprised it wasn't his daughters snooping. He's already texted me about grabbing dinner another night." Mom smirked.

The elevator doors opened, and there stood curly-haired Adam in his white button-down, and behind him was Victor with his dark eyes immediately on me.

"Lucy!" Adam said, racing straight from the elevator to scoop Lucy up in his arms. "Are you okay? Let me see it." He grasped her face in his hands and studied her bruise.

"I'm fine. No concussion, only a gnarly bruise," Lucy reassured him. Our family's little bodyguard was now in the arms of her own personal defender.

He kissed the wound, then left a trail of kisses down her cheek until they met her mouth. I looked away to find Victor walking toward me.

"We literally ran out of a meeting to get here. He threw me his phone and had me reading him every update you sent, so thank you for those. They probably saved us from running a few reds," Victor said. "She really okay?"

"She's going to be just fine," I said.

Our group crowded into the elevator.

Adam's eyes scanned us. "Why are you three in all black? Do I even want to know?"

"The Rhodes girls were up to something again." Victor shook his head. "I'm betting it ties into winding up in the hospital."

"Basically, I make a terrible spy." Lucy pointed to her bruise.

"Spy?" Adam's brows furrowed. "How does that include minigolf?"

"I'm going to need a long phone call tonight after you get home with the full story," Victor whispered low to me.

I gave him a little nod.

The doors opened up to the first floor, and we sorted out the rides home. Mom had her own car, but Adam took Lucy, who'd driven with Gracie and me. Gracie drove me and Victor in her old Jeep Wrangler.

I sat in the back with Victor. Gracie's eyes periodically glanced at us in the rearview mirror.

"So, you three attempted spying on your mom's date at Big Fun but left learning pretty much nothing about the guy?" Victor rubbed his jawline after Gracie and I had filled him in on our evening.

"He drives a motorcycle," Gracie said before hitting her blinker.

Then Victor leaned in closer to me and lowered his voice. "Liv, did you eat any dinner?"

"Oh." I chuckled, realizing right then how empty my stomach felt. "I completely forgot about dinner."

"Gracie, you two need food. Swing through the What-a-Burger drive-thru," Victor called up.

"Victor, I can make myself something at home." I glanced out at the houses glowing in the night out the car window.

"This way you can start eating now," Victor said. "Plus, you're probably a little traumatized. You watched your sister collapse." His eyes assessed me intently, like checking my vitals.

"Oh my, I'm fine. She only has a bruise." I pushed him away.

"It was kind of terrifying," Gracie said as she turned into the What-a-Burger drive-thru.

"See?" Victor said pointedly.

"And hilarious." Gracie snorted.

We ordered our food, and the second I took the salty, warm bite of french fry, I was grateful for pushy Victor.

"Hey, how's Watson?" I said, my voice low, matching Victor's from earlier.

"He's right back to his normal self. It's as if he never stepped on anything. It's crazy," he said, the two of us ducked down in the backseat, dark and cozy, while Gracie hummed along with the radio from the driver's seat.

"I think he needs me to take him for another pupchino," I said.

"You and the pupchinos." He laughed, playing with the strings hanging from his navy hoodie. I popped another fry in my mouth. "You've given him a taste for whipped cream now."

"Everyone has a taste for whip cream, sir," I said.

He stole a fry.

"Hey, those are mine."

Gracie's eyes peered from the rearview mirror. "You two know you don't have to look like a couple for me, right? We're not on campus right now, but you're looking awfully cozy back there."

"Gracie." I rolled my eyes. "He's this close 'cause he wants my fries."

He stole another. "Guilty."

I ignored the way I wanted to kiss the salt off his lips right here in my sister's car.

"Yeah, yeah." Gracie didn't sound convinced.

After we dropped Victor off at his truck at city hall and began weaving through the quiet, dark streets of downtown, Gracie turned down the radio. "Even if you and Victor really are just best friends, it's pretty sweet how he takes care of you. Not even a lot of boyfriends go as far as he does," Gracie said. "The way he looks after you is ... well, it's special, whatever you want to label your relationship."

I fidgeted with my seatbelt. "I know."

"You two back there whispering in your own little bubble? It's rare I see my big sister acting like a dorky teenager. I don't think you even acted like that when you were a teenager, so credit to Victor for bringing it out in you."

"Well, I'm glad you find my complicated, messy situation with Victor entertaining," I said.

"It's not that complicated. Take it from a girl in a very complicated situationship." Gracie pulled up in front of my house, putting the car in park. "What you and Victor have is pretty simple—you're just *making it* complicated."

I swallowed. "Easy to say from the outside looking in."

"What, are you embarrassed or something that he's younger?"

"No, not at all," I said, shaking my head vehemently. "I'm scared because he's never had anything serious before."

"Just because something wasn't long-term doesn't mean he hasn't been in love."

"Gracie, he's never even said the *L* word," I said. "I heard his mom and sister talking about it. It would be so new for him, but we'd be serious right away. There's no getting around it."

"Well, what's so bad about it being new for him?" Gracie grabbed her plastic cup from the cupholder.

"I don't want to be his first love and lesson learned, while he's the one I've been waiting for," I said, my voice breaking on the last words. "I've been through some heartbreaks, but I don't think I could recover from that." Tears burned at the images playing out in my mind of letting myself love Victor, letting him in, bravely naming what it was between us ... then losing him. Knowing exactly what I was missing out on.

"But who says his first love can't last forever? What makes you think it has to end?" Gracie asked as I reached for the door handle. "And hey, maybe it'll be the first time *you* feel love that big, too?"

# Twenty-One

When I got home, Gracie's words lingered in my mind.

I'd voiced my worst fears out loud—the fear I'd let myself love Victor just to watch it fall apart the way first loves often do.

But, instead of agreeing or commiserating, Gracie looked at me with hope in her eyes. An earnest, contagious kind of hope I hadn't allowed myself to feel in so long.

When she asked what made me think first love couldn't last, a door in my heart cracked open, just a little. Enough to let the hope in.

The wind was blowing hard outside my window, bringing in a fall cold front. As I wandered into my kitchen in the dark to turn on my kettle, trees clattered against the window. I pulled my robe's sash tighter, leaning against my kitchen counter as I waited for the water to boil.

I looked down at my fuzzy socks. They were the pumpkin ones from Victor. The night he gave me these, I thought how he was so different from the other men in my life—men who let me down, who didn't show up, who walked out the door.

Victor showed up. He was something sturdy I could rely on.

*A couple of weeks before Ryan showed up on campus, Victor and*

*I had been putting the finishing touches on my downstairs bathroom renovation. I was in overalls and a burnt orange tank top, with my messy ponytail coming undone. Victor was in a black T-shirt and ripped-up jeans. Both of us were a mess, crouching down on the bathroom floor, trying to put the finishing touches on my new sink.*

*Victor was digging through his toolbox. "Oh, man. I left the wrench we need at my place." Victor's place was a quaint brick townhouse on the other side of downtown. He had an attached garage and a cute front stoop. I knew this because I'd picked up Watson at his house many times but never been invited inside.*

*We'd spent so much time together, but never once had I seen Victor's house. His bachelor pad, as my mom would've called it.*

*"I'll need to run over there. It'll be like twenty minutes," he said, standing up.*

*"I'll come, too!" I bounced up.*

*He shook his head. "You don't need to do that. It'll be quick."*

*"I want to come," I said, trailing behind him out of the bathroom.*

*He was looking around for his wallet and phone. I grabbed them from the entryway table, placing them in his hands. "Oh, thank you," he said, looking down at his hands, then his eyes lifted to mine. "You sure you want to tag along?"*

*"I'm sure," I said, slipping my feet into my sandals. "It's about time you show me your place."*

*He had plants on his front stoop, and I liked imagining him thoughtfully watering them throughout the week. Victor barefoot on his front porch, checking the soil in the pot.*

*While I was looking around, Victor unlocked the front door for us. "Well, here it is. My house."*

*I ran in behind him. Watson's paws clicked across the tile floor to greet us. "Hey buddy." I scratched behind his ears.*

*I glanced around the living room as Victor messed with something in his kitchen. A worn-in black leather couch sat in the living* room with a round wooden coffee table that looked like a Victor Hernandez original. Black-and-white family photos hung on the walls. I walked into his kitchen and spotted a couple of photos hanging on his fridge: pictures of Ireland and Greece.

"Have you visited here?" I asked him, pointing to the pictures.

"Not yet," he said, grabbing a treat from the jar on his kitchen counter. He held it out for Watson.

I smiled to myself, thinking of the maps hanging in my office.

I glanced around. Minimally decorated, unsurprising for busy Victor. He was rarely home, and if he was, he was usually tinkering with some woodworking project. But I soaked in the little pieces of him around the house. The finger paintings from his nieces and nephews on the fridge. A work belt slung over a dining table chair. A tiny Latin dictionary on his bookshelf. A box of his favorite cereal by the sink. His leather jacket, which smelled like him, on the coat rack. The sneakers that were once white kicked off in his doorway.

"My wrench is in the garage. I'm going to go grab it—" he started, but I cut him off.

"I'm coming, too."

"My messy garage is part of the house tour?"

"It's the main attraction," I said, heading for the stairs to the garage.

The garage was really Victor's work shed. This place was not minimal. I didn't have to search for hints of Victor. The place was full of his touch. The walls had built-ins where he hung his tools and were lined with shelves. A worktable covered in sawdust. A sander. Chisels. A table saw. It smelled like smoke and cedar.

I took a few slow steps inside as Victor brushed past me to pick out the wrench. I touched a few different projects he'd recently finished. A maple chair wide enough that I could sit cross-legged. A dark mahogany vase that I immediately wanted. A freshly sanded table that looked like a nightstand.

"You do so many of these. But they must take a while to make?" How was Victor juggling these projects alongside the projects at my house?

"Yeah. Some take longer than others. Some of them can take months, but I don't mind waiting. I kind of like taking my time." He scratched his chin.

I pulled open a drawer and looked at the shiny tools I didn't understand. "You like the long projects, huh?"

"Well, I'm not starting something I'm not sure I want to finish. I don't like to waste my time." Victor's voice was warm, sanded down.

Victor wasn't just a playful guy. I'd already learned this, but now, looking at his work shed, the place he came to blow off steam and work on his craft, something about him clicked in my mind. He knew when to be playful, to bring light and laughter, but he also knew when to be serious. Like for a project, or a relationship, or his family.

I walked over to the cedar chair, running my fingers across it, feeling the raised edges of his ornate carvings. "You're kind of an artist, aren't you?"

"I don't know if I'd say that, Liv." He ran a finger through his hair, a blush coloring his cheeks.

"What would you say?"

"I'd say"—he took in a deep breath, thinking—"I like to build things."

"You're good at it." I clasped my hands, looking around the shed again. It was dark and cozy in here.

Victor headed toward the switch to open the garage door, ready to head back to my house. I stood back for a moment, watching him.

He was steady and solid, like the things he built. Like the tiny, ornamental details you'd notice when you looked at his creations a little closer, there was so much more to Victor once you looked a little closer.

Twenty-Two

"I think something that I noticed is how often we get an FMC that is really doubtful and questions not only the obviously amazing hero, but also *themselves*," said one of our book club members, Tamara. She was also an English major. "Like, *I relate*, but also, I want to throw my book across the room sometimes!" She huffed and blew a little strand of brown hair out of her face.

"I wanted to shake the character and say, *grow up and go get your man!*" another student exclaimed.

"I'm fairly grown up, at twenty-nine, and I hate to say it, but doubts and questions will always be there. You don't grow out of those," I said. "Hopefully, over the years, we get better and better at handling them, though, instead of letting them take over."

"And I feel like ..." Our conversation about our latest book kept bubbling, but my mind lingered on the doubtful main character.

How fear and doubt always popped up, but it was no match for what was meant for you. What was destined for you had a way of persisting like waves crashing to shore. God created a current that kept pulling you closer and closer to what was meant for you.

Because as daunting as creating a new class around romance novels felt, here I was sitting in the middle of a campus romance book club. I even had students showing up at my office hours to discuss things I was desperate to bring into the classroom.

And as terrifying as it was to admit everything I felt for Victor, I was still drawn to him. Never terrified enough to run away.

The two of us were unable to resist the pull of the current—the pull to each other.

Even in the midst of my hesitation and doubts, what was meant for me kept rolling in like a wave to my feet, until I was brave enough to reach for what I really wanted.

*Could I ever muster up the courage?*

"Guys, what would you think if some of these books weren't only book club picks anymore? What if they became assigned reading?" I asked, watching them perk up. "Would that take the fun out of it? What would you think?"

"Are you kidding?" Tamara said, eyes wide. "That's the dream!"

I left book club on a bravery high. I felt like I'd finally dipped my toes into the salty, foamy sea and realized it felt *good*. I plopped down in my office chair and gave it a spin. My phone buzzed, and my mind thought, *Victor*.

It wasn't him.

So, I clicked over to our text thread and typed up a message.

ME

you know, there are some great benefits to being your pretend gf

VICTOR

go on

ME

for starters, being Watson's dog mom

and care packages when I'm cramping

you're a top-notch dinner date

but, really…it's how you push me in the right direction. The right direction for me. you encouraged me to remember WHY I'm doing this job—and it really inspired me today.

so, thank you to the best pretend bf ever

VICTOR

if you think being my pretend gf is good, imagine being my real gf

My face felt hot. I pulled on my cardigan to let in some cool air while I waited for his reply, watching as three dots pulsed in our thread.

My phone buzzed. Victor's name lit up the screen—an incoming call, not a text message.

I stared at it like it might combust.

After a moment, I picked up the phone with sweaty hands. "Hey?" I said, out of breath as I sprinted to my office door to slam it shut to Sonny's prying eyes.

"I want to ask you something, and I thought it deserved a phone call, not just a text."

"Okay," I said, trying to sound calm, even as my heart thudded in my chest.

"You just sent me all those messages about how much you like being my fake girlfriend, right?"

"Right?"

"Well, I think it's time I show you what it would be like to be my real girlfriend. Can I take you on a real date?"

I shot up from my desk chair, sending it rolling backward. *A real date?*

A thousand tiny doubts prickled at the back of my mind.

But then I thought about last night's talk with Gracie and standing in Victor's garage, realizing he might be the steadiest thing in my life.

*Who was I kidding right now?* Yes, I wanted to go on a date with Victor. I wanted to kiss Victor. I wanted to call Victor freaking Hernandez *mine*.

I was so tired of pretending that we were just pretending.

"Yes, I really do," I breathed.

"Are we finally doing this?"

My chest buzzed. "I think it's about time."

"Olivia Rhodes is my date tonight?" he said, his voice striking a tone of awe as if he were meeting an idol tonight and not a tiny red-haired history professor. "Hmmm, so I get to show you what it's like being my girlfriend."

Hot, rough memories of his fingertips on my waist, his lips pressing into mine, flooded my mind. "With ground rules," I blurted out.

"Give 'em to me, Rhodes," he said without missing a beat, as if this was to be expected. I mean, the man knew me well.

"No kissing," I said quickly. Because, somehow, his lips had become my biggest weakness. I needed my wits about me tonight.

"Well, okay." He cleared his throat. "There goes the first thing on my list."

I bit my lip, grinning so wide I could barely stand it.

"What else is on this list?"

"It's a surprise," he said. "That's part of the fun of being my *real* girlfriend, by the way. I'm full of surprises."

"That comes with being your best friend, too, you know."

My workday dragged by slowly, like a long plane ride. *Could I just get home yet?* Five minutes before my workday ended, while I was packing up my tote bag, Victor sent a photo.

It was the top of a legal pad, just the top line showing. It said in messy handwriting I'd recognize anywhere:

*1: Meet me at the Sweet River Market.*

I threw the tote over my shoulder and called him as I locked my office door, with my phone cradled between my shoulder and ear.

"Yes?" he answered, all business.

"What should I wear tonight?" I half whispered, rushing down the hallway, passing open office doors.

"Oh," he said, his voice a low rumble. "This is a powerful position to be in. I have a lot of ideas, actually. Not sure how practi—"

"Victor, stop." I snorted. "It's you, so I'm assuming jeans and a T-shirt or something."

"Yeah, that'll do." I could imagine him grinning into the phone, his brown eyes twinkling.

I wore jeans, a loose long-sleeve white top, and my favorite worn-in brown boots. I did my makeup with crimson lip stain and the perfume Victor always told me made me smell delicious.

The Sweet River Market was tucked into one of the downtown buildings, on the street corner. It was small, but it had everything you might need, from fresh produce to laundry detergent. When I walked in, big orange pumpkins lined the entrance, sitting on stacks of hay.

I found Victor browsing the market aisles, casually pushing along a shopping cart like this wasn't a big deal. Like we weren't about to go on our first real date.

I tapped on his shoulder, and when he turned, an immediate smile spread across his face.

"There's my date," he said, his voice nearly giddy.

I felt giddy, too.

I peeked over his shoulder into the cart. A loaf of sliced sourdough bread, grapes, and a pack of peppered salamis. I raised a brow. "This is looking promising."

"I thought I'd let the grilled cheese master decide on the cheese selections." He gestured toward the other end of the store.

I led us toward the fancy cheeses, walking side by side, our arms not quite brushing. The air between us felt more electric than ever before.

I grabbed a wheel of brie and a block of smoked cheddar and dropped them into the basket. I added a case of nutty crackers and tossed that into the basket. "These are my favorite."

"See, I need your expertise. I'd have just grabbed some Triscuits and called it a day," Victor said, stepping closer.

Our fingers collided on the box as he reached for it. We exchanged a loaded glance.

"I'd have loved the Triscuits, too," I said, swallowing. I'd have loved anything he chose.

We grinned at each other, standing there in the middle of the market. His eyes were intent on me, like I was something he was finally letting himself want.

After a beat, I cleared my throat. "So, what's next?"

"Next, I need your expertise on the wine selection." He leaned his forearms on the shopping cart as he rolled it through the aisles.

Victor disappeared while I perused the wines, torn between two different red blends. I held both up—one bolder, one smoother. I chewed on my lip, glancing around for Victor, wanting to ask his advice.

A moment later, he reappeared behind me. "Where'd you disappear to?" I asked.

He dropped something in the shopping basket. His cheeks flushed. "I might've called ahead to the florist across the street, and she just called to tell me these were ready."

My eyes fell to a bouquet he'd set carefully on top of the groceries. Big and beautiful. Burgundy dahlias, golden sunflowers, and toffee-colored roses.

I scooped it up, eyes wide in wonder. "You chose these?"

He shrugged bashfully. "Kacey helped."

"They're perfect," I said, my voice quiet.

My fingers brushed the petals. I'd never realized toffee roses were my favorite until right then, when Victor gave them to me.

The moment hung between us, like it was important. This was the start of something.

The delicate, sweet, honeyed scents of the flowers tickled my nose. The fluorescent light blinked overhead.

Our fingers brushed as I lowered the bouquet back into the cart. "How's the date going so far?" he asked.

"I have a cart full of good food and beautiful flowers, so I'd say it's going well," I said. "Though my date isn't very sneaky."

"I should've been slyer, huh. Left them in my truck?" He snapped his fingers. "I'm never sly."

"I don't like a sly date, anyway," I said as I grabbed the bottle of wine with the coolest label and dropped it in the cart. "Let's check out."

W e drove down the backroads that led toward the Hernandez property, the truck bumping along. Kacey Musgraves crooned through the speakers. I rolled my window down, letting the moody Texas fall weather dance through my hair.

"You know, I said I wanted to go on a date, not to another Hernandez family dinner," I joked. We might be on a real date, but we were also us. It could never stay serious very long.

"Oh, my bad. Mom's fired up the grill out back." Victor winked.

I winced. "I don't need her judging my guacamole-making skills again." Last time I joined for a family dinner, I'd offered to help in the kitchen.

I'd started making the guacamole and asked if they had any mayonnaise. *The whole kitchen skidded to a stop.*

*"Did you just say ... mayonnaise?" Linda said, drawing out each syllable of mayonnaise.*

*I'd glanced toward Victor for help, and he'd slapped a hand to his forehead, shaking his head.*

*"My mom always adds a few scoops," I said.*

*"A few scoops?" Katie gasped.*

*"Honey, let's just keep you on dish duty," Linda said, scooting me away from the bowl of mashed avocado and toward the sink.*

"I wouldn't worry about that, Liv. My mom will probably never let you touch another avocado in her presence again, anyway. So, there won't even be the opportunity."

"Hey, I've seen you eat nearly a whole bowl of *my* guacamole before," I defended our Rhodes recipe.

"I eat, and love, whatever my girlfriend makes me," Victor said, his voice warm, eager, trying out the word. "Pretend or not."

I cocked my head to the side, watching him, letting myself really take him in as we barreled past his family's house down the country road. His tan, caramel skin. His deep, chocolate eyes. How his jaw ticked when he was focusing, like he was now, turning the car onto the rocky property trail.

I leaned into him. Our arms brushed. "Where're you taking me?"

He smiled. "You'll see."

I tugged on his shirt, finding any excuse to make contact. "You've got some tricks up your sleeve today."

He took his hand off the wheel and set it gently on the top of my thigh. His eyes were on me for a heated second. His eyes were serious, wanting. His fingers were warm through my jeans. My stomach fluttered as he rubbed a circle above my knee with his thumb.

A new kind of cozy silence fell between us as we made our way down the grassy fields.

He put the truck in park right by a bubbling, winding stream shaded by elm trees. There was a grassy clearing a few steps away. "This is my reading spot."

Victor collected an old quilt from the back of his truck and the basket he'd set our grocery haul in. A perfect picnic.

It was quiet out in the middle of the country, except for the fall breeze rippling through the swaying trees and the creek rushing. The sun streaked with hazy pinks and purples as evening came.

Victor reached his hand out for mine. Just us. No students or faculty eyes watching. Only his eyes on mine. *Is this a thing we can do now?* I slipped my hand into his. His fingers were calloused from years of woodworking, rough against my skin.

He led me toward a grassy spot beside the creek. We laid out the blanket, laughing as we tried to smooth it out for our picnic.

"Usually, it's just me here, and often, I don't even bring a blanket," Victor said. "But I've got to bring the nice blanket for my *real* date, you know."

We broke into the food, buttery brie cheese and soft sourdough bread, and we passed the bottle of red between the two of us. We watched the sun's setting rays glimmer through the trees, changing leaves.

"Try these," Victor said, handing me a cluster of grapes. "These are my favorite kind. Champagne grapes."

I popped a tiny, blue-black grape in my mouth. A burst of sweetness. "You really haven't ever brought anyone else out here?"

He shook his head. "This spot feels like my secret. I grew up with a billion siblings—"

"Five," I interjected.

"Which can feel like a billion. We've got a big house, but not that big. I still shared a room. I was always looking for a place to call my own. Sometimes, woodworking has felt like a place I can hide in, not just a thing I do." He took a swig of the wine, then gestured out to the creek with the bottle in his grip. "And here. I was a teenager, pissed off about something. When I got like that, I'd blast Dashboard Confessional in my truck and just drive the backroads. I parked out here that day. It was quiet."

"I'm honored you brought me here." I crawled closer to him, grabbed the bottle from his hands, and took a swig. "Everyone needs a place they can go."

"You're one of my places." His face was soft, open.

"Me?"

"Since I met you, I don't have to be anything but *me* when I'm with you," he said, grabbing at a loose thread on the blanket. "And I feel like … like you don't want it any other way than that."

"Well, you're right about that. You can always be you with me." Victor, with his guard down, was my favorite place, too. Still sweet, still funny and goofy, but tender and vulnerable and rough underneath in the best way.

"Just me?"

"That's all I want—just Victor."

"You *want* me?" His voice was quiet, but strong, like a pulse.

The sun was gone now. Starlight twinkled overhead, and Victor's eyes glowed in the dark.

"Well, I'm always inviting you over, aren't I?" A breathless, vulnerable laugh escaped me.

Somehow, along the way, Victor became a coping mechanism, his arms a restorative place, his voice a healing balm, his presence a need.

Was it always like this, and I was only now seeing it? Or was it a development over months of caring friendship? "You're a favorite place to me, too. A safe zone."

"You're my safe zone, too," he said.

"I'm better with you next to me, you know that?" I admitted, my head tilting to the side, a piece of hair falling in my eyes.

His eyes crinkled. "Every Olivia is the best Olivia." He looked down at his hands, the grape in his fingers. "I'd probably obsess over any version of you."

The feeling was achingly mutual, but I was still trying to tread carefully, walking the shoreline between us, with my dress hiked up, careful of the waves even as the tide came rolling in.

"You know what's funny?" I said. "How my mom picked you out for Lucy. What if you two had worked out?"

He grimaced at the memory of our mothers setting him up on a blind date over the summer with my sister, Lucy. I laughed at what a failure that date had been. "What's hilarious is how excited

I was for that date. I knew I thought one of those Rhodes sisters was hot—the tiny sexy librarian one with her dark red hair."

My whole body flushed.

"And those freckles." He said the last the word like he was gasping. "And instead, Lucy sat down across from me. Lucy's awesome, but ... she's not you."

"But, what if?" I pressed. "What if the date went so well and she made you forget all about me?"

He shook his head. "Nothing will ever get you out of my head."

I rubbed my arms. The temperature was dropping.

Victor tracked the movement, asking, "Are you cold?"

"A little," I admitted.

He shrugged off his jacket. Then, scooting closer to me, he wrapped it around my shoulders. It was heavy, leather, and smelled like sawdust and him. I slipped my arms in, tugging it closer like a blanket on a cold night.

His arm brushed against mine, setting off a ricochet in my heart. I slipped my fingers into his. I caught his eye, the corner of his mouth curving into a side grin. My mouth tasted like red wine. My chest felt warm, all aglow.

"Your mouth is dark purple." Victor chuckled. "Looks like you had a popsicle."

I touched my mouth. "It was the wine."

He reached over and brushed my lips with his fingertips. "I feel like you do things like this on purpose to drive me crazy."

I looked up at him, his fingers still on my mouth. "No kissing, remember?" My chest was heaving, every breath heavy.

He nodded, silently. Our eyes locked, memories of the two of us meeting like magnets, hot on my skin. I swallowed.

"Let's get you home, then?" Victor offered.

## Twenty-Three

Victor walked me up the front porch steps with his hand on my lower back, warm and steady. The pull between us was weighty, heavy, like it could drag us under any second.

I toyed with the house keys in my hands, but neither of us seemed ready to end the night just yet.

"Thank you for letting me take you on a real date," Victor said, his voice quiet. His eyes searched mine. He tucked a strand of my auburn hair behind my ear. His fingers grazed my skin and sent goose bumps down my neck.

I took a breath. "Thank you for tonight." I curled my hands around his forearms. I still wore his leather jacket, the creak of it breaking the silence as I moved. "For sharing your spot by the creek with me."

"It's even better with you there," he murmured, with his hands finding my waist.

I tugged him closer, the distance between us shrinking, our chests grazing.

I licked my lips. His eyes dropped to them, darkening in a way that made my heart flutter.

I was having trouble breathing, in a really fun way. He leaned in, resting his forehead on mine, letting out a low grumble—half desire, half restraint.

"You're a pretty good date," I said, pushing my forehead against his. This version of the two of us felt so easy, so sweet. I wanted to stand here on my front porch with him under the moonlight for as long as I could.

I rose on my tiptoes, snaking my arms around his neck.

"Am I allowed to hold you?" he asked roughly. "What do the rules say about that?"

"That's very welcomed," I whispered.

He slid his big hands around my waist, pressing my body into his, so close my feet lifted off the ground. With me up in his arms, he buried his face into my neck. My skin tingled against his hot breath.

I dragged my fingers through his jet-black hair, and he leaned into my touch. His eyes fluttered shut for a beat before opening again.

Both of us were breathless, nose to nose.

"We're no good at not kissing," I whispered, my lips a breath from his. My body and my heart begged for the space between us to disappear. To not miss this moment.

"Maybe that means we should be kissing?"

"I'm trying to be careful. To keep my heart out of the driver's seat," I said. Because that had been my rule of thumb since I was just a kid.

"I get that," Victor said, his voice not pushy, but vulnerable. "But maybe our hearts know better than us?"

Our eyes locked.

And for a moment, I let go of the rules. I let go of the fear. And I trusted my heart.

I crashed into him, lips against lips, hands twisted in the fabric of his shirt. His hands slid beneath the jacket, pressing me against him closer.

A kiss I'd find again in my dreams tonight.

Our breath was hot and uneven as we slowly pulled apart. My feet landed gently on the porch again, barely steady.

We stood there, eyes searching each other, searching for answers.

*What do we do now?* hung between us in the blinking porch light.

"Do I get another date?" His voice was a low rumble I could almost feel.

I looked down at my boots, biting my lip. "Can I think on it?" My heart was pounding in my ears. As much as I was a planner, I hadn't planned on our date. I'd let impulse take over. And I definitely hadn't planned for post-date.

It was spontaneous and out of my element.

Victor takes a step back. "Hmmm."

I snuck a glance back up. "I'm not saying no. Tonight was just ... a lot. It was big. I need to think on it."

He shook his head. "Okay. You've got my number." He walked down the porch steps.

I watched him go for a beat before letting myself inside my house. I rested my head against the door, burying my face in my hands. The leather of his jacket creaked. All I could smell was him.

*What are my next steps here?*

Someone knocked at my door.

I opened it up to Victor standing there, hands on the door frame, gaze anguished. "Why are we treading water?"

"What do you mean?"

"Why are we treading water when we're supposed to be together?" He sounded frustrated, nearly angry.

"How do you know we're supposed to be together?" I crossed my arms, feeling emotional whiplash that we were even having this conversation. Last night, another kiss felt like a disaster I was intent on avoiding. "How can you be so sure?"

"Hasn't it felt good to let our guards down a little? To finally act on our feelings? To stop pretending there's not something more here." Victor took a step closer to me. His arms were on either side of me on the doorframe. I could wrap my arms around his waist.

"But this isn't reality, Victor," I said, my voice barely above a whisper. "These past few weeks, we've been living in a fantasy. That isn't the nitty gritty of a relationship. We haven't had to deal with the hard stuff—the real stuff. We have to think about what the *real* us looks like."

"Why can't this be reality?" he said, his eyes ablaze. "We decide our reality. I choose this. *I choose you.* I want you to be my reality. I want you to be my whole world."

I shook my head. "Reality is how different we are. I have this demanding job, and I've had my heart broken too many times to let it happen again. And you ... you're still figuring life out. You've never even been in a serious relationship—"

"*I'm serious about you.* Our relationship is serious to me." His voice was sharp but hurting. "Living in a fantasy? None of it was fake for me. Nothing I said, nothing I did. Every word, every look, every touch has been agonizingly, torturously real for me." He exhaled, his arms dropping. "Sure, maybe it started for your coworkers, but for me ... I just wanted a reason to finally call you mine. To finally pull you close."

My heart was throbbing in my chest. Tears stung my eyes. "It felt real for me, too. I didn't have to act at all," I admitted, pausing for a moment. "But ..."

He stepped closer to me. "But you're afraid of me," he whispered. He swallowed. "Afraid I'm too much of a hot young buck?"

I snickered despite myself, shaking my head. Leave it to Victor to make me laugh in the middle of this emotional conversation.

He placed his hands around my face, lifting my chin toward him. "You don't have to be afraid, though. I'm in this for real, Liv."

"Victor, you just matter so much to me, and our relationship, I want to handle it delicately." I took a shaky breath. "I can't let us break it. I want to handle it with care. I'm sorry. I need us to press pause. To think it through. It's just how my brain works." *How my heart works.*

"I like you and your brain. If you need me to go through the Olivia system of checks and balances, I'll do it. But I'll ace it and then finally get to call you mine *for real*." He kissed my forehead.

"So, we can press pause?"

He nodded. "We can do whatever you need, Olivia. I'll give you some space."

I stood in the doorway, watching as he turned and took a few steps across my veranda. The porch light was a spotlight on him. He stopped for a second, standing still, his hand on his chest, and turned to look at me. He opened his mouth to say something.

I stood up taller, intent. I wanted to hear whatever he might say.

Then, he shook his head, never mind. He continued down my porch steps.

He left me standing in the doorway, watching as he drove off in his truck.

I sat in my doorway, my back against the door, knees to my chest, cheeks wet. How'd I go from a preliminary first real date with Victor to crying in my doorway, terrified we might make a mistake? And why, when my heart said *grab him, pull him in closer,* did my mouth ask for space?

## Twenty-Four

My phone rang in the night, after an already fitful couple of hours of sleep, startling me awake in my fluffy bed. I patted around on my nightstand, with my eyes still closed, until I found my phone and pulled it under the duvet to my cheek.

"Hello?" I mumbled, my mouth dry from sleep.

"Olivia, it's me." Gracie's voice was small, tired. I blinked at my phone—2:07 a.m.

"Gracie," I said, sitting up, suddenly alert. "Are you okay?"

"Yes," she said quickly. "Mostly. Austin and I had a long, tearful talk, and I'm so confused."

I rubbed my eyes. "Tell me about the talk. What happened?"

"Austin and I have been talking again, as you know. We've also hung out here and there. We were sort of acting like we're old friends who wanted to catch up. I guess we were trying our best to avoid having the talk we had tonight." I could imagine her pinching the bridge of her nose, eyes closed in frustration. "Maybe I was fooling myself that I wasn't hoping we'd find our way back." She took in a deep sigh. I waited for her to continue. "Last night, we were with a bunch of friends watching movies and eating fast food. After everyone left, he stayed behind. We started talking about our lives, and it progressed into talking about *us*. We admitted that there was still something between us."

It seemed as though two Rhodes sisters were having tearful conversations tonight.

"You talked about your feelings, but did you also talk about your history?"

"Of course." Her voice broke. "That's when the tears happened. He says he wasn't ready then, but he's ready now."

"Hasn't he said that before, though?" I was pretty sure I'd asked this question about Austin so many times before.

"Yeah," she groaned. "I just wish he meant it."

It was quiet for a minute. I switched on the lamp. "Why did you call me?"

"You're my big sister," she said. "I need sage advice. Wisdom from my elders."

"Maybe you also knew what I would say. Maybe part of you wants me to remind you that he's said all this before. You two have sat on that very couch and talked about your feelings, over and over again. And it always ends the same."

"Do you think ..." Her voice trailed off. She already knew what I thought.

"Did he even say he wanted to make it official and give a real relationship a try?"

She cleared her throat. "Sort of." Which, from conversations past, meant he'd admitted to feelings and wanting all the relation-ship benefits sans any of the relationship commitments. "We kind of got stuck talking about our problems from the past."

"Should we call Lucy and add her to our conversation?" I offered, knowing full well that Lucy was even more intense than I was at giving it to Gracie straight.

"No, no. It's late, and she has to deal with rowdy five-year-olds tomorrow," she said.

I winced. Lucy would be handling a room full of kindergart-ners in five hours.

I pulled the duvet up under my chin. "Gracie, you know

Austin. You know what a relationship with him looks like. You don't need me to tell you any of this."

"Actually, I *do* need you to tell me this. It's easy to get lost in the fog of my feelings and the sweet—*like, you have no idea how sweet*—things he says. I question if I'm being dramatic about our history. If I'm not giving him enough credit for how he's grown. I start to doubt my own instincts," she said. "That's why I call you up, even if it's two a.m. I need my sounding board."

I thought of my own emotional, tearful talk with Victor only hours ago. How easy it was for me to get lost in the fog of my own feelings—feelings of fear and doubt—and lose sight of what's right in front of me, forgetting my own instincts.

Yet, I didn't call anyone up.

I always sat in it alone, turning off the light and wiping my tears as I fell asleep, never calling up my sisters to have a sounding board to talk me through it.

I always answered their middle-of-the-night phone calls, but I never made those calls myself.

*What would Gracie say if I told her about my kiss with Victor?* I opened my mouth to share, but the words stayed heavy on my tongue. Instead, my lips formed a firm line.

Gracie started talking again, sniffling on her end of the line.

It was so late. And Gracie had her own problems. And I could handle my problems myself. It was the way I knew best, anyway. Why heap onto Gracie's bad night? It was better to just listen to her and deal with my stuff another time.

For the night, I had a good excuse to push my feelings off to the side.

The October morning air was cool as I walked onto campus. I tugged my gray cardigan closer. Signs for the upcoming Fall Seminar Panel were plastered everywhere—my name billed as a lecturer alongside Ryan's. I'd completely forgotten this event was so close, a week away. And now, with mine and Victor's pause, he wouldn't be there in the audience. I chewed on my lip. Part of me was tempted to send him a message telling him to un-pause solely for this last fall event. I couldn't imagine looking out in the crowd and not seeing his supportive grin, the way his eyes crinkled when they looked at me, full of pride.

I'd worked my whole career without Victor around. Why was I suddenly acting like a kid without their security blanket? Except Victor was even better to be wrapped up in. I shivered at the thought, pulling open the heavy doors to my building.

The workday that followed was quiet. I wasn't distracted by silly text messages from him and thinking up witty replies, or making plans for dinner, or renovation projects to take up my night. I had to ignore my habit of noticing little moments throughout my day and bookmarking them to talk to Victor about later. Instead, my day was quiet.

My night was quiet, too.

Every day and night the rest of the week was quiet.

Victor had become the rising and falling playlist of my life. And now, the volume was turned down. The music that once flowed through my life, sweet and rhythmic, was on mute. On pause.

Quiet.

*I can finally think clearly now*, I lied to myself.


F riday night was the one ray of light on my calendar— margarita night with Lucy.

"Let's go to Chauncey's for our margaritas tonight," she said, bellowing through my car speakers.

I hadn't been to Chauncey's in a while. It was one of the closest things we had in Sweet River to a bar. Dim lighting, pub-style food, and good drinks, sometimes live music. A favorite spot to host book clubs and birthday parties. It was always crowded, but in a warm, friendly way.

"I'm down," I said, pulling into my driveway.

I threw on a mauve knit sweater dress and black ankle boots, yanking my copper hair into a snug ponytail before heading downtown to meet Lucy for dinner and margaritas.

Lucy had beaten me there and found us a booth. I stopped by the bar on my way in to pick up my icy margarita. When I found Lucy, I saw she'd also ordered us truffle fries.

"You're the best," I said, popping a cheesy, garlicky fry into my mouth as I slid into the booth.

"Well, it's been a long day," Lucy said, shaking her head. "Today was a field trip day." She said the last sentence with an implied *enough said* in her voice. I imagined her leading an army of kindergartners around a museum.

I clinked her margarita with my own. "Well, it's Friday, my dear."

I took a salty, limey sip. Lucy eyed me across the table. "How was your week, Liv?"

"Same ole, same ole." I shrugged. Which, workwise, was true.

"How's the Victor charade going?" she asked, her voice clipped with suspicion.

"Oh." I stuffed another fry into my mouth to buy time. I hadn't planned to talk much about Victor. I'd intended to distract her with reality TV gossip, then bring up Mom's dating life, avoiding my feelings altogether like I'd been doing all week. "It's going fine. Just fine."

"I know it's been kind of confusing for you," Lucy said, leaning in, elbows on the table, her curly red hair falling over her shoulders. "How are you feeling now?"

A loud, familiar laugh erupted from a table several feet away. I glanced over. Victor's brother, Gabriel Hernandez, was sitting at a table with his fiancée, Emma Brown, and their sister, Katie, and her husband, Terrence. My heart sped up. Was Victor there? Would he show up later?

Lucy's gaze followed my eyeline. "Oh, how fun. I bet they're all in town for the upcoming wedding," she said.

The wedding was in a little over a week.

"You're going with Victor, right?" Lucy asked.

I swallowed. "I'm supposed to, yeah," I said. That was something we'd un-pause for, right? *Unless the pause leads to a full stop* ... I rubbed my forehead. I didn't want to think about any of it right then.

"Are you okay?" Lucy pressed.

"I'm fine. Long day." I took a drink of my margarita.

"You remember how I'd talk through my Adam drama with you this past summer?"

"Oh, how could I forget?" I chuckled. "I have vivid memories of you resting your face down on my kitchen island and clutching a pillow to your chest dramatically."

"We're long overdue some good girl talk," she said, setting her hands on top of mine between us on the table. I knew what she was doing.

Lucy could sense something was off with Victor and me. She was gently checking on me. But I couldn't open up about everything right now.

I was afraid if I started unpacking my feelings, I would start crying right here at the bar. Or worse, say something I couldn't take back that encouraged Lucy to push me to go for it with Victor.

My heart tightened in my chest. Or I'd tell Lucy everything, and she'd shake her head at me, telling me I never should've pressed pause. That now I'd gone and ruined everything with him.

"Agreed." I wiggled my eyebrows, ignoring the ache in my chest. "What's the latest with Adam?"

Her face fell, just a fraction. Only a sister would be able to tell. I'd ignored her nudge to share. "He's adorable as usual. His mom is actually coming to spend Thanksgiving here in Sweet River. He's excited and anxious, in pretty equal measures."

"Meeting the mom," I said, my eyes wide. "Big step."

"That is a big step, huh?" Lucy said. "I thought I'd feel more nervous to meet her, but really, I feel more anxious for Adam. I know he wants this visit to go well for his family. He wants the kind of closeness we have."

Late-night phone calls. Heart to hearts. Family dinners. Little rituals. Group messages. Every holiday was decorated with their voices and their faces. My family, the Rhodes women, were close —the four of us with our lives so intertwined it would be unraveling tapestry to try and pull us apart.

They were undoubtedly my safe space.

Then why did I freeze when it came time to ask for help? Unable to open my mouth and verbalize my feelings, my needs.

I knew Lucy would listen, eyes intently on me.

Mom would do anything for me. She'd race across town. She'd drain her bank account.

I'd been this way since I was just a kid.

I thought back to my childhood years, right after Dad left. How exhausted Mom would look when we were at home in our tiny rental house. She was working long hours as a nurse and trying to juggle the demands of a mom to three. She refused to let any ball drop. I could see the tiredness.

Lucy and Gracie were too young to notice. I wasn't sure they even remembered those years clearly. But I saw. I saw the weariness in her eyes, the tears on her cheeks. *I was scared for her.*

Lucy and Gracie would ask every question in the way little kids do. They'd incessantly ask for more. They were loud. They were wild. They were needy. Mom would give her all, and then some.

I couldn't do much. I was still so young myself. But I could help by keeping my mouth shut. I could meet my own needs, so Mom didn't have to. I could try to rush ahead and help my sisters, so they didn't ask Mom.

I could be one less thing she worried about.

Lucy grinned, rambling on about Adam, and I smiled at her, knowing she'd love nothing more than for me to break open my chest and lay out every feeling I was battling. But it was in my training to keep it locked up. I wasn't even sure I knew where the key was.

I flinched at the loud laughter coming from Gabriel and Emma's table. I hated how tuned into them I was—every single scrape of their chairs against the floor, wondering, *had Victor shown up?*

After a couple of margaritas, I wasn't hiding it very well, and Katie noticed my eyes on them. She and Emma waved at me, then Lucy twisted in her seat, calling them to come join us for a minute.

"You guys having a little girls' night?" Emma asked, sliding into the booth beside me, her long blonde hair hanging in a loose, messy braid.

"Yes, a girls' night was needed," Lucy said, scooting in to make space for Katie.

"We're on a double date," Katie said, nodding toward the boys, Gabe and Terrence, at the table, talking in depth about something. "The boys get so into their conversations, though, they'll probably take a while to notice we're gone."

"You guys working on wedding prep?" I asked. "I know the countdown is on."

"Oh, actually, no. We're mostly catching up on Sweet River gossip," Emma said, sipping on the glass of rosé she'd carried over. "I needed a wedding talk break."

"Oh, what's the Sweet River gossip?" Lucy asked, resting her chin on her fist, ready to listen.

"It is girls' night, and girls' night needs gossip." I lifted my palms up.

Katie and Emma exchanged a glance as if asking each other, *who would start the story?*

"Well ..." Katie leaned in conspiratorially. "Did you guys know Violet and Tristan back in school?"

"Oh, definitely," I said. "Those two were inseparable." Violet and Tristan were best friends all through high school. If you saw one, the other wasn't far behind.

"I always thought they would get married." Lucy sighed dreamily.

"We all did," Katie said emphatically, patting the table.

"See, Gabriel and I went to this writer's conference in Seattle for journalists—and you know, they're both writers. The main difference is that Tristan stayed in Sweet River while Violet travels all over the world. Somehow, they both wound up at the conference," Emma said. "And the two were avoiding each other the entire weekend. And I brought Tristan up to Violet, and she said the two haven't spoken since their senior year of high school."

"There had to be some massive falling out for a friendship like that to end like that," Katie tried to whisper, but failed, making me giggle.

"I'm in shock," Lucy said. "I thought those two were bound to end up together. I mean, they were 'best friends.'" She made air quotes with her fingers. "But I thought they were one of those couples who aren't together yet, but there's that big implied *yet* at the end."

"I know." Emma leaned back against the booth. "Tristan and Violet were inevitable."

I wondered if this was how these same people talked about Victor and me. If they made air quotes when they said we were best friends. If they said *Victor and Olivia are inevitable.*

My stomach dipped low, my cheeks going pink at the thought. I hated how I made another thing about Victor. And even worse, how badly I hoped they said that about us.

Twenty-Five

S unday night was Halloween. Jack-o'-lanterns lined my neighbors' front porches, and large fuzzy fake spiders clung to their bushes. Kids were racing down the street in princess dresses and superhero capes long before the sun went down. The sound of children giggling carried in through my open windows.

All week long, I'd tried to push the looming holiday to the very back of my mind.

Over the past several weeks, Victor and I had text messaged costume ideas back and forth: Kim Possible and Ron Stoppable, Ross and Rachel when they were in Vegas, Ferris and Sloane. Or Victor's favorites, which were a cheeseburger and fries or tequila and lime, since he'd been rooting for some kind of food-based costume.

What started as a joke about our "pretend couple costume," much like everything we pretended was a joke, easily slipped into something more real. Now I had our salt and pepper costumes hanging in my closet. These silly costumes would go sadly unused.

I stood in my closet, rubbing the soft fabric of the salt costume between my fingers, wondering how I could believe I had a chance of keeping Victor neatly compartmentalized in the friend zone? *How did I believe he was in the friend zone at all anymore when I ordered us these matching costumes?*

I'd envisioned the two of us passing out candy to trick or treaters together, sitting on my front porch side by side. *I've been fooling myself.*

You can't force something to be safe just by taping a less intimidating label on it. Calling dynamite a birthday candle might make it sound innocent, but in the end, it only makes it even more dangerous. It makes it something mislabeled, misused, a disaster waiting to happen.

*Denying the chemistry—the dynamite—between Victor and me was always a disaster in the making.*


Lucy, Adam, and my mom showed up on my doorstep dressed up in costumes and their arms loaded with pizza boxes.

"I need a slice of pepperoni pizza, stat," I nearly whimpered as they walked through the doorway. The spicy aroma of pepperoni wafted by me.

"Where's your costume?" Lucy asked, in a tone of surprise. She and Adam were dressed as Lucy and Ricky from *I Love Lucy.* My mom had thrown on a pair of felt orange cat ears. "You're Olivia. You always win the costume competition."

I *was* known for how seriously I always took my Halloween costume. I deliberated for weeks, months sometimes, and narrowed down the options until I finally landed on the costume. And I always made sure to have my costume secured on time. I didn't want to risk being costume-less on the 31st.

Last year, I dressed in a historically accurate medieval bliaut and headdress, which was the talk of the history department the entire week after. The year before that, I wore the lime green Isabella Parigi costume from the *Lizzie McGuire* movie that I'd won in a charity auction. I'd worn it to a costume party, and every millennial woman present recognized it on sight.

Yet, here I was, in a pair of baggy gray sweats and a white T-shirt, on the 31st.

"Weren't you supposed to be, like, paprika or something?" Adam asked, setting the pizza boxes down on my kitchen counter.

I reached into the cabinet for paper plates. "Salt. I was going to be salt," I said, leaving out the pepper counterpart.

"Salt?" Lucy raised a brow. Then, keeping her judgments on my costume to herself, she asked, "Did it not come in on time?"

I tapped the counter. "No, it came in. I had second thoughts about it, though. I'm not sure I like it."

"It's got to be better than nothing," Mom said, grabbing a plate from me. She opened the pizza box, and the scent of marinara and cheese filled the kitchen.

"Is that why you only have on a pair of cat ears?" I asked.

"I have on a striped shirt," Mom countered. "I'm one of those cute little striped cats. Like Garfield."

"It's just surprising because you're *you*," Lucy said, sitting down at my kitchen table. "The idea of competing with whatever you were going to have on is part of the reason I amped up my own costume so much."

I looked over her blue and white polka-dot dress and pinned-back curls, and Adam's suit and fedora. They had amped it up.

The doorbell rang, giving me an escape from this costume inquisition. I grabbed my big wooden bowl of candy and ran to the door.

As I gave the tiny trick-or-treaters handfuls of candy, I searched the faces of the grown-ups standing behind them. *What if Victor and his nieces and nephews were trick or treating on my street?*

My heart climbed up my throat as the trick-or-treaters skipped down my porch steps. I looked out into the busy street outside my house. The streetlamps were aglow, and red and orange leaves were underfoot. I searched the crowd for his face, but he wasn't there.

*I was the reason he wasn't here.*

The sun set in oranges and pinks while my doorbell kept dinging, and the bowl of candy slowly dwindled.

My house slowly started to smell like crisp apples, oranges, and cinnamon. I walked back into the kitchen after changing into my saltshaker costume to find my mom stirring mulled apple cider on the stove, a canister of my cinnamon sticks open beside her, and the leftover bits of an orange—a tradition from my childhood. Every Halloween, my mom's house would smell like mulled cider and candy.

I walked over to her and rested my head on her shoulder.

"How're you doing, honey?" she asked me with a Texas drawl.

"I'm …" I felt myself open a little. A crack. "Okay."

"Only okay?"

I heard a movie start from the other room. I peeked over the kitchen island into the living room. Adam stood in front of the TV, holding the remote, while *Halloween Town*'s opening credits rolled across the screen.

"There sure are a lot of Snickers bars in the candy bowl," Lucy said, walking back into the kitchen after handing candy out. "And you know what? I think I like the saltshaker costume. It's just missing something."

I closed my eyes, my head still resting against my mom. *Something was definitely missing tonight.*

"Oh, you know, it would be cute if someone else was the pepper!" Lucy said. "You should've had Victor over tonight, and he could've been your pepper."

A knife in my chest. Being twisted.

"Why isn't Victor here?" Mom asked.

"It's honestly weird he's not," Lucy mused. "He should be here and have built some table for us to set the candy bowl on or something."

Mom chuckled at this, echoing against my temple. I lifted my head.

"Is he with his family tonight or something?" Adam asked from the living room.

"He's been MIA lately," Lucy said.

"It's just been a week," I said defensively, my voice high. "He's been MIA for *one* week. It's not that crazy."

"One week, for you guys, is a little crazy," Lucy said, her voice lower, softer.

Tears prickled against my eyes. *Oh, no, was I about to cry?* "Fine, Lucy, the truth is ... we're on a pause. I told him we needed a break, *a pause*, okay?" I said, bursting into a small sob. Too many questions. Too many feelings.

My mom's hand found my shoulder, giving it a gentle squeeze.

"A pause?" Lucy repeated, her brow furrowed.

"Yes, a pause," I said. "It was dumb. *So dumb*. I wanted time to get clarity—to be sure I was making the right choice with him. I care about him and our relationship, so much. I thought I was being smart. Now, I think ..." I took in a shuddered breath. "I think I was just pushing him away. I probably hurt him. We haven't spoken this whole week."

"Oh, Liv." Lucy stepped closer, placing a hand on my arm.

I shook my head. "He was supposed to be the pepper to my salt. He was supposed to be here. He was why I bought all those Snickers bars. They're his favorite."

Mom and Lucy enveloped me in a big hug. I felt another sob rising in my throat. "I'm the one who made us pause, but I'm the one crying. It's so dumb."

"Sounds like you pressed pause to check how you're feeling?" Mom said softly. "Seems to me like these tears are the answer."

I wound up curled up on the couch watching *Halloween Town* after the trick or treaters started to slow down. I had a warm mug of cider in my hands, and Lucy and Adam were cuddling on the other end of the sofa. She'd put on his fedora.

A cathartic kind of relief had expanded in my chest since I'd finally cracked open and shared how I felt. A sense of comfort I hadn't expected.

"You know," Adam said, talking over the movie. "I'd been wondering if something happened between you and Victor."

"You had said that." Lucy nodded from her spot in his arms.

"What made you think something happened?" I asked.

"Victor gave it away, honestly," he said. "My usually happy-go-lucky, smiley employee acted so blue this past week. His smile gone. Shoulders always slumped. He looked like he wasn't sleeping. And he kept asking me about you."

I let out a breath, like all the air had been taken from my lungs. Heart ripped right out of my chest.

*Oh, Victor.*

"Okay, so hold your laughter," Mom shouted from the staircase, interrupting our conversation. Her steps padded across the floor.

She stepped into the living room, and a smile immediately broke across my face. She was in the pepper shaker costume.

There was a shy smile on her face. "So, it's not exactly my size," she said softly. "But you've always got the pepper to your salt in me."

My heart melted. The pepper costume in a men's large completely hung on Mom, but she was still the cutest pepper shaker I'd ever seen.

I set my mug down on the coffee table. "Thanks, Mama." My voice was wobbly with tears again. I jumped up from the couch and wrapped her up in a hug.

# Twenty-Six

Early Monday morning, I had an unexpected email from Dean Oates in my inbox with a request for a meeting with her when I made it into the office. *Dean Oates, the head of our department, wanted to meet with me right away?* I scanned the email for any clue I could find to determine what this meeting was about, but she'd given no other details, only an invitation to meet when I got to campus.

She'd popped into my office casually sometimes, and we'd had pre-scheduled meetings, but a random email requesting to see me right away wasn't normal.

I swallowed, my throat suddenly dry, as I tried to focus on getting ready for the day. I sleeked my hair back into a ponytail, threw on a black cardigan, and grabbed a bagel, holding it between my teeth, as I juggled my tote and keys on my way out the door.

I didn't bother putting on a podcast or audiobook to distract me during the drive. Instead, I wallowed in my anxious thoughts about every possible reason Dean Oates might want to meet with me so urgently.

*Maybe it was something good. Maybe she wanted to discuss my upcoming class. Maybe she was making an effort to meet with the faculty more.*

*Or maybe I was out of a job.* I couldn't help but feel a slow-building sense of foreboding.

The bagel I had for breakfast sat like cement in my twisted stomach the entire drive to campus.

"Dean Oates asked me to make sure you head over to her office after you arrived," Sonny greeted me as I whisked past her desk.

I shot her a thumbs up before dumping my stuff on my desk. I took a steadying breath, imagining Victor's warm hands around my shoulder, just the way we practiced. *I can handle however the meeting goes. Good or bad.*

Dean Oates greeted me with a soft smile after I knocked on her office doorway. "Come in, come in." She gestured toward the burnt orange chair across from her desk. "I've been wanting to touch base with you."

"You have?" I asked, trying to keep my voice professional and calm. I took a seat.

"I want to really discuss your future here at the school. I know you're taking on a new class. You have a lot of ideas we've briefly touched on." She swallowed, shuffling through a stack of papers on her desk. "But before we can start there, I do have a few questions about things that were recently brought to my attention."

"I'd love to answer any questions you have," I said, scooting to the edge of the chair.

"Well, are you familiar with our rules and regulations regarding relationships between professors and students?"

"Yes, of course," I replied, caught off guard. *Relationships between professors and students?* My mind raced. Did this refer to my book club with the students? Was it too close, too casual?

"We have a strict policy against romantic relationships," she said, an edge to her voice.

"I'm confused," I stuttered. I'd never had a romantic ... *anything*, with any students.

She cleared her throat and leveled me with a gaze. "It was brought to my attention that you are dating a student, Dr. Rhodes."

My jaw dropped. Of all the ways I imagined this meeting going, being accused of dating a student, which was a big no-no in our faculty rules and regulations, was not one of them.

"I'm not dating a student. I've never dated a student and would never date a student," I said firmly. "I don't know who is saying otherwise, but they're entirely mistaken."

A groove appeared between her eyebrows.

"You've met the man I'm dating, or might be dating," I stumbled over my words for a moment, "at the department dinner a few weeks ago. His name is Victor. He is *not* a student."

A memory flashed through my mind: Ryan accusing Victor of being a student following me around, as a way to belittle him. *He wouldn't start this rumor, would he?*

"I do remember meeting him." Her shoulders dropped, the tension in the room melting away. "I didn't want to believe you would do something like that, but I'm also not one to let the education and care of our students be compromised in any way. If a matter is brought up to me, I have to face it head-on."

"I can assure you. Someone was sorely mistaken." I placed a hand on my chest. "The education and care of our students is my biggest priority, too."

She gave me a small smile. "I see that in you. You're one of our best professors. I know the students love you. Our whole department loves you."

I felt my breathing regulate for the first time all morning. "I really care about our students."

She cleared her throat, then with a smile said, "Let's talk about the next steps for your class. I know you've been considering taking on Dr. Lewis's course idea, and I think that's a fine idea. We've wanted to offer that course for a while."

There it was, an easy route I could take: avoid putting myself out there, avoid the chance of making things more complicated or difficult, avoid any chance of rejection. I could nod along and teach a course already approved by the department.

It would make Dr. Oates happy. And it didn't mean I would *never* explore my own ideas. I would just postpone a little while longer until I had more seniority.

Until the timing felt safer.

"Dr. Lewis's course sounds great …" I began but stopped. The same part of me that cracked open to my mom and Lucy last night cracked open again. My real, honest feelings pushed to the surface. "But I actually have an idea for a class that I think our students would love. I got the idea from our campus book club."

Her eyes lit up. "This sounds interesting. Tell me more."

I took an excited breath before digging into the details of what I envisioned. My stomach fluttered as we spoke. We spoke at length. She got as excited as I did and helped answer even my smallest questions or doubts.

Before I left her office, she said, "I've seen your passion for your students and have been waiting to hear what you had up your sleeve, Dr. Rhodes."

After my successful meeting, I was too giddy to stay indoors. I stumbled outside for a breath of fresh air. It was cool and crisp outside, with the sun hiding behind thick gray clouds. I walked down the sidewalk toward my favorite tree. Its leaves were shades of gold and red. I sank down to the ground, resting my head against the rough trunk, and closed my eyes. A breeze rustled the leaves and brought goose bumps across my skin.

My meeting had gone so well. *She's been wanting unique classes like the one I had on my mind. She was hoping my class was just the first of many like it.* A smile pulled at the corners of my mouth.

I reached for my phone—an urge to share the news. On pure instinct, I pressed on Victor's contact.

He'd been the one encouraging me to chase my passion, my inspiration, whatever it was I *really* wanted.

My finger hovered over his contact.

A few students plopped down beside me, unzipping their backpacks and pulling out thick textbooks for a study session. Chit chatting about an upcoming test that seemed like it was going to be *painful*. I got up so they could have the whole spot by the tree to themselves.

I wasn't ready to go back to the office yet. I wandered over to the bulletin board I'd shown Victor weeks ago, when he accompanied me on that first date. I eyed the pinned-up anonymous love notes.

Some of them were old, the edges faded, and I'd nearly memorized them after all these years.

There were a few new ones now, though. I read the one on the upper right corner:

*Dear Ivy, your blue eyes are brighter than the sky. Love, your secret admirer.*

Another beside it read,

*Dear Sutton, I like your laugh and the way you think. Want to get a drink?*

My eyes dropped to a yellow sticky note I hadn't seen before on the bottom of the board. It was in Latin—my favorite language. The note already had me smiling.

The greeting and signature were both in English.

*Dear Pretend GF,*

*Quid non est pretensione? Quantum ego te desidero.*
*Your Pretend BF*

My breath caught in my chest. I mulled over the words in my head.

*Dear Pretend GF, What's not pretend? How much I miss you. Your pretend BF*

I knew that handwriting. I knew that pretend boyfriend who'd been studying Latin for me. This was from Victor.

He'd come by campus just to leave a little note on my favorite bulletin, respecting me and my requested space by not showing up in my office or blowing up my phone, but still finding a small way to show up for me.

To make me smile.

And in Latin. I could imagine him working with his Latin dictionary and Google Translate to find a way to string this message together.

It was definitely against the unspoken rules of the bulletin board, but I tore the note down. Holding it in my fingers, I imagined him pinning it up for me, his dark hair falling in his eyes as he found a free corner of the board to hang it.

I snapped a photo on my phone, tears pooling in the corners of my eyes. I typed up a message with the photo for Victor.

ME

Found this today! When were you on campus?

I headed back toward my office, not watching where I was going as I hit the send button and bumped into someone. "Sorry," I said, glancing up to realize it was my student, Chloe.

"Dr. Rhodes." Her eyes lit up when she saw me. "Fancy meeting you here." She waved a pink paperback book in front of me.

I took in the group of girls sitting on the steps of the arts building with the book in their hands.

"We're having an impromptu book club meeting!" Ashley said, sitting cross-legged on the bottom step, her white Converse had Sharpie hearts scribbled on the top. "We've had a lot of thoughts while reading this one and needed to discuss stat."

I chuckled.

Ashley's eyes dropped to the yellow note in my hand. "Is that from the bulletin board?"

I looked down at the note. "Oh, yeah, it is. It was left for me, though, so I think I'm allowed to take it."

"I saw that one this morning," Chloe said, then her cheeks went pink. "I'm a hopeless romantic, so I might check the anonymous love note board every morning while I walk to class."

"Me, too," another student admitted.

"Wait, wait." Ashley held up a hand. "Who is leaving you notes in Latin?"

I chewed on my lip, thinking through my words. I could roll past it and say a friend of mine posted an inside joke. Or ...

"Someone I've been afraid to admit I've fallen in love with," I confessed, and then the story of Victor and me came tumbling out as if something that was wound tight in me had become completely undone.

The students listened, enraptured, peppering in their "oohs" and "ahhs" and shaking their heads in judgment when I told them about how I asked for a pause.

"A third act *pause?*" Ashley said, covering her face with her palm. "Dr. Rhodes, the agony."

"And then, I found this." I handed over my note, and they passed it around. "I just sent him a message about it."

"Has he replied to your text?" Chloe asked, holding the note in her hands.

I stole a peek at my phone. "Not yet."

"It's Victor. You know he will," Ashley assured me, as if she really knew him after my long story.

The sky was gloomy and gray overhead. I felt a light sprinkle of rain falling on us. "I know he'll reply. I'm mostly worried about what comes next. What do I say now? How do I ... un-pause?"

"You're a romcom reader." Chloe tapped her book. "You know what you're supposed to do next. It's time to get your man."

A smile broke across my face. "It's time to get my man, huh? Well, I'll have to get him after the conference in a couple hours." I glanced at my watch, knowing it was time to get back to my office and use the time I had left to finish preparing for the conference.

A knot formed in my stomach knowing Victor wouldn't be in the audience, and that was my fault.

I checked my phone again as I walked into my office—still no reply.

## Twenty-Seven

Our panel had to arrive early at the auditorium to review our seating arrangements and the flow of the presentations and discussions. I'd changed into a nicer but still professional black dress and blazer.

I was on stage across from Ryan and the other professors, going over what to expect with the moderator, Alexis, while the stagehands bustled around us, adjusting lights and microphones.

Ryan's eyes kept roaming over to my seat. I crossed my arms over my chest, doing my best to ignore him.

As he asked Alexis a few questions, I bit the inside of my cheek. The conversation from this morning still rang in my ears. *It was brought to my attention that you are dating a student, Dr. Rhodes.*

Our eyes met for a moment, and he swallowed hard, tugging on his collar.

Later, backstage, just before we were scheduled to go on, someone handed us water bottles. I made small talk with a colleague, but I could feel Ryan's eyes on me again, so I glanced his way. *Is he sweating?*

Ryan rarely sweated. He didn't fidget or tug at his collar, especially not before he was about to step on a stage under a spotlight. That was where he thrived. Always composed, always in control. He took everything in stride, even feelings he might hurt along the way. He was frustratingly proud that way.

The only times I'd seen him sweat were when he felt bad about something. Like how he kept wiping his sweaty brow the day he told me he was taking the job in Ohio.

My nostrils flared. Ryan was sweating and staring at me because he started the rumor that Victor was a student and wasn't sure if I'd been approached yet. *Why would he do that?*

I turned toward him, not even trying to hide the anger in my eyes, but then the stagehands began ushering us toward the stage. The announcer was welcoming the crowd as we huddled on the side of the stage, waiting for our signal to walk out. A boom of laughter from the audience echoed through the room.

"Now, let's welcome our Classics and Antiquity panel to the stage, starting with Dr. Olivia Rhodes," the moderator said into the microphone.

My heart raced as I took the first steps out onto the brightly lit stage. I smiled toward the audience, giving a slight wave.

In a sea of people sitting and clapping, there stood Victor, in the front row with the proudest grin. Even from the stage, I could see the crinkle around his eyes.

The way he looked at me, you'd think he was watching me win an award, not listening to a lengthy panel discussing the Middle Ages. All the anger and frustration about Ryan left me like vapor, as if there wasn't room for me to feel anything but the bubbly joy from seeing Victor in the audience.

I sat down in my seat, trying to contain my grin. *Focus*, I reminded myself. *Oh yes, clap for my colleagues as they walk on stage.*

Throughout the panel, Victor was like my own pep squad, clapping the loudest after every one of my answers. I felt his support like a physical, tangible thing. My own extra dose of confidence, like I'd taken a shot of whiskey before I walked on stage, warm flooding under my skin.

Except Victor on the front row was better than a shot of whiskey. His eyes were solely on me the whole night, like I was the band at the concert he'd paid to see.

After the panel, I didn't wait to shake hands with everyone and make small talk backstage like I normally would. Instead, as the lights came back on across the room, I rushed down the stage steps. Victor was already weaving down the aisle toward the exit. I slipped through the small groups of chattering people throughout the aisles, trying to avoid any collisions.

"Victor," I called out over the murmur of the crowd.

He didn't hear me, walking through the glass doors. I jogged after him.

I followed him outside in the soft glow of twilight. "Victor!" I shouted.

This time, he stopped in his tracks on the sidewalk.

"Oh, hey," he said, with a tentative smile. Almost polite. "I thought you'd be busy after, talking with everyone—"

"No, no." I shook my head as people brushed by us, exiting the building. "I want to talk to you. I ran out here because I need to talk to you." I tried to catch my breath, placing my hand on my chest.

"You do want to talk? 'Cause I didn't show up here to manipulate you or pressure you into talking to me before you were ready. I was torn about whether or not to come." He put his hands in the pockets of his leather jacket. "But I wanted to make sure you felt supported tonight. That's all, I promise."

"I did feel supported. It meant a lot to look out in the crowd and see you there." I tucked a piece of hair that had gotten loose from my ponytail behind my ear. "Did you get my text earlier? I found your note on the bulletin board."

"I did see the text, right before I left to come here. I didn't mean that to put any pressure on you; I just wanted to make you smile—"

"It did make—"

Victor's eyes narrowed at something behind me, right as I felt a large hand on my shoulder.

"Olivia," Ryan said.

I felt my heart sink. "Ryan?" I turned around. *The timing of this guy.*

"Hey, I think we need to talk," Ryan said. I wondered if he was about to admit to going to Dean Oates. "I think it's long overdue."

I looked toward Victor, frustrated. "We were right in the middle—"

"It's okay." Victor took a step back. "Go ahead."

Ryan grabbed my hand in his. "We have unfinished business."

"What does that even mean, Ryan?" I asked while Victor walked away from us, disappearing through the maze of autumnal trees lining the campus.

"It's been tense between us since I arrived," he said, his voice low. "I know you've felt it. The undeniable pull between us even at that first dinner."

I felt my jaw drop a little.

"It's been hard to be on this campus without feeling ... as if there's so much unfinished and unsaid between us. I've been trying to stay professional and swallow my feelings, but ..." He gripped my shoulders. "I regret how I ended things with you. Back then, I was trying to put my career first and remove any distractions. Now, as I'm sitting with you on stage, I know you're so much more than a distraction. We could be a power cou—"

"Wait, wait." I held up a hand, stepping backward out of his grip. "You're seriously trying to tell me you think there's still something romantic between us? That's what you want to talk about right now?"

"Yes, I—"

"You're not apologizing for telling Dean Oates *that I was dating a student*," I cut in.

His eyes grew wide.

"Or even apologizing for how you dumped me like I was an inconvenience, without an ounce of empathy or respect, after dating for years."

"I am sorry. I'm sorry for how I ended things. I've felt a lot of regret since I got here," Ryan stuttered. "Anything I've done ... I've not had my head on straight. I know I'm not handling seeing you again very well."

I laughed humorlessly. I thought I would be the one not handling Ryan well. I was terrified I would need a human shield in Victor.

"Olivia, I didn't tell Dean Oates you were *for sure* dating a student. I told her ..." He looked down at his feet. "I didn't tell her anything for certain. I can promise you that."

I pressed my lips into a firm line, nodding my head. I didn't actually care to hear him apologize or explain himself. I just wanted to get back to Victor. "Okay, fine, Ryan. Good to know. I'm sorry you've had regrets. I was right in the middle of something, so I don't have time right now." I turned to leave, but he grabbed my hand. His fingers were cold.

"Olivia, you can't walk away when I'm pouring my heart out." He held my hand between both of his. "I think we should try again."

I shook my head. "I disagree. Wholeheartedly. The only regret I've felt about our relationship is regret over the time I wasted believing you."

He dropped my hands as if I'd physically burned him.

"I'm not looking for any type of reconciliation with you," I said, trying to hold onto the fraying fragments of my patience. "You lied about me to my boss, Ryan. *I don't want anything from you at all.*"

He didn't say anything for a beat, sticking his hands in his trouser pockets. "I am sorry for what I said to Dean Oates. I couldn't stand seeing how ..." He was quiet, eyes downcast. "I am sorry, though."

"Thank you for saying sorry," I said. The word *sorry* sounded strange coming out of his mouth, as if he wasn't quite sure of its meaning, but he was saying it anyway. "But I've got somewhere to be."

I followed the path Victor took down the sidewalk, finding him standing by my favorite tree. The evening sky was a navy blue around him. His form was softened by the glow of the streetlamps. His back was to me, his hands in his jeans pockets. He'd taken off his jacket, thrown it off to the side.

With my steps closing the distance between us, I was breathless. My hands shook from an emotional overload. But I wasn't going to hold back anymore.

His shoulders were visibly tense as I touched his back. "Victor."

He turned to me, his eyes full of hurt, and it felt like a punch to my gut. "I'm sorry we were interrupted," I said. "I didn't expect him to show up like that."

He shook his head. "Is that why you wanted to take a break from me? Has being around Ryan," he spat out his name, "brought up old feelings, and you were afraid to tell me?"

"What?" I nearly laughed at the idea. Having Ryan on campus had only shown me how much I'd moved on. I'd underestimated myself and how far I'd come.

If my history with Ryan left a permanent mark on my heart, reminding me what I'd never settle for again, these past few weeks with Victor were a blazing revelation of just how happy, how seen, how deeply cared for I could be.

"Maybe it sounds crazy to ask that." He shoved his hand through his dark, wavy hair. "But are you torn between us or something?" He looked away.

"Absolutely not, Victor Hernandez," I said firmly. I stepped closer to him, pulling on his gray button-down. He'd dressed up for the conference, probably for *me*. "I haven't had feelings for Ryan in years. I only have feelings for *you*."

His eyes shot to mine right after my confession. He blinked like he wasn't sure he'd heard me right. "Feelings ... for me?"

I nodded.

Something in him softened, like my words melted some of the tension in his shoulders. He exhaled. "I just hate seeing you with him. How he looks at you. It made me wonder if this was part of why you needed space. Maybe I didn't know the full story like I thought I did."

This pinched at my heart. I blinked back tears. "You want to know what I feel about Ryan? *Relief* that I didn't wind up stuck settling for him and missing out on everything good that was waiting for me." *Missing out on you, on us.*

"I've been stewing over here, so angry at your dumb ex. Angry at myself for how much I've been missing you." He let out a rattled breath. He looked down, his voice low. "I need to calm down."

Then his eyes met mine again. "It's been hard not hearing from you."

"It's been hard for me, too." This week had been a grueling lesson in the depth of my feelings for him. "Harder than you probably realize."

A couple of students screamed with laughter a few steps away.

"Come on, Liv." He licked his lips, jaw clenched. "It's been agony for me *for months*. You know, I've wanted you all this time. I've *always* wanted you."

"I knew you had a crush," I offered feebly, with my palms raised.

The crush was evident in the way his eyes lingered, the little gifts, the blurriness around the edges of our friendship. Maybe it was another safer label I taped up.

Victor's eyes would find me across a room, eyes soft on me, and I would think, *It's just a crush.*

Victor would switch my light bulbs and tinker with my leaky faucet, and my sisters would shake their heads when I told them, and I would say, *Fine, maybe he has a little crush. But we're just friends.*

I would wake up in the morning, my first thought would be about him and his stormy, dark eyes, and I would tell myself, *It's okay, you just have a little crush, too.*

"Crush?" He laughed, running a hand down his face. "It was always so much more than a crush. There's no comparison. Crush was watering it down to make it easier to swallow. Nothing about how I feel about you, from the moment I saw you, has been small."

My heart was beating out of my chest. My hands wanted to grab hold of him, pull him against me, but I needed to finally, finally, finally get this all out in the open. To tell him exactly what I wanted.

"I see that now," I said. "Maybe I was afraid to see it before, but I do now. I see what's between us—what's *always* been there."

He grabbed my wrists, drawing me closer until our lips were a breath apart. "Do you feel it now, too?" he asked in a low murmur.

I nodded, looking up into his eyes. His gaze pinned on mine.

"Oh, I feel it. How I feel about you—how badly I want this— has lodged itself in my head." I laced my fingers through his. "I think, even though I was in denial, I felt it all along, too."

"I don't care how long it took you to get here," he said, pressing his forehead to mine.

The night was cold, but my body was radiating with warmth, his heat.

"As long as you're here now."

"I'm here now." I could smell his spicy cologne mingling with the scent of crisp leaves swirling around us. "I'm terrified and giddy and crazy about you—and *finally* here."

"I want to try this thing for real." His voice was a rasp I felt all the way down to my toes. "Tell me what you want."

"I want to try this for real, too," I said, light, breathless.

"You whispered that." He dragged my wrists around his neck, lacing them over his shoulder.

I could grab his hair if I wanted.

"Say it again."

My heart thundered in my chest. "I want to try this for real," I said louder.

He growled in response, warm in my ear. He kissed my neck, leaving a trail of kisses up to my lips.

My stomach somersaulted.

He kissed me hard like a wave crashing to shore, intent on pulling me under with him. I was lost in him.

My fingers dragged through his hair down his neck, his hands on my hips pressing me flat against him, like I couldn't be close enough.

I'd finally let my feelings free, saying exactly what I wanted aloud, unraveling the tight stitches I'd sewn over my vulnerabilities and needs long ago with each word.

I ran my hands down the backs of his arms, feeling the muscles I used to watch him flex while he built things in my backyard under my hands.

"Pauses." He kissed under my ear, goose bumps everywhere. "Are." He kissed my jawline. "Stupid." He found my mouth again.

# Twenty-Nine

VICTOR

I think I'm getting worse at saying goodbye
to you

ME

It's always been a problem for us

I woke up before my alarm, restless and excited like when I was a kid on my birthday or the morning before I left for summer camp. I pulled the covers up under my chin, grinning to myself in the dim morning light. *Was last night real?* I touched my lips. Victor had kissed them so assuredly, so confidently, as if he'd meant to be kissing them all along. Last night, as the night stretched on and the campus quieted, we walked hand in hand toward the parking lot. We couldn't shake the smiles from our faces. Victor kept his arm around me, and my arm snaked around his waist. No doubt, we looked like a couple. *We were a couple.*

But when we got to our cars, we didn't want to go.

*Is it really that late?* I'd asked, wrapping my arms around his waist, looking up at him from my chin on his chest.

He'd pushed me against my car door, kissing me breathless under the moonlight. He'd hoisted me up, my legs around his waist, whispering against my ear, *Think the security guards are gonna bust us?*

I blushed at the memory this morning, palms over my warm cheeks. Victor had always made my pulse race, but this new side of him made me blush, made my stomach flutter.

My phone vibrated on my nightstand. I leaned across the bed, sliding open my phone.

VICTOR

check your doorstep

I jumped out of bed. I only had on an oversized T-shirt, so I quickly stumbled into a pair of baggy white sweatpants. *What's Victor left for me this time?*

I skipped down the stairs with bare feet, throwing open the door to find Victor standing on my faded doormat with a large to-go coffee cup in his hand, with the word *chai* written in Sharpie. A sleepy grin tugged at the corner of his mouth.

"Morning delivery," he said, stepping inside and giving my forehead a tender kiss. Now the coffee came with a kiss. *I could get used to this.*

My hair was a slept-on, tangled mess. And my face was still puffy from sleep. "I'm a mess this morning," I said.

"You're adorable," he corrected me.

He headed into my kitchen. I spotted a cap folded into his back pocket. "How's things? I know it's only been a week, but it feels like we haven't talked in a year. Give me the update." We'd been too distracted with things like kissing last night to play catch-up.

He wiggled his brows, reaching into his other jeans pocket for his wallet. He whipped out a business card, dropping it on my kitchen island. I peered down, reading the name printed in bold font.

### HERNANDEZ WOODWORKING
### VICTOR HERNANDEZ
#### Woodworking & carpentry

"I'm so proud I could burst." I grabbed the shirt over his chest.

He grinned down at me. "I had to do something to get my mind off you. I went all in on the paperwork and legal stuff I'd been dragging my feet on."

"Are you calling me a distraction?"

"Oh, no doubt." He reached behind him, grabbing the cap I'd spied earlier from his back pocket. "I wanted to show you this, too."

He set the navy green cap with the name *HERNANDEZ WOODWORKING* stitched across the front and his name on the back. I could already see a row of these hats hanging in a future shop downtown with matching shirts. I could already see the beautiful things Victor would build and ship around the country, and this was just the first step. I was so proud of him for taking that first step.

I stole the cap from his hands and tugged it over my messy bed head.

His eyes twinkled with pride. No longer downcast eyes while talking about this passion of his—he was proudly stitching it on a cap. He reached around me, unbuttoning the back and snapping it tighter around my head so it fit like a glove.

"I'm definitely keeping this."

He cupped his hands around the back of my head. "My name's sewn on the back," he said, running his finger over where the name *Victor* was stitched.

"That doesn't mean you're getting it back," I said, grabbing the bill, grinning up at him.

"Keep it," he said, his eyes like melting butter watching me wear his hat.

I grinned victoriously.

"Now." He leaned against my kitchen island with his arms crossed, eyes serious on me. The morning sun glinted through my window blinds, dancing over him like a spotlight. "Give me your update, baby girl."

Victor and I used every bit of morning time we could before he had to head to city hall for a meeting with Adam, and I had to race upstairs to throw on real clothes. We walked out onto the front porch, with his hand tangled in mine.

He pulled it up to his lips and gave it a light kiss. "Hey, what do you think about coming to Emma and Gabe's rehearsal dinner and wedding as my *official* date?"

I hummed in interest. Birds chirped in the copper-colored trees in my front yard.

"I got an in with the groom, you know. I could make a call and get you seated right by me and all that good stuff."

I was pretty sure they were already going to seat us together, but I played along. "A real live wedding date?"

Victor's forehead wrinkled. "Oh, you know, there's no pressure. I don't want you to feel rushed or pressured," he reassured me. "I know my Dr. Rhodes might want to take this slow, keep it in the research period, before you're sure about it all."

My young, playful Victor handled me with such intention and care. "I *want* to go as your date."

His shoulders dropped in relief. We kissed goodbye, and as he was driving away, all I could think was how *sure* I was about us.

After work the next day, I met Lucy at a dress boutique in downtown Sweet River. We piled our arms with gowns in autumnal colors for the November wedding. Both of us were humming along to the early 2000s pop music playing from the speakers overhead.

"I like you in this emerald green color," Lucy said as I twirled in front of the dressing room mirror in a shiny green satin slip dress that fell right under my knees.

The two of us were crammed into the same dressing room. We'd shared one since we were preteens and never stopped.

It was a benefit of having a sister—real feedback right away, without having to leave the dressing room.

"How cold is it supposed to be this weekend?" Lucy asked, sifting through the dresses hanging on the rack in our room. "Do we need jackets or shawls?"

"We should double-check the weather. You know how it is in Texas." The weather was moody and unpredictable.

I shimmied out of the green dress, ready to try on a burnt orange one next in my lineup.

"How dressy should Adam be? Is it like a dress shoes and slacks wedding, or a boots and button-downs type wedding?" Lucy asked, slipping a long-sleeve, flowy dress over her head.

"I can shoot Victor a quick text to double-check."

"You know, I was at Coffees and Commas this morning and overheard Katie telling a customer all the Hernandezes were bringing dates," Lucy said, eyes wide. "I can't believe I'm just now telling you. Do you know who he's bringing?"

"Me," I said, trying not to smirk. I could literally feel the twinkle in my eyes.

"Like ... officially? A real deal, proper date?"

I nodded excitedly. "I'm Victor's official, real deal proper date."

"Olivia Rhodes." Lucy's chest puffed, dropping the hanger in her hand. "When did you two decide this?"

"He asked me yesterday."

"How did you not immediately text me this information? I thought we were making progress with your sharing." Lucy collapsed onto the small bench in the corner.

"It's been one day since he asked me, Lucy." I cocked my head at her theatrics. "Plus, I told you about the kiss right after it happened, didn't I?"

"You texted me." She pulled open her phone, clearing her throat before reading my message aloud, "'Hey, FYI, Vic showed up at my work thing tonight, and we kissed again. But I'm not freaking out this time or anything. I think it's a good thing.'"

"That's pretty vulnerable and open," I said, raising my hands defensively. "The kiss was a good thing, and I *openly* admitted that."

"I replied, 'WOW! I'm so glad it feels like a good thing. Does this mean the pause is off?' *To no reply.*" Lucy cast me a glance from over her phone, then resumed reading. "I sent a follow-up, 'Hey, how are you feeling now since the kiss?' Still no reply, until you called me this evening and invited me to shop for dresses."

"Baby steps, okay? I'm getting better at sharing in person. It might take time for that to translate over the phone, if it ever does." I checked myself out in the mirror. I was usually a decent texter, but I'd been highly distracted by Victor since the kiss. I'd felt like I was floating on a cloud these past couple days, and he and I had been trading text messages and phone calls in all the spare non-working moments.

"I'm not asking for a play-by-play via text. A simple 'I'm going to the wedding as Victor's date' would've sufficed."

"You knew we'd kissed. I would've thought you would assume if Victor was taking a date, he was taking me," I said, pulling down a zipper on the back of my dress.

Lucy was by my side in seconds to assist me with the zipper—another perk to shopping with my sister. "You guys have been such dorks the past couple months, so for all I know, you two had kissed but were still in denial, and maybe he'd given up and gone for someone else."

"Well ..." I spun around to face her. "We're not in denial. The pause is thankfully over, and we're most definitely *on.*"

She clasped her hands together in front of her chest. "Adam and I have been waiting for this moment."

"You know what? The kisses are …" I shuddered happily. "Amazing. But one of the sweetest moments of the night was when I looked out into the audience and saw him sitting there in the front row. My heart melted, and I realized, who am I kidding, this is the guy for me."

Lucy sighed.

I chuckled. "The next morning, he showed up at my door with coffee, and we were chatting. And I realized, I'm getting all my favorite parts of our friendship, but even better now. No more resisting the urge to grab his hand or tell him he's adorable."

"Wait, wait, no zipping forward to the next day until after you've told me everything I missed from Monday," she said, laser-focused on me and waiting for the story.

As we walked out of the store together, giggly like we were in high school again, Lucy squeezed my hand and said, "I'm so happy to see you so happy."

Cars zoomed past us on the downtown streets. People bustled by on the sidewalk. The sun had set, streetlights glimmering overhead. "I am happy," I said.

"For what it's worth, I think Victor is worth taking a chance on."

"It feels like more than taking a chance on him," I said, my voice wobbly. I'd been circling around these thoughts since we confessed our feelings the other night, but they were big and something I could've easily shoved away for later. Maybe past versions of me would've done exactly that.

But here I walked, arm in arm, with my sister, walking down the street toward dinner. I felt safe. I felt ready. "I'm in love with him, Lucy."

Lucy stopped our quick pace. The two of us were at a standstill outside the Mexican restaurant. The air was cold around us. "Love?"

"Love." I turned to her. "I love him. I'm in love with him."

"Have you told him?"

I shook my head. "I've only thought about it so far. I had to process it—"

"Of course, you're Olivia. You've got to let it simmer for a minute."

I chuckled. "I'm going to tell him. I mean, I don't see how I could go on without telling him with the way he kisses. If I don't find the right moment, it's going to slip out accidentally."

That night, after I showered and wrapped myself up in my plush pink bathrobe, I called Gracie. We'd both been so busy. We hadn't caught up in a while, and I wanted to check on my little sister. I put the phone on speaker.

"Hey, Liv." Her voice echoed through my bathroom from where I had my phone sitting on the bathroom counter.

"Gracie," I squealed. "You picked up." Gracie was a busy college student, so it was a rarity to get her to answer a phone call.

"I mean, I've been waiting for your call. I've heard from Mom and Lucy today that you have *news* ..."

I ran a brush through my wet hair. "That's correct. I do have news. Victor and I are no longer just friends. We're taking it to the next level."

She cheered on her end of the phone. I reached for my vanilla lotion.

"I'm happy for you, and honestly, relieved. You were two little idiots pretending you weren't head over heels."

I snorted, rubbing lotion down my arms. "Honestly, Gracie, I wanted to check on you, too. We've barely spoken, except for a few text messages checking in, since your call about Austin the other night."

The memory of Gracie sniffling on the other line was still fresh in my mind.

Gracie groaned. "I'm sorry I woke you up the other night just to talk about boy drama."

"You can call me at four a.m. for all I care. If it means talking you out of getting back with him, I'm answering."

"You did a good job. The morning after our phone call, Austin and I talked, and we broke up. For good. I deleted him off socials. I blocked his number. I can't keep playing this back-and-forth game."

I hummed in agreement.

"It hurt." Her voice was throaty, like she was holding back tears. "But it was necessary to end it for good. Make a clean cut."

"I'm sorry it hurt, even if it was necessary. Even if it will be good for you in the end, I'm sorry for how it hurts right now," I said, my heart aching for my sweet, bubbly little sister. I hated how Austin dimmed that bright light in her.

"I'm going to be fine," she said. "I can distract myself with studying for finals. They're coming up before Thanksgiving break. I have a giant paper due that I've barely started."

The conversation broke into a long discussion about school, professors, and studying tips. I wound up curled up in my bed, the phone to my ear, before we started to say goodbye.

Gracie yawned. "Thank you for calling to check on me."

I propped my pillow under me, the wind rustling outside my bedroom window. "Of course, Gracie."

"I'll talk to you later, then," she said. "Remember to send me pictures from the wedding."

"I will," I said.

But, before we hung up, I quickly added something I'd had in my head since our call began. "Gracie, I hope you know that someday you'll find yourself with someone who treats you so well that it'll be hard for you to believe that you ever considered settling for someone like Austin."

I felt it coming for my sister like thunder before a storm—she would find the one who made her realize why it didn't work out with anyone else. Like I did.

"I do know that," Gracie said softly. "Sometimes."

## Thirty

It was a few days until the wedding, and the prep and excitement had kept Victor busy amid our budding new relationship. We took to finding free hours here and there, like during my lunch break. I'd brought a long Italian sub sandwich I'd made the night before for the occasion.

"Forget this," Victor says, forgoing his attempt to scoot the big chair from the middle of my office over beside my rolling chair behind my desk.

He plopped down in my desk chair, yanked me into his lap, and said, "Let's just share a seat."

"Comfy." I leaned against his chest for a second, feeling his heartbeat against my back. I had our sub spread out on our desk before us and started slicing it.

"How's your day been?" he asked, his hands resting against my waist.

"Good, good," I said. "We're preparing for finals looming ahead, but it's the quiet before the storm. Plus, things have settled down as the fall events are coming to an end. We're all done except for the last panel seminar on Friday, but I'm thankfully not working that one."

"Yeah, you've got a hot date on Friday." Victor snuck his arms around me, hugging me from behind.

"A rehearsal dinner date, that's serious stuff," I said, biting my lip. My heart picked up pace. The rehearsal dinner felt like the real launch to sharing our relationship with friends and family. So many people would be there, and this would be their first time seeing us as an *us*.

I felt giddy.

"I'm really grateful you'll be there. I'll need kind eyes in the crowd," Victor said morosely, leaning his head back against the chair. "I'm nervous about this toast."

I twisted in my seat so we were face to face. "Victor, you'll be amazing." My outgoing, charming, irresistible, life-of-the-party Victor had been spiraling about the toast since his brother had asked him to be the best man.

He moaned in reply, hands over his eyes.

"You're great at speaking. You have amazing jokes. A great balance of sentimental but hilarious." I put my hands on both sides of his face. He looked at me. "I've read this thing like twenty times. It's good."

He swallowed. "This toast is a big deal. It's important to Gabriel. He's my big brother, and I want him to be proud and to be glad he picked *me* to be his best man." Emma and Gabe had recently explained how they wanted their toasts shared at the rehearsal dinner instead of the reception.

"Even if you flopped up there, he'd still be glad he picked you. He picked you because he loves you, not because he thinks you'll deliver the best performance." I brushed back his floppy, dark hair. "Though you will."

"At least I can look out and see you and know that at the end of it, I get to kiss these lips and nothing else will matter." He rubbed a thumb across my bottom lip.

"I'll be right there, waiting for the kiss at the end," I promised right before the fire alarm started ringing.

Victor's brows knitted in confusion.

"Not again," I moaned. Someone had been pulling fire alarms across campus this whole fall semester. And now they'd pulled it in the history building.

We started for the door when I heard shoes pounding down the hallway, and a blur ran past us with a backpack bouncing against their back.

Victor and I exchanged a knowing glance, and then we ran after the blur like two detectives on the case. As we got closer to him, details became clearer. It was a male student with shaggy blond hair and a big red hoodie. A backpack hung loose off his shoulders.

People were crowding behind us as we hurried down the staircase, feet pounding down the steps.

The door opened up to the outside, and the shaggy-haired blond picked up his pace as we ran out into the sidewalk under the sunshine.

"Hey," Victor shouted.

"Wait," I said loudly in my professor voice. "I work on this campus!"

The guy skittered to a stop, glancing back at me with fear in his eyes.

I narrowed my eyes in recognition. He was a back-row kid in one of my introductory courses. "Peterson?" I said his last name.

He swallowed. "Shane Peterson."

"Did you?" Victor interjected, pointing toward the history building.

He looked down at his white Converse shoes, with hearts drawn in Sharpie on top. I blinked, a flash of memory. Ashley from the book club had the same hearts on her Converse.

"Do you know Ashley Forde?" I felt like an investigator grasping at any pieces I could put together.

He glanced up quickly, in surprise. "Yeah?"

People were flooding around us, griping about the fire alarm stopping classes and interrupting tests and meetings, a loud murmur around us.

"She has the same hearts on her shoes." I pointed to his shoes. "Are you friends? Does she know you're pulling the fire alarms?" I was suddenly worried this fire alarm saga involved my book club members.

"I never said I pulled—" Shane tried to defend himself.

"You were running down those halls like you were running from the law—*from the direction of the fire alarm.*" Victor shrugged, like we had him caught.

"I could've been running for my life. There was an alarm going off," Shane said. His eyes snagged on something behind my shoulder. I turned to see Ashley skipping down the building steps, hand in hand with a tall, dark, and handsome type.

Shane winced, like he'd just been shoved. "It doesn't matter, anyway."

"Pulling the fire alarm definitely matters," I said sternly.

"Whatever." He kicked the ground with the top of his shoe. "You know, she drew these hearts on my shoes to match hers. We did everything together for a while, until she met him." He pointed toward the guy she was holding hands with. "They're in the same class. That's where they just came from. She even picked up his favorite candy on the way to class today." He said this last part like it was the most heartbreaking detail.

I nodded. Puzzle pieces aligned. "Did they hang out after class for the first time in September?"

I remembered the first fire alarm happened a couple of weeks into the beginning of the fall semester back in September.

He didn't answer, just swallowed.

"Maybe another time you saw them coming home from a date late at night? Got her whole dorm running outside to interrupt the potential of a goodnight kiss?" I crossed my arms, narrowing my eyes.

"Fine, fine." He gave up, sounding exasperated. "It's been me. The first time was a stupid idea that came to me when I heard they were getting coffee after class. I hoped it would interrupt class and mess up their plans."

"Then it became a habit?" Victor asked.

"Yeah," he said, embarrassed and red-faced. "It worked okay in the beginning. Now"—he looked over at where they'd stood, wistfully—"it's too late."

"I get being stuck as a friend when you desperately want to be more, but ringing alarms isn't going to help," Victor said. "It's not about what happens with her and that guy. It's got to be about what happens between her and you. Talk to her."

"But, also, stop ringing the alarms." I narrowed my eyes at him. "I know your trademark now."

He nodded. "I hear you, Dr. Rhodes."

I glanced over and saw Ashley looking our way with a curious gleam in her eyes and a small smile for me and Shane, unaware of the effect she had on him. Unaware that the fall fire alarm fiasco had all been an elaborate ruse inspired by her.

"Wait until Gabby hears about this," I whispered to Victor.

"Man, I sure do love visiting you on campus." Victor sighed wistfully, slipping an arm around my shoulder.

After we were finally let back into the building, Victor was grabbing his things from my desk, slipping his wallet and phone into his pockets, while I plopped back down in my office chair.

"How late do you think you'll be out?" I asked. Victor and I had been talking on the phone every night this week until we nearly fell asleep, but I knew tonight he had Gabriel's bachelor party.

"Probably pretty late. All of us took off work tomorrow or at least took a half day," he said, as I stood up from my spot. "Maybe you could text me when you're going to bed, and I could step away from the guys and give you a call?"

I wrapped my arms around him in a tight hug. "That sounds good."

"You know," he said, his voice sly in the way it got when he was about to share an idea with me. "We could go back to pretending for one night. We could pretend to run into each other ..." His arms were still wrapped around me. "Maybe I'll give you the bachelor party agenda? You happen to show up where we're having dinner."

It was tempting. I considered it for a minute. A little extra Victor time sounded nice. But ultimately, I knew better. I scrunched my nose and shook my head. "No. I can't. That's a bad girlfriend look. I can't be the girlfriend ruining guys' night and crashing bachelor parties."

He pressed a goodbye kiss to my forehead as I spoke. "Plus, no one even knows I'm your girlfriend yet."

"My girlfriend," Victor said slowly, drawing out each syllable against his tongue.

It made my stomach flutter. "Your girlfriend." I nodded, leaning a hip against my desk. "And a good one. The kind that makes you sub sandwiches and listens to you recite your best man toast almost every night *and* over lunch."

Victor laughed warmly as he walked toward the doorway. "Girlfriend of my fantasies."

He stopped in the doorway, giving me a final grin—the kind that made me ache in a really good way, the kind that made my heart catch in my throat, and I felt the words, *I love you*, almost slip out.

I opened my mouth but hesitated. So close.

"See you later," he said.

And then the door was closing behind him, and the word *love* was still there on my tongue.

After he left, my heart sank. I'd almost told him, and I felt so deflated for holding it back. I grabbed my phone and texted Lucy.

ME

Isn't it karaoke night at Chauncey's tonight? I'm free. Wanna girls' night??

# Thirty-One

I didn't know how much Victor had shared with his family about *us* since we became an *us*. So, when I bumped into Emma and Katie and Emma's giggly bachelorette party at Chauncey's, I tried to choose my words carefully. I knew the family was days away from the wedding, and updates on Victor's love life were probably low on the priority list, and it should come from him.

Not as a tipsy slip from me.

"Join us for our toast." Katie grabbed mine and Lucy's hands, pulling us toward their table. "To Emma Brown, who's always been my sister, but now, in a few days, it'll finally be legal!"

The party raised their salt-rimmed margaritas in the air as Katie spoke, and Lucy and I lifted our glasses, too, clinking them together.

"To Emma!" we shouted.

All the partygoers donned matching white tank tops with their bridal party role embroidered across their chests in hot pink.

Emma's said *BRIDE.* "Did you know Victor's with the bachelor party right now?"

I nodded. "I did hear about that."

Lucy and I exchanged a loaded look.

"*Of course* you did." Emma took a sip of her drink. Her tone dripped in insinuation, and I bit my lip trying to resist saying, *yes, we're together.* "I'm pretty sure he'd be jealous if he knew I was the one sharing a drink with you tonight and not him."

I adjusted my slinky, long-sleeve black top. "I kind of wish he was here, actually." I sighed. I swirled my glass of white wine in its glass.

A small grin pulled at the side of her mouth. "Yeah?"

I nodded, giving a shrug.

"Some people just have that effect on you sometimes, huh," she said thoughtfully, tucking a long strand of blonde hair behind her ear.

"Truly," Lucy emphatically agreed, eyes wide. "You can't resist the pull even from the very beginning, even if it's someone you really do not want to draw you in."

"You're telling your heart, *no, no, we can't like this person,* but your heart is already stuck on them like Velcro," Emma said, raising her voice over the noise around us.

I leaned in closer to hear while someone belted out Backstreet Boys from the stage.

"Sometimes, we make things way more complicated than they need to be," Lucy said, with the two of us nodding in agreement.

I sipped my wine. Someone pulled Emma away, and she smiled her goodbye, running off.

"His family isn't going to be very surprised when you and Victor tell them you're together. Honestly, they're probably going to be relieved. I feel like they're anxiously waiting for you two to finally make a move," Lucy said, scooting closer to me.

"They weren't always this obvious. I'd blame Emma's on the tequila," I said, though, part of me wondered if they were always that bad and I'd just gotten really good at ignoring it. Always playing pretend.

"How do you feel? Relieved?" Lucy asked.

"I feel more than relieved. I feel so ..." I felt the smile all the way up to my eyes, my ears. Warmth spread across my body. "I feel so happy."

Victor made me happy. It was as if I'd been keeping myself locked up in my house all the time, and then I'd finally let my doors open and stepped outside to feel the sunshine. My whole body was aglow. *Why did I keep myself locked away all this time?*

Lucy reached her hands across the table to grab mine.

I felt giddy and warm and had had a few sips of wine, so without thinking, I leaned on my elbows across the table and said, "I almost said *I love you* to him."

"You did?" Lucy flung her arms excitedly, almost knocking over our wine glasses.

I nodded. "It was right there, on the tip of my tongue. I opened my mouth to say it and ..." I mimed my mouth zipping. "Zip. Zero. Nothing."

"You said nothing?"

I nodded. "I said nothing." The crowd roared their applause for the latest karaoke performance.

"Why do you think that is? Are you scared?"

I took a deep breath. "I don't feel scared. I think he loves me right back."

"Then what's the holdup?" Lucy's wild red curls fell in her eyes as she tilted her head in question.

"Old habits die hard. I can't quit being Careful and Cautious Olivia overnight," I said. It was hot and humid at Chauncey's as people filled the space. "I want to throw caution to the wind for him, though. He deserves it."

"You're going to have to make the words come out—get all Dr. Rhodes on it. Command the room!" Lucy said, all bubbly and happy.

Dr. Rhodes did command the room and felt confident and assured because she was always speaking in her area of expertise. When it came to my new boyfriend? I did not consider love to be my area of expertise.

Glimpses of the creases around Victor's eyes, his warm laughter, and the way his whole body relaxed when I wrapped my arms around him filled my mind. Maybe love wasn't my area of expertise, but Victor sure was.

I could teach an advanced course on How to Cheer Victor Up or Intro to Hernandez Sibling Dynamics.

Lucy patted the table, waking me from my thoughts. "We're up next!"

"Up next for what?" I blinked.

She shimmied her shoulders. "Karaoke, of course."


After Lucy and I had sung our hearts out to Whitney Houston's "I Wanna Dance with Somebody" and then an encore performance to Sabrina Carpenter, I jogged off stage sweaty and giggly and in desperate need of another drink. I made my way through the crowd when my eyes landed on Victor Hernandez.

It felt like I'd taken a shot of espresso, a warm giddiness straight into my veins. "Victor!" I called out.

His gaze cut straight to me. His face broke into a smile as he waved his arms for me to hurry over to him.

I ran right to his side, like a puzzle finding its piece, and laced my arms around his waist. His leather jacket was stiff under me.

He squeezed me close, tucking my head against his chest. "Hey, you."

"I missed you—" I started to say, but then felt the eyes of his brothers, Gabriel and Luis, on me. And I swear I saw Katie's ears perk up like a German shepherd's as I spoke. "Buddy," I added awkwardly at the end of the sentence.

His brows wrinkled in amusement as he looked down at me. "I missed you, too, *pal.*"

I wanted to pull him somewhere alone and ask if we should just tell everyone right now. Or grab his face and kiss him, so there was no other choice. But I also knew we shouldn't make it about us tonight with everyone there to celebrate Emma and Gabriel. "How'd the bachelor party get over here?" I asked.

He exchanged a glance with his brothers. "We heard it was karaoke night?"

"We enjoyed your and Lucy's song," Luis added. "You guys are actually pretty good."

"Oh, thanks!" I said.

"I'm actually about to take to the stage," Gabriel said. He kicked back a long gulp of his drink before striding off toward the stage.

Fall Out Boy's "Alone Together" thumped through the speakers as Victor and Luis told us about the bachelor party in between laughing at Gabriel's karaoke performance. We all cheered when he pulled Emma on stage with him.

Victor kept his arm around me the entire time, his thumb finding the belt loop of my light-wash jeans. I was basically floating, and his rough fingertips brushing against me were the only thing keeping me on the ground.

Emma and Gabriel joined us later. While we all talked, I noticed everyone's eyes darting to Victor's hand on my waist, my arms around him. How they'd exchanged glances when he said something sweet about me.

There was a note of concern in their eyes. *Do they think I'm leading him on?*

"Victor Hernandez!" a young woman shouted behind me.

Victor and I broke apart to turn around.

A tall woman with long, shiny brunette hair wrapped him up in an embrace. She had on a little black dress. "Where've you been?" she demanded as he pulled away, his eyes blinking in shock.

"I've been around." He laughed awkwardly. "Guys, this is my friend Georgie. Georgie, this is ... everyone," he said, because our group was probably too long to name.

Though I would've loved to hear him introduce his girlfriend, Olivia, right about then.

"Hi, everyone." Georgie gave a tiny wave. "I'm Victor's favorite fellow lifeguard from back when we worked together at the pool over the summers."

He snuck his arm back around me. "Ah, yes, the good ole life guarding days. Saved a lot of lives."

"Honestly, you risked a lot of lives. Victor, shirtless and watching over the pool, was the biggest distraction. Girls were flinging themselves into the water in hopes of getting mouth-to-mouth from him." Georgie gave him a playful shove. "Me, included."

"You were a lifeguard, too. That's just dangerous." Victor laughed.

"We were all willing to risk it all. What can I say?" She quite literally batted her eyes. And it looked good.

"I don't even remember you ever being a lifeguard?" Katie interjected.

It felt warm in this crowded space.

"I think it's that summer he turned so dark he actually looked bronze," Gabriel said.

Georgie chuckled. "You were bronze."

*Why were random beautiful baristas and lifeguards always popping up and flirting with Victor?*

Victor brushed his thumb back and forth against my arm. "Well, we're here celebrating my brother's bachelor party, Gabe." He nodded to Gabe. "*And* his bride's bachelorette, Emma."

Emma smiled.

Georgie clapped and told them congratulations. I chewed on my lip, and small talk dwindled until she left.

As soon as Georgie was out of earshot, Katie shoved Victor so hard he lost his grip on me. "How do these girls find you everywhere we go?"

"Hey, hey, drama. Not *everywhere*." Victor readjusted his jacket.

"We were willing to risk it all," Luis said, his voice pitched high like Georgie's.

My cheeks flamed. Probably my neck and arms, too.

"We were like nineteen that last time we saw each other, guys," Victor said, sounding annoyed. His hand found mine, his pinky brushing mine.

I glanced around the bar for Lucy, like she was an exit door.

"She obviously still remembers you." Emma was giggling.

Everyone was teasing him. I tried to drone it out. Bumping into these girls when we went out used to be one of my flashing warning signs.

My heart was beating frantically, like I'd just found leaks in a boat I'd buckled myself into.

"I'm going to the bathroom," I said, barely above a whisper, then made a beeline for the bathroom at the other end of the room. People were tipsy and loud as I made my way through.

"Liv." Victor's voice rose over the noise around us as he followed after me. "Liv!"

I stopped walking, his rough fingertips finding the crook of my elbow. I turned toward him.

His eyes narrowed in concern. "Are you okay?"

I shrugged. I didn't know how to tell him I felt like we'd taken something delicate, our new relationship, out and shared it carelessly with others. They'd shaken it up, not realizing what they were doing, not realizing they were messing with something fragile.

"Come on." His voice was soft as he stepped closer to me. Bad karaoke pulsed through the speakers. "Talk to me."

"It bothered me, you know?" Tears burned behind my eyes. I sniffed.

I cared so much. I was always the girl who cared way too much, who gave all the hoots.

"It hurt a little. Everyone joking about some other girl. About how girls always find you or whatever."

"Olivia," he said, his voice crumbling over my name, like it broke his heart to see me hurt. "They might not know we're together, but everyone knows you're the only girl I care about."

"Maybe that's true." I tucked a strand of hair behind my ear. "But it still hurt. I care what your family thinks about me—about us. I care if girls like Georgie, or the barista on my campus, know you're not available."

"You've got it," he said. "Stamp *Olivia's man* on my forehead."

"Or introduce me as your girlfriend," I offered. "That's also an option."

"You're right," he said. "Tonight, I was being careful because my family was there, since they don't know yet. Next time, it'll be clear."

Maybe after the past few weeks, my heart was ready for things to finally be clear.

Someone brushed past me, pushing me into Victor's chest. We were so close, my body pressed into his. I looked up into his eyes. "I care about how we handle this relationship." I swallowed around the lump in my throat. "I don't want us treating it like a secret. Or a joke."

"You know I'd never try to keep you a secret," Victor said, shaking his head. "Tonight was just bad timing. Things have been a whirlwind with the wedding. I've barely had a chance to talk with anyone."

I nodded, biting my lip. "I get it." And I did get it, in my head, but my heart would need a minute.

Everything between us felt so new, so delicate.

"I'll be right back," I said, taking a step back. Tears prickled against my eyes.

He held onto my hand. "I don't want you feeling sad tonight." Victor tugged on my hand as I pulled away.

"I just need a minute," I said and pointed toward the restroom with my free hand.

His face fell.

"I'm okay," I promised, before turning to leave.

I locked myself into a stall.

A few tears escaped. I took a few breaths. I hadn't wanted to escape Victor, but I'd wanted to escape everything else.

I hadn't realized how much it would matter to me to call him mine.

*We should've talked about this beforehand,* I thought. *We should've told his family.*

Over and over, I surprised myself with how deeply I cared when it came to Victor. I used to be so skilled at containing my feelings. With my exes, I used to be able to ignore anything that bothered me until it faded.

I couldn't ignore anything I felt about Victor. Nothing about my feelings for him ever faded. It only grew, spreading like a wildfire.

I wiped my watery eyes before exiting the stall.

A few tipsy girls gossiped at the sink.

Tonight was important to Victor, and I wanted to see him before he left. I washed my hands and wiped my eyes in the mirror before heading out to find him.


I stood in the toes of my black leather boots, squinting around the bar, but Victor and his brothers weren't anywhere to be found. Out of the corner of my eyes, I spotted Lucy walking out the door, and I followed behind her.

Once I walked out onto the downtown sidewalk, I realized Lucy walked away down the street with her phone pressed to her ear. I heard a familiar voice and realized in the opposite direction down the sidewalk, Victor was talking with his brothers, their backs to me.

The boys were standing in a huddle, facing downtown, streetlamps shining overhead.

I stepped closer but stopped in my tracks when I heard my name.

"You know, you've got to be careful with Olivia, man. She's dragged you along for a while," Luis said.

*Oh. If they didn't know about me earlier, they know now.*

We had been all over each other in a way we never were before, even when the lines were blurry. I'm sure that warranted a few questions once I'd fled for the bathroom.

"She hasn't dragged me along," Victor said, his voice strong, protective. "She's just a thinker. She doesn't dive into anything unless she's vetted it first. I'm fine being vetted first."

Gabe chuckled. "I'd vet you first, too."

"You sure she's really in it, though?" Luis asked.

"Yeah, I am sure. I'm sure about her," Victor said.

I bit my lip. I was sure about him, too.

"I'm just looking out for you." Luis slapped Victor's shoulder with a loud thwack.

"I'm not scared off by her feelings. They've never scared me. If she's scared, I'll be a little braver for her. If she's nervous, thinks we're moving too fast, I'll slow it down for her. If she's overthinking, I'll talk with her as long as she needs," Victor said as the crosswalk light a few steps away switched colors. "If her past is making her have second thoughts because of jerks who've only ever left, I'll show her a future with someone who'll stay."

The guys murmured something in response, but my heart was caught in my throat. I touched my fingers to my lips, wanting to memorize every word Victor said. He said exactly what I needed to hear, and it wasn't even said to me. It was just Victor talking off the cuff with his brothers.

It took me back to one of our early romance book club meetings. We'd been discussing the passionate declaration of love from a particular book's male love interest, and one of our club member's friends who'd tagged along to the meeting spoke up, saying, *These speeches are why romances drive me crazy!*

This had gotten the whole club's attention. Our eyes were on her.

"Men just aren't like this in real life. They don't say stuff like this!"

Now, overhearing Victor, it took me straight back to that memory, and all I could think was, *Sometimes they do.*

Victor sure did, without even meaning to.

I took the steps to close the distance between us. My boots clicked against the pavement. "Here you guys are," I said.

The guys turned to me.

"Olivia," Luis said, in a tone of surprise.

They knew already that we were at least *something.* And I was officially done pretending about anything.

I slipped my hand into Victor's. "I couldn't let you leave without saying goodbye."

"I was going to come find you inside before we left. I wouldn't leave like that." Victor squeezed my hands in his. His palms were warm against mine. "We just came out here to talk for a second."

I leaned up on my tiptoes, bringing my lips to his cheek. "Okay, good. I need a proper goodbye," I said, then brushed my lips against his cheek for a little peck that showed I was in this, too.

But Victor pulled me in eagerly, turning his face to make his lips meet mine.

The guys hollered and laughed. One of them clapped.

Victor's lips smiled right in the middle of our kiss, and a throaty giggle escaped me. He lifted me up off my feet and spun me around.

He was all mine, no hesitation. We were all in, for everyone to see.

When I landed back on solid ground, flushed and laughing, Victor whispered in my ear, "Everyone knows now, by the way. I couldn't wait to tell 'em anymore."

I glanced up, my voice barely above a whisper, "I figured. We aren't good at hiding it."

"No, you guys really aren't," Luis added.

I covered my face with my palm, laughing.

"I hate to break this up, but I've got a party to continue," Gabriel said.

"Okay, please bring him back to me in one piece," I teased, realizing just how natural it felt stepping into this role in Victor's life.

"Back to you?" Gabriel wiggled his brows. "Victor with a girlfriend. I'm liking this new development."

The boys headed back inside to round up the rest of their group, and Lucy walked over to me.

"I was on the phone with Mom and Gracie. Mom was trying to figure out how to end things with the motorcycle guy," she said. A group of giggly girls streamed out of the bar and filled the sidewalk. "What'd I miss?"

I tiptoed down my creaky staircase in the crisp November morning air. While I fumbled with my coffee maker, my phone rang. I blinked at the caller ID to find Lucy's name on the screen.

"It's barely six a.m.," I answered through a big yawn. My coffee maker bubbled to life.

"I know, but I'm about to leave for work. The kindergarten day starts early," she said. "Now, do you really think you have enough time after work to get ready for tonight?"

Tonight was the wedding rehearsal dinner. I was going as Victor's date. *As his real girlfriend.* "I'm leaving work early, actually, so you can come straight over after work."

"Which hair supplies do you want me to bring?"

"All of them," I said. "I want to let the ponytail down and have flowy curls or something."

Lucy squealed on the other end. "What are you wearing?"

"That red halter dress I got for the Henderson wedding last year."

"Victor's going to lose it," Lucy said. And she wasn't wrong. I looked really good in that dress. "Okay, so text me when you're heading home from work."

Victor rehearsed his speech with me again last night. I was ready for him to deliver the speech and see for himself how good it was and soak in how much it meant to Gabriel.

"Thanks, Lucy. I'm really excited to be on girlfriend duty," I said, pouring myself a mug of steamy coffee. A couple of lectures and then I'd be back home getting ready for tonight.

I was about to walk out of my office and head to the first of my morning lectures when Gabby rushed through the door.

"Olivia! Your new class is the talk of the department," she said, with her eyes bright.

I was standing by my desk, my tote already over my shoulder.

"You've had the most student interest in the shortest amount of time that the department has ever seen."

I had heard about this. Dean Oates had already sent me an email congratulating me on the student excitement late last night. "I can't wrap my mind around it, honestly."

"I was here for an early class, and I've seen myself how it's been the talk of the department all morning. *All morning*, Liv."

A warm rush of pride filled my chest. "I don't even know what to say. I'm thrilled the students are excited about it."

"It's not just the students. All of us are excited. I plan on attending." Gabby crossed her arms, with her bracelets jingling.

"Come as often as you like," I said. "You're invited to all of my classes."

"Do you know who has had a lot of questions about it?"

"Who?" A tight wrinkle formed between my eyebrows.

"Ryan." She dropped her voice low. "He was asking me all these questions about you and the class. About Victor."

I rubbed my forehead. "I'm sorry. That's annoying. *He's annoying.*"

"I don't care. I bragged on you. And the class." She chuckled. "And Victor."

"The audacity of that man—after spreading rumors about me

—to now try and gather intel." I rolled my eyes. "Can he just fly home now?"

Gabby put her hands together in prayer. "Please, Lord, send Ryan back home."

"Amen and amen," I added, heading toward my office door. "I have a lecture. Let's talk after."

I was wiping down the chalkboard after a lecture on early Greek life as the last few students trailed out of the classroom, when in rushed the seminar moderator, Alexis.

"Dr. Rhodes?" She had a short black bob that bounced when she walked and big blue eyes. Her eyes looked intent, like she was on a mission.

"Hi, how can I help you?"

"Ryan dropped out of the seminar happening this afternoon," she said, her voice high and stressed. This seminar was the big grand finale for the Fall Seminar Series. It was going to be packed. Almost the entire department was going to be there. Except for me. I was happily missing.

"Oh my." I leaned my hip against the podium in front of the room. "What are you going to do?"

"I'm going to ask you to take his place." She raised her shoulders up toward her ears in question. "Will you take his place, please?"

My eyes went wide. "I-I have plans tonight ..."

"This seminar's big plug was a closing lecture about a closer look at daily life in Ancient Greece. You gave a riveting and quite popular lecture on this topic a couple of years ago ... I still have notes from it. You'd be the perfect substitute." She took a few steps closer, her hands clasped at her chest. "Please."

"I truly do have plans." I twisted my fingers together. "A rehearsal dinner."

"Are you in the wedding?"

"No, but my boyfriend is." I shrugged

"Can you tell him your department is in a real bind and that the head of the department had been the one to specifically bring your name up to step in?"

I loved this department, this school, these students. *But Victor, and his toast.*

"I'll call him and get back to you," I said.


"Olivia, Olivia, don't worry about it." Victor's voice was a balm to the anxious ball in my chest. "There's a reason they asked for you to step up. They know they can rely on you. You're the dang heart of that department. Show up for your team, okay?"

I groaned, sinking into my leather office chair. "I want to be your date tonight, though, not be at school. Lucy was going to curl my hair. I was going to record your toast. I had big plans."

His laugh vibrated into the phone. I could almost feel it against my skin. "You're still my wedding date tomorrow, right? No school parade they need you to lead or something?"

"Yes, I'm still your date tomorrow, I promise."

"Then that's all that matters."

"I'm really, really sorry." I spun in my office chair until I was facing the window behind my desk that looked out onto the campus. Trees in reds and oranges blew in the breeze.

"You've got nothing to be sorry about. I'm proud of you. You'll be a million times better than he would've been. You should've been the first pick anyway."

"Well, I'm proud of *you*," I said. "Your toast is better than you realize. Don't worry about anything other than saying it straight to Gabriel, okay?"

"Okay," he said, like following orders.

"You're so much more amazing than you realize." I rubbed the tender place on my chest.

He cleared his throat. "Back at you."

We hung up, and I buried my head in my hands.

My body, my brain, would be here showing up for the school, but my heart was already driving back to Sweet River to show up for the guy who always showed up for me.

I spent the next couple of hours familiarizing myself with the lecture I was supposed to give tonight. I'd given it a few times, so it came back to me pretty quickly. I sent the slides over to the team.

And before I knew it, I was backstage. The other presenters' voices boomed through the speakers while I prepped and went over beats with the stagehand. And, admittedly, I kept checking the time and imagining what Victor would be doing right then.

While I hung backstage and sipped from my plastic water bottle at 6:44, Victor was probably practicing walking down the aisle with the maid of honor.

At 7:12, as I was about to walk on stage, Victor was probably finding his name card on the table for dinner.

"Well, here's our savior of the night." Dean Oates woke me from my visions of Victor's night without me. "I wanted to thank you for stepping up. I know it's not easy to jump into an event like this with only a few hours to prepare. It's huge, and the whole department is grateful."

It felt surreal. Weeks ago, I was angry that Ryan would be giving the grand finale to the Fall Seminar Series as a special lecturer, and now here I was, begged by the moderator to step in and take his place. With only a few hours to prepare, at that. Not enough time to really enjoy, *or* enough time to properly freak out.

"Of course, I'm happy to help. I want the whole night to be a success."

I stepped on stage. The spotlight was bright on me as I pulled the microphone to my lips with shaking hands. Once I began talking, it felt easy, natural even. This presentation was such a passion project that it felt more like a conversation, my excitement palpable to the audience. I recognized many of the students in the front rows, and seeing their interest as I spoke got me buzzing. Time flew by. The only thing missing was Victor grinning proudly in the front row.

Next thing I knew, I was backstage again.

They were preparing us for the ending Q&A panel. While Alexis was briefing us, I glanced toward the clock backstage. 7:50. Victor probably hadn't even given his toast yet.

If I left right now …

"I've got to go," I interrupted Alexis. She looked immediately panicked. "I'm so sorry. I filled the important slot, I gave my time, but I know these speakers can handle the Q&A panel. You guys will barely feel the lack of my presence, but there's somewhere my presence *really* matters."

Alexis took a beat, taking in the information. "Okay then. Go where you need to be."

I ran out the back door, slipping off my ankle boots, with my bare feet running down the cool sidewalk. The campus was quiet and dim in the fading sunlight.

I climbed into my car, turning it toward Sweet River. Toward Victor. With my gray trouser slacks and matching blazer and ponytail nearly coming undone, this was what I was wearing to the rehearsal dinner—so long red halter dress.

But I was going to show up for him, messy and late, but I would be there.

## Thirty-Three

I had to park a few blocks down from Coffees and Commas since the streets were lined with cars, probably because of the rehearsal dinner and the fact it was a Friday night downtown. I slid out of the car, letting the door slam behind me. I held my shoes in my hands again and raced barefoot down the cold street. It was 8:26 p.m. The dinner was supposed to be wrapping up soon.

The sky was sapphire with twinkling stars overhead and the air crisp. Streetlamps lined the street and passersby crowded the path as I weaved toward Coffees and Commas—toward Victor.

I swung the doors open, hit by the warmth of the close quarters filled with guests sitting around tables set up for the dinner. Candles at the center of every surface and twinkle lights strung overhead. Everyone was facing the center of the room, where Victor stood with a microphone in his hand.

The door swung closed behind me. No one looked my way. Every eye was on Victor, whose eyes were on Gabriel and Emma as he spoke.

"But I'm happy to share him with you," Victor said, his voice playful but still thick with emotion.

Emma nodded, wiping a tear away.

I took a few steps forward. A few guests glanced my way, and I smiled politely.

Victor's warm, booming voice filled the small space. "I used to spin my wheels, terrified I'd let down the people I loved. But lately, I've gotten an up-close look at love." His throat caught on the word love like rough sandpaper. "When love is good and right and *real*, there's no space for that kind of doubt because that kind of love lifts you up. It gets you reaching for things you never thought were possible before."

Tears pooled in my eyes. I'd heard this speech before, but each word still plucked at the strings in my heart.

"And that's what you two have—a love that lifts each other up." Victor raised his glass, casually glancing back out toward the crowd, his eyes stopping like a record scratch when they landed on me. His face melted into a smile like I was the best surprise.

I gave a small smile and perked my shoulders. His grin widened as he clinked glasses with the tables around him, everyone toasting the couple.

After he took a swig, he set his flute down and walked straight to where I stood in the center of the room.

People couldn't help but glance our way as his hands met mine, our fingers entwining.

"You made it," he said, his voice tender, quiet.

I chuckled. "I'm a total mess, but yes, I made it." My chest was rising and falling fast.

"It ended early?" Victor asked, his warmth wrapping around me.

"No, I left early," I said. "I skipped the last part."

"Liv." His voice was syrup as he tucked a fallen strand behind my ear. "You didn't have to do that."

"You always show up for me. I want to show up for you, too."

"You don't see it, huh? How you do more than just show up for me. You make my world go 'round," he said.

Our lips met lightly, and the room applauded around us. We

broke into a laugh in the middle of our kiss. I glanced over his shoulder toward Emma and Gabriel's table, where Gabe whistled.

Linda Hernandez was nodding, mouthing, *It's about time.*

I buried my face in his chest. I hadn't meant to make a scene. I'd only meant to be the smiling face on the front row, like he'd been for me, even if for just the last couple minutes.

Victor led me to his table with the bride and groom and their families. Linda grabbed my hand to give it a gentle squeeze.

"I'm glad you could make it," Katie said warmly. "You must've booked it from your event."

I'd definitely booked it down the winding roads between the school and Sweet River. "I didn't even stop to fix my hair." I gestured toward my falling ponytail.

"Well, now our table feels complete," Linda said sweetly.

I felt my cheeks go pink. Victor slung his arm around the back of my chair. I rested my tired head against his shoulder.

Gabriel stood up to thank everyone for making it to the rehearsal dinner, his voice loud and eliciting murmurs of laughter throughout the room as he made a joke. Victor's own laugh hummed under my cheek. A feeling of peace radiated through my body—a rare, warm feeling that I usually only felt with my family on lazy holiday mornings and late nights up talking in Mom's living room.

Now, as I sat at this table with Victor's family, with my head on his shoulder, that sense of home snuck up on me. A feeling Victor had more than earned.

He was so much more than a safe zone.

*Thirty-Four*



This wedding wasn't mine, or even in my family, yet I felt giddy as I slipped my silky burnt orange dress over my head. My auburn hair was in waves down my shoulders. I'd stayed up late last night with Victor's family at the rehearsal dinner, sitting around the table drinking champagne and laughing as they shared stories about Emma and Gabriel.

Everyone kept saying, *Tomorrow's the big day, we need to get home,* but no one moved from the table for hours.

Coffees and Commas was owned by Katie, so there was no closing time.

*I loved having you by my side tonight,* Victor had whispered after he'd given me a kiss on the forehead, his breath warm against my temple. *I love ...* But he didn't finish the sentence.

*He loves me, too.* I could feel the love in my bones, in his kiss, in the air between us, like it was a tangible thing, heavy between us. Something we carried together, shared back and forth.

I kept replaying that moment in my mind as I drove through Sweet River to the Grenseman Hotel. The wedding was taking place at an old hotel built during the roaring twenties. It had recently been refurbished back to its old grandness.

As I walked through the doors, it felt like stepping back in time to a lavish, grand party in the '20s with shiny wood floors, opulent mirrors, and art deco stylings lining the walls.

I slipped into the ballroom, searching the seats for Lucy, Adam, and my mom. The ballroom was lavish and filled with autumnal flowers and decorated in rich golds and copper tones.

Lucy caught my eye, waving her hand in the air. I nodded to her and made my way to the seat they'd saved for me.

I smiled at my mom when I noticed a fellow professor from my department was sitting next to her. I recognized that gray hair and thick black glasses. "Charles?" I said, in a tone of surprise. *How funny he was invited to this wedding.*

"Olivia?" Charles said, his mouth hanging open in question. "Olivia *Rhodes*." He said my last name slowly, like it was the answer to a question.

My mom laughed curiously. "You two know each other?" She said this as if *she* were the one who knew Charles.

I blinked at her.

Charles swallowed, looking at Mom. "We do."

*Oh.* Charles was my mom's date. My coworker was dating my mom. Charles, who was known for rambling during his lectures and absentmindedly leaving his things around the history building. I would try to avoid getting stuck in conversations with Charles because they were hard to escape and always went longer than I wanted.

"We work together, Mom," I said. *Why couldn't sweet Jeff be Mom's date to the wedding?*

"You know, you did put you were a history professor. Why didn't I think to ask which school you worked at?" Mom chuckled to herself. "Well, that's great. You know two people at this wedding now!"

Charles beamed, obviously smitten with Mom already. I shot a glance at Lucy, who gave me an apologetic wince. Adam was trying not to laugh.

"How'd you two meet?" I asked.

Mom and Charles explained what I'd already assumed, that this was another one of Mom's LoveLocal matches. I tried not to imagine a future where Mom and Victor carpooled to have lunch with Charles and me at the school.

We made small talk until a soft, sweet love song began to fill the room, and one of Victor's cousins walked tiny Grandma Hernandez down the aisle. Katie walked down in an amber-toned bridesmaid's dress on Terrence's arm. Victor walked out next, in a black suit and amber tie, his wavy dark hair swept back, making my stomach flip. He had a bridesmaid on his arm and his eyes straight ahead, but when he took his spot at the front of the room, his head turned.

His eyes searched the crowd for me. A grin spread across his face when he saw me. He dramatically clutched his hand to his chest, and he mouthed, *Drop-dead gorgeous.* I giggled in my seat. My cheeks and neck flushed.

The wedding processional continued, the room rising to their feet, as flower girls tossed flowers before Emma stepped through the doors, on her dad's arm.

Her blonde hair was swept back into a low bun at the base of her neck. She wore an A-line dress embroidered with lace and tiny beads. Her face was serene and intent on her groom, waiting at the front for her.

I stole a glance toward Gabriel, who was swiping a tear away. His eyes were so full of love.

Emma and Gabriel exchanged self-written vows that made the room break into laughter and tears.

The wedding ceremony came to an end. The wedding party

exited to prepare for photos, while the rest of us were to begin the reception in the hotel's garden with a cocktail hour.

I headed down a hallway, hunting for the restroom, when I spotted Victor walking off with the bridal party. He must've felt my stare, turning his head to me. We locked eyes, his caramel to my green. His grin was confident and cool. He shot me a wink that made me melt right there on the spot.

He turned back, keeping pace with the wedding party, leaving me standing there, shaking my head. *I loved that man.*

I pushed open the bathroom door to find Emma standing in front of the mirror, her wedding dress billowing around her like icing on a cupcake. "The bride needed a bathroom break," her friend said from behind her, laughing.

"It's a whole event when I go to the bathroom," Emma said, gesturing to the gown. "I require assistance."

"Well, you look beautiful. The wedding—your vows." I touched a hand to my heart.

Emma took in an excited breath. "I can't believe the ceremony is done. I'm Gabriel's wife."

Her friend squealed. I squealed, too.

"Oh, I'm getting a phone call from Katie. One sec." Her friend answered her phone, taking a couple of steps away from us. Katie was the maid of honor, and from what Victor said, had been running the show.

Emma looked back into the mirror. "It was fun to have you at the dinner last night. You had Victor glowing in a way I've never seen, and I've known him since he was a little kid."

I bit my lip, smiling down at my feet. "He makes me glow, too."

"I'm glad you two went for it. It's easy to get stuck in the What Ifs, holding back what you feel to keep things feeling safe and easy. But take it from a bride who is so glad she finally stopped hesitating: say how you feel when you get the chance."

"Say how you feel," I repeated. The friend was still on the phone. We were in the bathroom for a moment, so I cleared my throat and asked. "How did you stop hesitating?" The feeling of the word *love* stayed stuck in my mouth, fresh in my mind.

"Oh." Emma thought about it, eyebrows furrowed. "I guess I just forced myself to say what needed to be said. Like jumping off a diving board, you just make yourself leap."

That was the thing about love. It didn't come made to order, all safe and going out of its way to make you feel comfortable. It had a mind of its own. It showed up whether you were ready or not. It challenged you. Love asked you to be brave.

"That's vague, huh?" she said, her nose scrunched. "Does it help at all?"

"It does help. It's true. You just say the scary things," I said, running my fingers over my own satin dress, taking a glance in the mirror.

Her friend ended her call before I could say anything else, walking over, rattling off an update from Katie about the photo-shoot. She helped Emma with her train as they exited the bathroom.

Lucy walked in right after they left. "Hey, here you are. I was wondering where you've been."

"I was getting a pep talk from the bride."

# Thirty-Five

Twinkle lights were everywhere, even woven through the trees, heavy with copper and gold leaves. Taper candles glowed in golden candelabras at the center of each table. A coffee bar toward the back of the garden helped fight the chill in the air this November night, while guests clutched drinks spiced with apple and pumpkin flavors.

Happy chatter hummed around us, along with poppy love songs the DJ played. Adam grabbed Lucy's hand when we walked out and immediately spun her into a dance. Her wild red hair fell around her shoulders.

"Those two," my mom said, arriving by my side, Charles in tow.

"Those two," I said, grateful my sister found someone who made her so happy. Who made her *glow*.

"Your daughters both have such nice boyfriends," Charles said, waving the cocktail in his hand toward me. "I met Olivia's boyfriend weeks ago at our faculty dinner. Wasn't his name Victor?"

I nodded, swallowing. *Oh dear, that night was a total charade.* I tried to remember what we'd said to him. Charles must've bought whatever we were selling.

"I remember how he told us the story of how he met you at the coffee shop—how he got your help with milk alternatives? Right?" he said. "He'd had a crush right away. Something about liking your freckles."

The story he told came back to me.

All of it was true.

None of it was a charade. None of it was an act.

*We never even had to lie—not a word, not a touch.*

"I see where you got those beautiful freckles," Charles said, blushing at Mom.

"Oh, well, thank you." Mom touched her freckle-laden cheeks. Her blue dress swished at her ankles. "Did you recognize Victor up there in the wedding party?"

Charles's eyes lit with recognition. "Now, that you mention it, I do."

"Speak of the devil," Mom said, nodding toward Victor, who strolled into the garden. His eyes swept the place until they landed on me.

He grabbed my hands. "I've got to show you something." He led me farther into the garden, across the dance floor, to a corner with an ornate stone fountain, iron benches, and a beautiful wooden arch.

Victor's arch.

Two intertwined triangles, meeting together to make one beautiful arch. I touched it. It was wrapped with ivy. My fingers traced the carved ivy detailing, Victor's trademark.

My breath caught in my chest. "It's beautiful."

He bit his lip, looking down at his feet for a beat. "You think?"

I loved that I got to see the vulnerable moments of confident, cool Victor. I collected them like treasures I found along our life together.

I stepped closer to him. "I *know*. It's perfect."

"We took our photos out here," he said proudly. "Em and Gabe even did their first look out here by the arch."

"September" by Earth, Wind & Fire started pulsing through the speakers, filling the garden. Victor grinned immediately, reaching his hands for mine.

"Victor, Olivia, get out here," Katie shouted from the middle of the bridal group, which was forming a big huddle on the dancefloor.

Terrence had his hands on her waist as she swayed to the beat.

Victor and I jogged over, hand in hand. Luis and his wife, Rachel, were dancing, hands in the air. I caught him giving Victor a nod of approval. Victor spun me into the center of the dance floor. Sweaty and happy, we danced.

The night unfurled before us with a fiery pink sunset overhead, twinkle lights shining.

A slow song by Tim McGraw came on next. Victor pulled me close, his warmth wrapping around me on this crisp evening. His hand was on my lower back, the other interlaced with mine. I looked up to find him grinning down at me. It made me grin right back. Joy bubbled in my veins like fizzy champagne.

"I love being the one you dance to the slow songs with," Victor said, his voice a sweet rasp in my ear.

Goose bumps trailed down my neck.

The word *love* was on the tip of my tongue. "Well ..." I licked my lips, taking a beat, asking myself to be brave. "I love ... *you*, Victor." A lock on my heart fell open.

He pulled his head back quick as lightning. His eyes widened on mine, almost like he was wanting to check if he'd heard me right.

"I'm so in love with you," I said through a giddy, relieved laugh. "I've thought it so many times now. I had to say it."

"I've never known how to be anything *but* in love with you, Liv," Victor said, stopping us in the middle of the dance floor. People danced around us. "I've thought it a thousand times, but I've wanted to wait until you were ready. I didn't want to scare you. But I'm sure you, and everyone, can tell, *I love you*."

My heart was bursting. I grabbed his suit jacket, pulling his mouth inches from mine. "I'm not scared. I'm sure of us. I've never felt as sure of anything in my life as I am of you and me."

He planted his lips on mine, soft, tender. The music swelled around us. He lifted me up, with my feet dangling in the air for a moment. My body was pressed against his. His chest was warm and solid under me. He dropped my feet back to the ground, pulling apart from our kiss for a second, to look at me like he still couldn't believe he got to hold me in his arms like this.

"What are you thinking?" I asked, the two of us starting to sway to the music again.

He shook his head. "I'm just ... happy."

I nestled my head against his chest, a breeze ruffling through the garden, through my hair. "Me too."

It was as simple as that. I'd finally stopped pretending. Stopped fighting it. Let my guard down. Let my feelings out. Let him in. And let myself be vulnerably, wondrously, bravely *happy*.

## Epilogue

Two Years Later

It was the first day of the fall semester, and it was my first class of the day. The classroom was already full of students as I walked in, with my ankle boots clicking through the room with each step. Over the past two years, I had developed a few popular classes that studied ancient history through the eyes of different forms of literature. This class was the original class that started the others: the romance class.

I greeted the room.

"Hi, I'm Dr. Rhodes."

Setting my things down on the podium at the front of the lecture hall, I leafed through my paperwork and welcomed everyone to the class, having my student assistant hand out the syllabus.

I took the first five minutes of class to go over the syllabus, making note of the students in the front row who took notes eagerly, and the students in the back row who looked half awake. One guy was slumping so low, I could barely see him, and he had a hat tight over the top half of his face. *Definitely hiding something,* I thought to myself, my lips pursed. *Probably a hangover.*

"Any questions about the syllabus before we move on?" I asked the class, leaning against the podium. I didn't even look up from my paperwork, studying my notes.

"I have a question." A voice echoed through the lecture hall, vibrating against the walls. A voice I'd recognize anywhere.

I glanced up, searching the students to find the guy who was slumped in the back was *Victor*, now sitting straight up, his arms crossed behind his head.

I raised a brow.

I felt antsy, nervous butterflies in my belly. *What was he up to?* "You have a question?"

I knew Victor wouldn't do anything too wild. He'd never do anything to hurt me or my career. He'd been my biggest supporter the past two years. He was the person I'd grown to trust most in the world.

Heck, he'd not only won my trust, but my whole family's over the past two years. He and I were best friends with Lucy and Adam.

"I do, Dr. Rhodes." He took his hat off and threw it down on the ground at his feet. I realized that was one of his business's hats. His business had grown so much in the past two years. He'd had to stop working with Adam. He'd had to get his own shop, a place where he could sell products in the front but also work in the back. A huge success that kept surprising him, but not me.

"A big question."

*A big question?* I swallowed, my throat dry, my heart expectant. "Go on."

"Well, first of all, let me ask, how do you expect any students to focus when someone as gorgeous as you is standing in the front of the room? I don't think it's fair to the students to have a professor this distractingly good-looking."

I rolled my eyes. "Okay, okay—" Was this some joke? Was I missing something?

"But that's not the only question." He stood up, walking down the stairs that led from the seats to the platform where I taught. "See, I don't only think you're distractingly gorgeous. I *also* think you're intelligent, fierce, hilarious, fun." He ticked off the attributes on his finger as he walked toward me. "And the very best friend I've ever had."

He stood before me now. My hands were shaking. It felt like all the air had been zapped from the room. I couldn't breathe.

"I also think ..." He took a shaky breath. "I'd like to spend the rest of my life with you. Making you happy. Making you laugh. Helping you in every way I can. Taking you to those places on the maps in your office."

"And on your fridge." I chuckled softly. This felt surreal.

"I'd like to spend the rest of my life being the best friend you've ever had." His voice was shaking. His eyes were no longer playful, but intent and serious.

He dropped to one knee. I gasped. The whole classroom gasped. My hands covered my mouth.

"My question is not really in regard to the syllabus, I'll admit. See, I'd like to ask ... will you marry me?"

Tears dripped down my cheeks as I nodded my head. "I'd love to marry you!" I sniffled. I blinked through the tears to see he'd popped out a ring box with a shiny gold ring in it. "This ring is beautiful," I said with shaking hands as he slid the ring on my finger.

"It's antique," he said. "I know you love old things. So I thought you needed a ring with a little history as we write our own history."

*Our own history.* I'd read a lot of stories as I'd studied history for years and years, but my favorite story of all had to be mine and Victor's.

I stopped gawking at my ring and wrapped my arms around him. "Oh my gosh," I kept saying over and over. It felt like I was in the happiest, sweetest dream I didn't want to wake from.

Victor spun me around. "I'm not just your hot young buck anymore. I'm getting promoted to *husband.*"

We slowed to a stop, grinning at each other. Our whole lives ahead of us—*forever* ahead of us.

On the campus where I'd realized I was in love with him two years ago, I'd just agreed to marry him. I laughed into my hands in amazement.

"Um, Dr. Rhodes, does this mean class is canceled for today?" a student piped up in the front row with their hand raised in the air.

*Coming Soon*

Gracie's story will arrive in 2026.

Keep up to date on the latest book news on Instagram at @authorrebeccajojackson or sign up for Rebecca's newsletter at rebeccajojackson.com.

# Acknowledgments

Thank you to God for the beautiful story you've written me. Even when I keep throwing in ridiculous plot twists!

Thank you, Joseph, my own safe zone— there's nowhere safer in this world than beside you. My heart, my soul, my entire body breathes a sigh of relief when you walk into the room. And also thank you for being my own Victor, always saying, "I know you can do it yourself, but you don't HAVE to do it yourself."

Thank you to my mama, who is somehow even cuter and funnier than Mama Rhodes. And my dad who I know is going to read this romcom in between his westerns.

Thank you to my sisters for the inspiration for the Rhodes adorable sister dynamics. Can we have a margarita night soon??

A big hug of gratitude to Hannah, Ashley, India, Katie, and Dreama for reading early messy drafts and providing invaluable feedback and encouragement.

Thank you to my in-laws for your constant support! I didn't only get the best cheerleader in Joseph—I got a whole family of cheerleaders! Your love and support always means so much.

A big thank you to Jen Boles, my copy editor, for becoming such an important part of Sweet River.

And a thank you to English Proper Editing Services for your incredible attention to detail!

Another important part of Sweet River is my spectacularly talented illustrator, Melody Jeffries with Whim & Joy. I'm so grateful my Sweet River Series has you!

Sutton and Ivy, I write stories about messy, heartfelt, strong, hopeful women who know they've got their mama and sisters on their side no matter what—the kind of women you'll grow up to be.

Thank you to my amazing Core Team, Bookstagram friends, and wonderful early readers—your collages, reels, graphics, playlists and reviews (I screenshot these posts and read them to my husband all teary-eyed and happy) remind me why I took a chance and put these stories out there. Obsessing over fictional characters and towns with you is just SO MUCH FUN.

## About the Author

Rebecca Jo Jackson is a writer who grew up in a small town in Texas (hello, Sweet River inspiration), but now has a home in California with her bookworm husband, two adorable daughters and pup.

This is the next standalone book in her Sweet River series. She hopes her books feel as sweet and cozy as a warm cup of coffee from Coffees & Commas.

www.rebeccajojackson.com

instagram.com/authorrebeccajojackson.